THE FORGOTTEN SON

Copyright © 2024 by BJ Sloan

All rights reserved.

No part of this book may be reproduced in any form or by any electronic or mechanical means, including information storage and retrieval systems, without written permission from the author, except for the use of brief quotations in a book review.

Edited by Twyla Beth Lambert

Cover Design by ambient studios

Print ISBN 978-1-957529-20-2

Ebook ISBN 978-1-957529-21-9

Library of Congress Control Number 2024937842

This book is a work of fiction. Names, characters, businesses, places, events, locations, and incidents are either the product of the author's imagination or used in a fictitious manner. Any resemblance to actual persons, living or dead, or actual events, is purely coincidental. Brand names are the property of respective companies; author and publisher hold no claim.

To Steve
I picked him and wasn't wrong.

one

THE LAST TIME Bunny's head felt like this, he'd sat behind the barn breathing fumes from the lawn mower gas can. His vision cloudy, mind in a fog, not a care in the world. But this time, he'd sat next to a girl. The most beautiful girl in school. *Raquel.*

He's almost a mile from Raquel's bus stop before he realizes he's still smiling. When he'd made the snap decision to climb onto her school bus instead of his own, he hadn't considered the long walk home. But the time today sitting right beside her was magic. Heck, he'd trek that distance twice a day if he could feel like this. She listened when he talked, her smile so bright he'd forgotten to breathe. Raquel made Bunny feel like he was—*something.*

He takes out the homemade burrito she'd slipped into his pocket and begins to eat. His lunch tray had been knocked to the floor today, even before he sat down. How stupid he must have looked with cheese and macaroni dripping down the front of his jeans. Everyone had laughed. Everyone except Raquel.

Bunny picks up a discarded can on the roadside, tosses it up, and bats it forward, retrieving it again and again. The crumpled aluminum clangs and bounces skipping along the rocks at the edge of the highway. Bunny saunters after it, drunk with thoughts of

Raquel's silky dark hair and long ebony eyelashes. Out of nowhere, an ear-splitting horn blast knocks him backward. A speeding semi whooshes so close it almost lifts him off his feet. As the truck blows past, Bunny steadies his footing on the road's shoulder and tugs his cap into place. His daydream shattered, the memory of the mocking voices and laughter from school return to attack. His mind folds into its dark place. What would they think? Would they be sorry or even care? He could see it now, inventing the scene in slow motion in his head. The truck that had roared behind him. It draws closer and closer until he steps right in front of the speeding eighteen wheeler. People would shake their heads and say, "That boy sure had a reason." And why not, with the shit hand he'd been dealt. But then he thinks about how he'd felt looking into Raquel's mountain-green eyes. *Would she be sad that he was gone?*

    The sun balancing on the horizon shocks him to attention. It's late. Nan is going to be pissed, and he's still miles from the house. The familiar dread falls across his shoulders like a crushing weight. He begins to run. "You better get here on time, Bunny Boy," she'd yelled from the front door that morning. He squeezes his fist at the words now pinballing inside his brain. *Bunny Boy*. He hated that name. Nan had told him a hundred times the story of when she first laid eyes on her newborn son. "Your head looked like a VW van with both doors wide open." She'd hoot at her memory.

    The delivery nurse, struggling to hand off the baby, had tried to soften the new mom's dismay and offered, "Don't he look like a sweet little bunny?"

    "You know your father left us when he saw you," Nan always added. Then she'd squeeze his chin between her fingers, pucker her lips, and baby-talk the hard words. "Now that's a face only a mother could love." She'll never understand that Bunny is late because he got on the wrong bus—on purpose. He picks up his pace to make up some time and thinks about the ride with Raquel. Her bus today, without his usual tormentors, had felt like Disneyland. No name calling, no misery, just her heart-stopping smile.

Since his last birthday, Bunny had noticed Nan's nervous activity. She acts like she's cleaning the stove, the chicken yard, the boards on the porch. He knows it's because she can't keep still. Nan never tidies up anything. He can almost feel her unraveling, the loss of her control that he silently celebrates as a victory. "Two more years and I'll be eighteen," he'd announced, enjoying her pained expression. His birthday wish had been an overdue promise to himself. When he blew out the candles, his decision was made. He stopped letting her cut his hair. Within a few months, the sight of his unkempt red curls had pushed Nan's normal sour mood into overdrive. Unfazed by her snide remarks and looks of disgust, he liked the longer locks. Hair covering his ears gave him what he desperately needed: the gift of looking into a mirror without recoil.

He jogs off the gravel road shoulder and turns onto the blacktop toward home. Lights appear from behind, and this time, he moves from the road to the safety of the ditch. A black pickup slows beside him. "Need a ride?" TC Conway, the next-door rancher, leans down from the driver's side, looking out the passenger window.

"Sure, thanks." Bunny nods. Inside the spotless truck, TC's starched white shirt is brilliant even in the fading daylight. It almost glows. His jeans look stiff, with a heat-set seam and finished by ostrich boots that gleam with a fresh shine. Bunny has always thought TC to be a bit of a dandy. Everything about his neighbor is different. He doesn't talk like most farmers and ranchers, and he's not dressed like one, heading home from a long day's work.

"Coming from school?"

"Yes, sir."

"Little late. Bus breakdown?"

That smell? What is it? Bunny glances around the cab for the sweet, almost edible fragrance, like cotton candy. A paper-wrapped cone of white lilies rests on the seat between them.

"Nah, rode over to a friend's. Just walking back from there."

"Mmmmm... a girl?"

"No. I mean yes, well, sorta."

"A little stopgap angel?"

"What?"

"A little... you know." TC makes a fist and punches the air. "A little 'she'll do.' Nothing wrong with that. Shoot, that's healthy."

"Wish somebody would tell Nan," Bunny mumbles.

"Oh, Momma don't like to let go, huh? How old are you now?"

"Sixteen last birthday."

"Old enough. Just have to make it known—they's plenty of girls to chase."

"Won't work with Nan." Bunny frowns.

TC grins and leaves Bunny wondering how he keeps his teeth so white. "She'll come around. Mothers always do."

They drive on in silence with Bunny thinking hard about what he can say when he gets home. It doesn't much matter. No excuse he can dream up is going to help. TC slows the truck as they approach the narrow lane to Potts' house. "Right here is fine," Bunny says. "Thanks a bunch."

"Hey!" Bunny looks back as TC extends the flowers. "Give your momma these."

"Don't you need 'em?"

"She wasn't home." TC shrugs.

Bunny leans in to accept the wrapped blooms, thinking about what TC said. "You headed home?"

"You got it." TC gives a quick two-finger salute off the brim of his straw Stetson and drives away. This guy has a wife and three daughters, the middle girl is in Bunny's class. Four ladies at home, but the "she" he's talking about isn't one of them? Bunny shakes his head and starts a long-legged gallop across the field.

He can see the outline of the roof against the still-pink horizon, but closer to the house, there's no sign of lights inside. Nan never leaves home. Maybe she's asleep or maybe she'll be in a good mood. *Yeah, and maybe she won the lottery.*

The sweet fragrance of the flowers cradled in his arms fills his nostrils. Flowers for Mom. Couldn't hurt. He runs past a pile of brush and trips over a large striped cat, who springs from the tall grass, hisses, and bolts away. "Damn," Bunny mutters. This is Nan's doing. She mothers the orphan balls of fur, fawning over ever stray cat in the county. That's why kids at school call her the Crazy Cat Lady. Potts' place is the official dumping ground for unwanted felines.

Several of them Nan thinks are special because of unusual markings or, more rarely, a peculiar deformity. She elevates this select group to the status of inside pets. The Potts' house, with its fur-matted furniture and damp kitty toys, offers little comfort for Bunny. The four-legged inside crew often regard the sandbox with the same enthusiasm as a mass port-a-potty, and they know the best way to irritate him is by making a smelly delivery in his room.

When he reaches the house, the front door is locked, and it's dark inside. He raps on the window. "Nan, let me inside, would ya? Sorry, I'm late... Mom. Please let me in." Cupping his hands, he looks in the glass. Nothing but Mister Six-Toes and Diablo draped on the sofa. Their tails jerk, annoyed at being awakened from their nap.

But for Bunny, being locked out of the house is nothing new. He's spent many nights outside, finds it peaceful, and has learned how to adapt. At least tonight it's not raining or cold. He spots a half-buried jar in the yard, pries it free, and fills it with water from the hose before sucking in a big mouthful himself. Unwrapping the lilies, he sinks the stems to revive them. Across the yard, the 1960 Chevy sits in its normal place. "Mom's in the house alright, just teaching me a lesson," he whispers to himself.

He walks over to the once-blue sedan, Nan's original and only car. He knew the story of how she'd received the new car on her sixteenth birthday. But that was almost eighteen years ago and although it still ran, the time of it being a stylish ride had long since passed. The doors are locked—no surprise, with Nan guarding the key to that old beater like it's gold. She laughed when Bunny asked if he could drive to school. "What if I need to get to the hospital?" Lately, Nan's complained about her health even more than usual.

First she can't breathe, then she's dizzy. She plays the poor me card so often, he's grown numb.

Bunny steps on the bumper and pulls himself onto the hood. He stretches his long legs across the cool metal of the car and rubs his eyes, feeling very tired. Raquel's sweet smell lingers on his fingers, and he cups his hands over his face and breathes deeply. In the dim light of dusk, the gleam of the sky-blue polish dances on his nails. He smiles as he thinks about her musical laughter as they'd bounced willy-nilly on the bus seat, she struggling to brush the color. And the look on her face—pure amazement when he'd said yes to her painting his nails. But Raquel didn't know her power. She could've asked for a kidney, and Bunny would have agreed if it meant she'd hold his hand.

He dozes off, then wakes, surprised by the canopy of emerging stars that flicker in the darkness. In the southern sky, a familiar pattern grabs his attention and he stretches a hand, simulating a high-five to his mentor. Bold and confident, Sagittarius stands guard with a watchful eye and a fully drawn bow. Bunny had taken up archery himself after his science teacher revealed that his birth date fell under the sign. Watching his heavenly kindred spirit, he puffs his own chest. "You take the first shift, Archie. I'll relieve you halfway through the night." He closes his eyes as the words evaporate into the night air.

In the early morning. A rooster crows and Bunny wakes, cold and stiff. His stomach rumbles and he thinks about the chickens. If he's lucky, he might find a few eggs. The sudden and painful emptiness makes him hurry to the chicken yard. In the dark, he startles a sleeping bird that protests loudly before it flaps away. He rounds the side of the henhouse and feels the way to the nesting area at the back. Near the corner, something gives and rolls under his foot. Gasping, he jumps back. "Ahhhhhhhhhh," comes from the ground. And then a second, recognizable "Ooooooooh."

"Nan! Nan!" Bunny creeps forward, reaching into the darkness. "What happened?"

two

His truck climbs the hill with the ease of learned repetition, and TC rolls to a stop behind a sprawling rock house. He'd built the home on this prime point a few years earlier, capturing a view he never grows tired of. The rolling green of the Conway ranch land spills before him, as far as the eye can see.

Last year was a productive one, with cattle prices soaring. The extra profits had allowed TC to purchase the flashy new ride. Satisfaction brimming, a grin spreads across his face as he gets out, pats the hood of the truck, and turns toward the house.

TC is outnumbered, being the only man in a house full of women. He'd hoped for a boy each time his wife was pregnant. A son to teach how to turn a profit on a ranch and one day take the reins. But after the third try, he accepted it was not meant to be. None of the daughters favored their dad—a shame, really, because it would have been an improvement. Though all three girls are tall, two of them are also thick-bodied. Heavy women are not pleasing to TC, so he almost doesn't see them at all. Only Jodie, the middle girl, is rail thin like her mother.

It's Jodie who greets him at the backdoor. "Oh, there you are." Her words drip annoyance. Hands on narrow hips, she maintains a stern expression, but the girl's sparkling blue eyes deny her irritation. "Mom wouldn't let us eat without you."

"Hello there... favorite offspring. Nice to see you, too." TC smirks.

"Dad, we're starrrrrr-ving." She stiffens and drops against the wall.

"That so? Guess your mom knows who makes the money around here." The rich smell of seared beef rushes down the entry, making his own mouth water. "Besides," says TC, "I was helping a friend of yours."

"Like who?"

"Bunny Boy Potts."

"Dad!" Jodie makes a face. "Why would I be friends with him? Why would anyone?"

"That's not very neighborly," he says and pushes his daughter toward the dinner table.

TC glances into the kitchen where Bridget Conway hovers near the sink. He knows she's been watching out the window. Her shoulders are rounded in a permanent slouch, an unspoken apology for her prominent stature of near six feet. It's warm today, but Bridget is covered head to toe, with hands and face the only available skin. The long bib apron is double-wrapped around her narrow, shapeless middle, and her sturdy, black-rimmed glasses have slipped low on her nose. She notices his eyes on her and an unsure smile flashes on her lips, but she turns away, hiding the sudden heat rising in her cheeks. She's a reliable partner as a wife and mother, but TC's thoughts of Bridget have become like paint on the wall. The surface may be covered, but the color is just plain vanilla.

The family takes their places at the table and the dishes make it around before Jodie breaks the silence. "Dad, you gave Bunny Boy a ride?" With his mouth full, TC only nods. "He wasn't on the bus today," Jodie continues. "So... where was he?"

TC swallows, taking a gulp of tea. "Said he rode another bus... with a girl, I believe."

"I knew it," Jodie giggles. "I bet it was Raquel."

"Who?"

"You know, the new people that just moved here to work the Bosque Ranch. The Martinez family. They have like, seven kids."

"Does she like Bunny Boy?" asks little sister Amy, her face wrinkling like she just smelled old milk.

"Probably doesn't know better," Meredith chuckles. "Or maybe she's into the Ronald McDonald look?"

"Forget about the cartoon hair. How about those ears?" Jodie hoots.

TC slams his knife and fork to the table, interrupting the laughter, then backhands his plate away. Green peas and gravy flying, he shoves back to stand. His chair topples over and smacks against the floor like the blast of a shotgun. "Is this what you teach our kids?" he bellows, spraying a mouthful of mashed potatoes and shaking a finger at his wide-eyed wife. "That poor kid can't change the way he looks. And I sure as hell don't see any prize-winning beauties at this table, either."

Bridget lowers her eyes, staring into her lap as her husband stomps away into the kitchen. The silence around the table is thick as they hear a twist-top crack open and then the harsh slam of the back door.

He drops the tailgate, takes a seat on the back of the truck, sips the beer, and concentrates on lowering his blood pressure. The dim light of dusk is his favorite time. Come home, eat a good meal, and reflect on the day. The sound summons Rowdy, who appears, staring up from the ground. The animal cocks a fluffy black and white head and brings folded ears to attention, waiting for an invitation. His master pats the truck bed, and the dog easily sails up to lie beside him.

The hilltop view works a magical calm on TC. It's his place to reflect on what he's done right in the world, his own success, ten times that of his father. In his boyhood home, he'd watched the family struggle just to have food and clothes on a country preacher's pay. He knew his father was a good man, but not particularly a happy one. The preacher never spared the rod with his wayward son. Even so, TC had railed against his father's beliefs, making a vow to succeed and enjoy the things never allowed. "That'll send you straight to hell," was a familiar warning he'd received at home and from the pulpit. But a life shackled by fear and denial, TC knew, just spit in the face of God. Lots of beauty in the world, and he hungered to taste it all.

Across the meadow, at the far corner of his property, sits the run-down home of Nan and Bunny Boy Potts. There was once a time when he knew Nan was happy, full of life. But over the years, something had unraveled, and her mind became stuck in the gear of crazy.

Potts' place is dark tonight, no lights visible. The old house and surrounding three acres had once belonged to TC. When he gifted Nan the little place, it had seemed like a generous action and one he almost instantly regretted. During the still of evenings, he could hear the boy's screams across the still meadow. He'd grit his teeth, clench his fist, and tell himself that's just Nan's way, her business. He thought the boy becoming school age, surely things would change. The child would at least have an escape, an offer of normality, a reprieve. But listening to his daughters tonight, he understood for the first time—Bunny Boy's life both at home and at school is twisted and wrong. TC shakes his head and curses his blind ignorance. He should have known.

The sliver of sun sinks and the serenade of the night begins. Cicadas' shrill notes vibrate from the trees as mud-happy toads return the call with bass bravado from below. No sound tonight from across the meadow. "Maybe the old gal has hung up the strap?" TC muses as he scratches Rowdy behind the ears. But the sourness chewing his insides makes him tilt the bottle and pour the rest of the beer into the yard. "If she hasn't hung it up... I'll have to make sure she does."

three

"Nan, Nan!" Bunny shouts and kneels beside her as she moans and thrashes on the ground. "Mom, can you hear me?" No response as he fumbles in the dark. "I'll get help." He gulps and runs to the house, ready to break inside if necessary. Finding the back door unlocked, he grabs the phone off the cradle beside Nan's bedside and calls the sheriff's office.

With the help of a flashlight, Bunny brushes away the powdery barnyard excrement coating her face. Her frightened eyes wild, she grabs his hand as Bunny scrubs at the dried blackness in the corners of her mouth. Nan is still in her nightgown and has soiled herself, but in his search for injury, he finds only a small gash over her left eye. Her empty egg basket is upside down several feet away, and broken shells dot the ground surrounding her body.

"I'm sorry, I'm sorry… I… should have come home right away," he stammers. "I should have been here. Please, Nan, don't be mad." In the narrow beam of light, her eyes flash recognition. She works to move her lips, but the muscles only twitch. Her struggle escalating, Nan's arms flail, trying to push out the words. She swings erratically and strikes Bunny across the face and shoulders. He grabs her arms, setting off a series of moans and grunts. Nan's eyes plead for help until they overflow, making dust trails down her cheeks. He can do nothing but sit beside his mother, rock her gently, and wait for help. When the ambulance arrives, the sun has still not shown itself. But the sky to the east is ablaze with brilliant strokes of yellow, orange, and red.

It takes three of them to lift Nan. She protests loudly, but her nonsense noises fall on deaf ears. Bunny tries to calm her, taking her hand to walk beside the bed on wheels. Her body laps the sides, the extra parts of Nan jiggling freely as two men struggle to push the weight through the sandy chicken yard.

They load Nan into the back of their van. "You're... taking her?" Bunny stammers and steps forward to touch the arm of the man standing close.

"Sure. Doctor has to look her over."

"But why? Can't... can't you give her something?"

"We're taking her to the hospital. You want to ride along?"

Bunny shakes his head. How would he get home? There are animals to feed and then there is school. He watches as they slam the back doors and drive away. When the red taillights disappear, the panic of being alone hits him. It feels like he's choking. He must stop them, stop them from taking his mother. Bunny explodes in a dead run. Reaching the end of their road, he turns toward the highway. "Don't take her! Please stop, please stop!" But the strong headwind only pushes the words back into his face. Exhaustion numbs his brain, and the white van is nowhere in sight. Bunny slows to a walk. His head throbs. His lungs burn. Defeated, he slumps toward home. When he nears the house, the rumble of the school bus on the road catches his attention. He looks up just in time to see it pass by.

This will be the first day he has ever missed. Nan has been gone less than an hour, and he's already screwed up. But he can't think about that right now. His mom has been taken away, and that notion almost makes his head explode. She was out there since yesterday morning, gathering eggs in her night clothes like she does early every day. Bunny can't let go of that image. "What a worthless piece-of-shit son," he whispers, her words a familiar refrain.

When he reaches the yard, his legs are numb. It's as though his feet are stuck in deep mud, and it takes all his strength to move forward. New daylight burns away, the early morning cool and the sudden heat making him shiver. With his stomach past empty, the blinding sun causes his head to swim, and he staggers. "Food," he whispers. "I need food."

Bunny hopes Nan has restocked his food shelf. But that's unlikely as she was lying on the ground since yesterday morning. The day before, all he had left was a jar of pickles and half a bottle of mustard. He'd made himself a plate of dill chip slices, each with a squirt of yellow mustard he carefully positioned in the center. He'd sat on the porch and thought about a scene from an old black-and-white movie where a pretty girl offers her guests tiny bites of food from a tray. But the make-believe dinner had given him stomach pain, and when Bunny opens his pantry today, only the same two items sit on the shelf.

The memory of the broken eggs from this morning comes back to mock him. Exhausted, he sinks to the floor. The house is so quiet. It's weird being here alone. He lies down and tries to relax his back against the floor, closing his eyes.

Something tickles his face, and Bunny's eyes fly open. Mister Six-Toes paces back and forth so close his tail brushes against Bunny's lips. Startled, Bunny sits up as the cat folds his hind legs, sitting still as a bookend. "What do you want, Sixer? Food? That makes two of us." But the feline moves to the refrigerator, rises on his back legs and kneads all twelve toes against the door. "Something in there? Sorry, Bud, that's Nan's special stuff. That's for people with a gland problem. Besides, see that padlock? I've got no key." He shrugs. But the cat wails and returns to pacing, this time in front of the off-limits refrigerator.

Bunny checks the animal's food dish and it's licked clean. The fifty-pound bag of kitty chow is empty, with only the scoop left inside. He refills the cat's water bowl and sets it down. "Best I can do, unless you'd like a little mustard?" But now, Six-Toes is joined by Diablo, who also paws at the locked white box.

"You guys are trying to get me in trouble." But... maybe Nan will understand. "I doubt there's anything in there you want," he says, pulling a screwdriver from the junk drawer. He works to back out the screws that secure the hasp, thinking he'll be able to reattach the lock so Nan will never know. He applies so much pressure on the last screw, rusted in place, that he only strips the screw head. In desperation, he pries off the hasp, hoping he can straighten the metal. Door free, Bunny pulls it open and sinks to his knees.

He kneels before the open door, bathed in the light and cool air, and worships in disbelief. His brain refuses what is right before his eyes. Every available cranny is crammed with colorful boxes, cartons, and packages. Twinkies, Oreos, honey buns, caramel corn, and root beer line the inside. Jars of chocolate-covered raisins, peanut butter, jam, loaves of bread, and bagels, bags of salty chips, and crackers crowd the shelves in the door. In the freezer, Bunny's hand shakes as he touches frosty tubs of ice cream, frozen pizza, and Fudgesicles.

He attacks the food. Tearing the packages with his teeth causes an explosion of chips and cookies over the room. The two hungry cats sniff at the scattered morsels, but Bunny scoops them from the floor and shoves them into his mouth.

His primal need to satisfy his hunger is so strong he forgets about Nan. The eating frenzy slows just long enough for him to chug a quart of root beer before returning to grab a half-gallon of Neapolitan ice cream. He sits in front of the open door of the refrigerator, shoveling in the cold sweetness, and dreaming about what he can eat next. Down below in the meat tray, he discovers plastic-wrapped tubes of refrigerated cat food. Bunny slices a couple of fat wedges and tosses them into the food dishes.

About an hour passes and, with Bunny's stomach now resembling a ripe watermelon, he stops the gorging. Bunny doesn't bother to straighten the hasp or reattach the lock on the refrigerator. He remembers begging Nan for Twinkies when he was younger. Kids at school brought them in their lunch, but they never shared. His mother said they cost too much and besides, she told him, she only bought healthy foods. But this is what Nan eats while he's at school... or maybe the nights when she locks him outside.

He finds a seat to stand on and climbs up to examine himself in the bathroom mirror mounted high on the wall; it's the only one Nan would allow in the house. Bunny takes off his shirt to look at his body and almost falls off the stool. He can count every rib. His shoulders so frail in appearance they're bird-like. Arms no bigger than a small child's, his face drawn and hollow. No wonder his ears look huge. "Is this what you want, Nan? You proud of your boy?" he shouts.

Bunny takes Nan's framed photo, the one she keeps by her bed, and goes outside to the porch. He sits with his legs over the side, his feet swinging free. The photograph of Nan was taken years ago, even before he was born. The girl in the image is laughing. With long hair across her shoulders, she looks like summer in cut-off jean shorts and a yellow tank top.

He's never seen his mother with long hair. And the clothes. There's no way now she could fit into shorts. Heck, he can't remember the last time he even saw her smile. Could she really have changed so much? The girl in the photo couldn't be his mother. How can this possibly be Nan?

It's surprising she kept the picture. Just looking at it has to make her sad. But maybe that was the last time she was truly happy. The pretty girl looks like someone he'd like to know. But after what he found today, he's sure of one thing. Bunny doesn't know the person his mother has become.

four

IF SHE HAD ONLY BEEN BORN with the face for it, a career as a runway model would have suited Bridget Conway. Her body grew tall, but her curves did not. Even now, as a mother with three daughters, her shape is often compared to a flagpole. But looks being what they are, she knew well her limitations. Thank goodness her daddy had money.

When her husband walked by on his way out this morning, Bridget performed the ritual she'd adopted over the years. When TC is near, she lowers her glasses and notes the dancing chain looped from belt to the watch pocket. The watch was a gift, he'd said, and that was all the explanation she got. It was such an old-fashioned style, but TC was never without it. In truth, the dangling loop of gold was the first thing that'd caught her attention when he'd asked her to dance.

At the Spring Party, when she was just a girl, she was standing with a group of others along the wall of the gymnasium when TC walked over. At first, certain he must be talking to her friend, she kept her eyes down, fixed on the watch chain. But when he reached forward, pulling her by the hand to the dance floor, Bridget thought she was in a dream. TC Conway was the tallest and best-looking guy in school.

That was nearly twenty years and three children ago, but even now, Bridget feels a rush whenever TC looks at her. "That Conway boy is after my money," her father, a retired oilman, had ranted when they started dating. And Bridget saw the sideways glances. She knew what the pretty girls said behind her back. But when she was with TC, she no longer felt invisible. She didn't care about the gossip or Daddy's money or any of that. She felt special and proud, and if that was the price, she would gladly pay it for a life with him.

This morning, after the girls got off to school and TC left for the day, she went out to tend her lily garden. Bridget has a way with the flowers, having learned from her mother. She surveys the blooms and takes a deep breath, filling her lungs with their sugary sweetness. Tall, graceful stems of red, white, and yellow wave from elevated beds under the trees and along the edge of the house.

She works steadily, removing the weeds and spent blossoms. It's easy to see by the number of cut stems that someone has been gathering her blooms again. She figures TC. Still, it's hard to understand why he needs to take flowers to the ladies in the office at the cattle auction every week. "Always recognize the folks who help you," he'd told her. When she straightens to rest her back and dry her face with the back of a gloved hand, she sees a trail of smoke rising across the meadow. The yellow flames of a fire are near Nan's house. That's weird. Nan doesn't spend time outside, and she certainly burns nothing. Bunny must be in school—if that fire is unattended, their house may be in danger.

When Bridget turns onto the lane to the Potts' house, a tomcat with one thing in mind chases his love interest in front of her car. She jams the brakes. Stopped in the middle of the road, Bridget grips the wheel and looks ahead to the house, where fire dances from an open-top barrel. She drives on and rolls to a stop in the front yard as Bunny runs out from behind the barn, carrying something toward the fire.

But when he sees Bridget getting out of her car, he comes to a dead stop several feet away. The appearance of the gangly scarecrow boy is comical. It's been years since she's seen her neighbor, back when he was only a small child. But now his shirt hangs from his shoulders like it's pinned to a clothesline, and the mass of hair pushing from under his cap is the color of bricks on a street. It's easy to see why the girls were making comments at dinner. TC was right about what he said. His anger was misplaced, but his actions made her proud he'd stand up for people challenged in the looks department. People like herself.

"Bunny... right? I'm Bridget Conway—TC's wife."

"Wow, you're tall." He gawks.

"Well, yeah, so are you."

"But, you're a lady."

"My daddy was tall. How about yours?"

Bunny shrugs. "Didn't know the man." He sets the bucket at his feet, the bail clanging against the metal side, fueling a chorus of high-pitched protests from inside.

The boy's reaction unsettling, she gets to the point. "Saw the fire. Burning trash?"

"Getting rid of some stuff."

"Worried me. I thought you were in school."

"Missed the bus."

She nods, pointing to the pail. "What's all the commotion?"

Bunny glances down. "Been finding these in the barn."

Bridget walks closer to see the reason for the screeches. "Kittens! Oh, my goodness, four... six... ten... you got half a bucket full!" She bends, touching the squirmy bodies and selects a particularly pissed-off red and white fur ball. "Oh, look," she says, holding up the pink-faced baby. "They don't even have their eyes open yet." She returns the kitten to the bucket and asks, "Your mom in the house?"

"Something happened," Bunny says quietly.

"With the cats?"

"No, with Nan. Last night. They took her."

"They?"

"Hospital, I think."

"Is she there now?" He nods, moving the bucket slightly with his foot.

"Don't you want to see her?"

"Don't have a license." Bunny gestures toward the old car parked in front of the house. Knee-high grass forms a solid fence around the wheels and makes Bridget wonder when the rusty thing was last driven. But a son needs to be with his mother. His sick mother.

"Is it bad, you think?"

"She didn't say. Don't think she could talk." His voice cracks with the telling, and he seems embarrassed. He stares across the meadow, seeming uncomfortable with Bridget being so near. "You live up there?" He points to the sprawling Conway house on the hill.

Now it's her turn to be uncomfortable. By comparison, his own home a few feet behind them is made of weathered grey wood complete with sagging porch and yard art of ancient, discarded farm implements almost hidden in tall grass. Stinging with guilt, Bridget says slowly, "I could take you... to see Nan."

"Really?" he says and looks up, his eyes finding her face for the first time.

"Sure." Bridget smiles, hoping to put him at ease. "I just need to change out of my gardening grubbies." She starts to her car, then remembers something and turns back. "You better put those babies where you found them or else a bunch of momma cats are going to be pretty unhappy with you."

"Thing is..." Bunny says, looking across the field again. "I... don't want more cats."

"I see." Bridget shakes her head, realizing it is Nan who collects the animals and Nan is not here. Growing up on a ranch, she knew all too well the unspoken rule for animals who've become too old, too injured, or just not needed. For a moment, she thought about grabbing the bucket and taking it home; But then, her daughters would fall in love and TC would do away with the kittens when the girls were gone to school. No, she didn't need to invite more drama into her own house. Her stomach twisting, she knew it wasn't her place to judge this boy. "I'll be back in an hour and give you a ride to town."

five

BUNNY'S BUS is the first one to arrive at school. It's early, so he takes a seat on the rock wall out front to wait for Raquel. Other kids in late-model trucks and sporty coupes hurry past him to claim prime parking spaces. Engines race and two girls bounce with the latest dance moves beside a red jeep with radio volume turned to annoying. A few kids driving hand-me-down rides creep to the back lot and park, then walk up to join the party in the front.

No one takes notice of Bunny perched on the wall, watching. He swings his long legs to his own imaginary rhythm, as boy-girl crushes greet each other with hugs and laughter. He thinks about Raquel and how he longs to wrap his own arms around her and show the world she belongs with him.

Filling the time, he fishes a pencil from his pouch and applies pressure at an angle to rub the lead against the cement cap of the wall. Soon the pencil is sharpened to a fine point, and he tests it against his own fingertip, drawing blood. Nothing worse than a dull lead in math class. Satisfied, Bunny stows it in his shirt pocket.

More kids arrive as two additional buses unload beside the school. They lean against the sandstone building in groups or pairs to make the most of the last minutes of freedom. The ill-mannered blast of the first bell upsets the morning tranquility and jars the reluctant students into motion. They shuffle past Bunny ascending the steps to the front door, but there's still no sign of the last bus or Raquel.

Clouds collect overhead, darken the sky, and stir a fresh smell of rain that swirls on the cool breeze. The sudden weather change and the no-show for Raquel is making Bunny anxious. He climbs up on the wall for a better view to watch for the late bus. Minutes tick by, and just as he turns to go inside, a yellow blur roars into the schoolyard and snaps open the folding doors.

When Raquel descends the steps, the clouds break and intense sun streams down, giving her hair a movie-star, blue-black shine. Today, she's wearing a white blouse that contrasts with her warm, flawless skin. She's so lovely that even watching from a safe distance makes him feel light-headed. Bunny waits for her to look up. He needs to measure her reaction, understand her eyes, before he approaches. And there it is—her beautiful smile that warms his heart. "Your bus was almost late." He grins.

"I know. We waited behind some road workers for maybe ten minutes," she says, hugging books to her chest. "I didn't see you yesterday."

He shakes his head. "I missed the bus. My mom got sick."

"Oh, sorry," Raquel says. The two bump shoulders as they go through the door at the same time. "What happened to your mom?"

"A stroke, doctor said," he shouts over banging lockers and loud voices that echo down the hall. She touches his arm, her eyes full of concern, but then the second bell blasts and sends Raquel in one direction and Bunny in another. He won't see her again until lunch, but just the thought makes his stomach churn with excitement.

All morning, Bunny pretends to be a model student. He fixes his eyes on the teacher at the front of the classroom, opens his books to the correct page, but he speaks to no one. Bunny gives a masterful performance, pretending to pay attention.

His thoughts drift to his hospital visit yesterday. Nan the color of cotton, her eyes afraid, distant. The left side of her mouth drooped like she has a cheek full of ball bearings. She could move the first two fingers of her right hand, but what good is the peace sign when her legs don't work, and her voice is missing? The body lying in the hospital bed hardly seemed like his mother at all.

Afterward, it was strange how good he'd felt on the ride back with TC's wife. She had surprised him with an invitation to dinner at their home tomorrow night. He'd closed his eyes and thought about what it would be like to bring Raquel to the big house on the hill. He would show her off, introduce her to the family. It would impress them he could attract such a girl, and for a moment, the tall, sweet lady behind the wheel was the person he would call Mom. But the memory of Nan's eyes, frightened and alone, had shattered his daydream, and the imaginary family melted into the black pool of his own life.

When noon time finally arrives, Bunny leans over the trash to finger-comb the morning collection of spit wads from his tight red curls. He's become so accustomed to it he hardly reacts unless a juicy ball is a direct hit to his exposed neck. That always sends a shiver down his spine. Even the teachers turn a blind eye to what must look like a sideways hailstorm directed at Bunny's head.

In the lunchroom, he forgoes the line, grabs a milk carton from the box, and finds a seat on the far side of the room. Working to control his excitement, Bunny takes some deep breaths to calm down. He has something special to give Raquel. When she comes through with her tray, Bunny waves to her. "I've got something for you," he says as she takes a seat, then pushes a package of Twinkies across to her.

"I love Twinkies, but... where is your lunch?"

"I have some," he says, holding up another package. "And milk." Bunny smiles.

Across the room, the muscle morons of the varsity football team huddle together, having noticed the couple. Suddenly, Mean Man

Watson and his favorite sidekick, Fast Eddie, saunter toward the table where Bunny and Raquel sit alone.

"So... Bunny Boy." The 300-pound Watson scowls down at him. "Who said you could have Twinkies?" He snatches the cellophane-wrapped treat, rips it open, and in one motion crams both pieces into his mouth.

Fast Eddie, dwarfed by his hulking companion, giggles uncontrollably. "What about her?" He points to the package sitting in front of Raquel.

"Today, we'll let this pretty girl slide," Watson says, blowing cake crumbs over the table. He swallows and leans across, spreading his fingers to support his intimidating weight, while addressing Raquel. "But, honey, you really shouldn't hang around with this clap-ridden loser." His mouth an evil grin, he leans in close to share a secret. "People will get the wrong idea." The big man whispers loudly, the advice a poorly veiled threat.

Like ignited gasoline, Watson's words explode Bunny's hidden anger. The gall of this clown, talking to his girl. Bunny eyes the jumbo-sized paw spread on the table to his left. In one motion, he snatches the dagger-sharp pencil from his pocket and drives it completely through the soft flesh of Watson's hand.

The nasty smirk on the big man's face distorts into an open-mouthed howl. Watson grabs at his impaled hand as Bunny quickly jumps out of reach. Fast Eddie yells, "Oh my God, Potts has a knife!"

With an ear-splitting scream, Watson extracts the wooden stake, exposing a gaping hole. A red stream pulses, covering the table and his shirt. He bolts from the lunchroom, cradling the hand, but is slowed by the stampede of terrified students running for their lives. One girl is knocked to the floor in the logjam and can only cover her head as the surge of flying bodies trample her.

Raquel doesn't run but looks on with wide, unblinking eyes, her mouth hanging open. Bunny reaches to reassure her, but she quickly backs away. "Raquel... I couldn't just let him... don't you see?" Her eyes lock on him defensively. Stunned into silence, she edges back even farther.

Soon as the crowd clears, Principal Pemberton yells from the safety of his position behind the food service door. "Put down the weapon, Potts! The police are on the way."

He only wanted to share lunch, give Raquel something special, be in her company. This girl is what he needs, dreams of, and longs for. He can't sit by and let his chance be ruined. Raquel's frightened eyes say so much. She's upset with him, and that was not supposed to happen. Bunny hangs his head and stares down at the blood-covered table where his yellow #2 pencil rests peacefully in a pool of red. "Next time," he whispers softly. "Next time, it will be a knife."

six

THIS IS the third time he's changed shirts, and the one he has on now feels big enough for a second person. Invited as a dinner guest is a new experience, and Bunny wants to make a good impression. He understands collared shirts are more acceptable, and although he's unsure where Nan found this blue one, it has a collar and sleeves. Bunny stands on a chair and looks in the mirror. The shoulder seams hang halfway to his elbow and the sides bag out, but it'll have to do.

He'd read that a dinner guest should bring a gift. Bunny looks around the house, searching for an acceptable item for his hostess, Bridget Conway. There is no liquor in the Potts' house, so the bottle of wine the article suggested is out. He thinks about the half-dozen eggs he'd gathered this morning. Fresh eggs would have been nice, but he'd scrambled them for breakfast. He looks into Nan's refrigerator and considers a half gallon of ice cream, but by the time he walks to the Conway's, it'll be slush.

Bunny wishes for some flowers or a box of chocolates, like the guys in movies give girls. But then his eyes lock on the ever-present blue bottle of perfume on his mother's dresser. The smoky, sweet smell called *Boy's Club* is the only fragrance Nan wears. Bunny picks up the blue container. "Almost full." He smiles and pockets the star-shaped glass bottle, promising to worry about Nan missing it later.

He travels across the meadow up to the big house. Being early, he walks along the creek bed collecting branches from ash trees to make ammunition for his bow. He's never owned any of the slick, brightly colored arrows he'd once admired in a sporting goods store. Tipped with metal, they looked lethal. Researching in the library, Bunny had learned how to work the wood into an acceptable projectile for his handmade willow bow. His ash arrows were not as menacing, lacking color and razor tips, and might be mistaken as a simple bundle of sharpened sticks. But fashioned under his patient hand, they were accurate for marksmanship and taking down small game.

By the time he masters the climb up the hill to the Conway's, Bunny is hypnotized by the graceful sway of the long-stemmed flowers wind-dancing near the house. He stoops to run his hands over the intensely green and very soft grass of the front yard. Feeling small in the shadow of the massive two-story home, he twirls with arms out like a pinwheel on the breeze. "Someday, Raquel," he whispers. "Someday." Suddenly, he bends low to peek under the fat limbs of the big oak at his own tiny house. The distance makes it feel far away, but like a wart on an elbow, it's there when you go looking. He picks up the bundle of sticks he's collected on the walk and makes a tidy pile just outside the back door, promising to retrieve them on his way home.

Bridget Conway appears, offering a smile. "Bunny, come in, come in," she says and holds the door wide. An intoxicating aroma fills the house, and led by his nose, he follows her down the hallway. "I hope you like fried chicken," she says, showing the way into the kitchen. His stomach rumbling, he stares wide-eyed into the bright and tidy room. A pan sizzles over a flame next to a tray of shiny-topped biscuits ready for the oven. The white counter is lined with platters and bowls of various colors beside a small army of glasses and a pitcher of iced tea. The rich smell makes his head swim, and he clutches the edge of the counter to steady himself. Bridget pulls out a stool from the island. "You're the first one here, so have a seat and I'll get you a cold drink."

While she fills a glass with ice, Bunny fumbles in his pocket, retrieving the blue bottle. "I brought you... this," he says and slowly pushes the small container across the counter.

Bridget eyes the bottle. She seems unsure, then picks it up. "What's this? Perfume?"

He nods and looks down, heat climbing up his neck. "Didn't want to show up empty-handed."

"How nice." She smiles and lifts the cap, bringing it to her nose. "Mmmmm... smells different." She sprays a squirt on each wrist. "Smoky and sweet at the same time. What's it called?" She turns the bottle, looking for a label. "Never smelled anything like it."

"*Boy's Club*," Bunny says.

The back door swings open, and female voices sounds from the hall. "Mom, Jodie left a pile of sticks by the back door."

"Liar!"

"Ouch! Mom!"

"You deserve it, cow."

The girls round the corner, look into the room, and stop dead. TC, close on their heels, bumps into them as now four statues stare into the kitchen.

"Um, Mom... what's going on?" Jodie asks.

"Supper is almost ready." Bridget waves a pair of tongs in the air and smiles at her family. "Remember, I told you Bunny is joining us for dinner."

"But, Mom, he got kicked out of school." Jodie protests. "Tell her." She points accusingly at him. "Tell her how you stabbed that guy in the lunchroom."

Suddenly, it's so quiet you can hear chicken bubbling in the grease on the stove. Every Conway eye turns to the dangerous dinner guest sitting on their kitchen stool drinking iced tea. Bunny puts the glass down, wipes at the water collecting on the outside, then presses wet fingertips against the back of his neck. "I... can go back to school in a week."

"You got expelled?" Bridget frowns at him, but there is relief in her voice. Still, the disappointment in her eyes is painful. He has upset the evening, made them all uncomfortable.

Bunny stands, "Sorry. I, probably should go."

"Wait a minute," TC puts up a hand. "If that's true, why weren't you arrested?"

Bunny shoves hands in his pockets and looks at the floor. "Wasn't a knife. Just a pencil."

"Is that so?" says TC. "Have a good reason?" Eyes down, Bunny nods. "Figures," TC chuckles. "Just some high school hijinks. Come-on, everybody." He pats little Amy on the head and points toward the dining table. "I'm hungry."

TC claims the chair at the head as Bridget loads a platter with fried chicken and pulls biscuits out of the oven. TC gestures to the chair on his immediate right. "Why don't you sit here, Bunny?"

He obediently takes the space as Meredith and little Amy eye him like a coiled snake and quickly move across the table. Jodie, left with the space next to Bunny, moves her chair away. She notices her father's look and makes an elaborate show of scooting all the way to the corner. Satisfied, she plops in her seat and breathes out heavily. "What? Who knows if he brought a pencil with him?"

As the food makes it around the table, Meredith chimes in, "So, what's with the bundle of sticks outside?"

"Probably some type of weird voodoo curse he's putting on our house," Jodie snaps, making Amy giggle and almost choke on a mouthful of tea.

"I make arrows out of 'em," Bunny says.

"Arrows? What?" Meredith says. "Why?"

"For my bow," he says and demonstrates with an imaginary draw.

"Don't they sell those?" Meredith stares, but Bunny, busy with a big bite of chicken, only nods.

"You seem to have a thing for sharp, pointy sticks," says Jodie.

"So, Bunny," TC says, ignoring the snark from his daughters. "You're out of school for a few days?"

"Until next Wednesday."

"You like to make some money while you're on vacation?"

Jodie grunts and drops her fork clanging to her plate. "Dad?"

Bunny gulps down a mouthful of mashed potatoes. "Money?"

"You know, a little cash for arrows or whatever."

"Sure... guess so."

"The feed mill in town where I'm a part owner can use help unloading grain trucks. It's hot, dirty work, but since you're not busy, what do you think?"

"So, Dad," interrupts Jodie, "if I do something bad enough to be expelled, you'll offer me a job?" She glares.

"Depends," says TC.

"On what?"

"Right now, your mouth is about to over-load your ass, so rein that in." Her dad's cocky grin says *try me*, but his icy-blue stare sends the no-shit warning. Turning his attention back to Bunny, he adds, "I can give you a ride to the mill tomorrow. Eight o'clock work for you?"

Bridget passes between them with a basket of biscuits fresh from the oven. She offers the hot bread to Bunny, who helps himself, taking one off the top. "Here, have another," she says, placing a second on his plate. "Looks like we need to put some meat on those bones."

Bunny stops chewing, swallows, and looks up into Bridget's face. "Best food I've ever had."

Her soft, grey eyes turn down at the corners, and her bottom lip quivers. She stares at him for a beat, then sucks in a breath, her cheeks a patchy red. "Oh my, that's quite a claim," she gushes. Her voice breaks, lips straining a smile.

"Thank you for having me," he adds, hoping to ease her discomfort from the attention.

Bridget, standing close, gets a reaction from TC. He wrinkles his nose and narrows his eyes, looking confused. "That smell? Perfume? Where did you get that?"

"Do you like it? Bunny gave it to me."

"Why are you giving my mother perfume, weirdo?" Jodie lets the caustic words slip, but a threatening look from her father causes a sudden interest in the chicken leg on her plate.

"I think it's sweet," Bridget says. "Oh, TC, please drop by the hospital tomorrow before you come home. You know, so Bunny can see his mom."

seven

"Make sure you throw that bottle of perfume away," TC demands. It'd been almost seventeen years, but it all came back last night when he'd smelled that scent. Every disturbing memory taunted him. The old gal just refused to let go.

"But why?" Bridget protests. "Bunny was just trying to bring something. Not like he had many choices at his house."

"Don't care, get rid of it." TC grabs his Stetson and positions it squarely, then checks his image in the hall mirror on the way out. He'd promised to pick up Bunny this morning, and he hurries to the yard to cut a few blooms for his day plans. As he turns onto the lane to the Potts place, he checks the time and breathes, "This kid better not make me late."

TC rolls to a stop in front of Bunny's house. "Well, I be damned, he's outside."

"Good morning, young man," he says as Bunny climbs in. "Dressed and ready—I like that."

"Got dressed last night."

TC spins the wheel with one hand and gives Bunny a side-eye look. Wrinkled T-shirt and jeans. Yep, looks like it. Really a great way to dress for a job interview. He sees Bunny checking out the flowers in the seat. "Sale day. I treat the office ladies," TC says. "You got a pair of work gloves?"

"No sir."

"Well, you're gonna need 'em. Look in that glove pocket there. Should be something that'll fit."

Bunny pulls out several, tries them, and seems happy with a tan leather pair. "You get plenty to eat last night?" TC asks, smiling.

"Oh, yes, sir. Your wife is a great cook."

"That she is. That she is."

On the way, they pass green fields with thick rows of cut grass waiting for a baler to turn it into hay. A group of speckled, red-and-white steers gather under a shady tree near the highway. Their long horns make a signature silhouette, their tails busy swishing flies. A pond brims with rainwater, reflecting a mirror image of willow trees near the bank.

"Say, Bunny, you like your name?" TC asks.

"Truth? I hate it. A nurse named me."

"Yeah, I know the story." TC stops at that, but immediately regrets doing so. Bunny's shock is obvious when he turns in the seat to stare at him. "She sure didn't do you any favors with that one," TC says, making a face. "I was thinking, you need an edge."

"A what?"

"An edge, a better name." TC steals a glance from the road to judge the boy's reaction. Bunny's brows like house-tops, his mouth pulls together in thought. "You know, something short like BB, or even Red, or Slim."

"Really?" Bunny smiles at the idea.

"I knew a guy in school we called Red. I think his real name was Robin." TC smirks, letting a laugh slip out. "That old boy was one tough son of a bitch."

"Red... you think so?" Bunny's eyes are big, his voice full of hope.

"Hey, you got the hair."

Getting into Willow Creek, TC winds through the streets to the feed mill. He bounces over railroad tracks and turns into a gravel lot with a sizable white building and loading docks out front. Already, there are three eighteen-wheelers in line at the back of the property. Silver silos of varying heights point like rockets above the roofline. "Going to be busy today." TC smiles and glides the truck under a tree to park. "Come on," he says. "I'll introduce you to Laguin. He runs things around here."

They start across the dusty lot to the building, and Bunny stops walking. "What if he doesn't want me? Maybe I'm not strong enough?"

Truth is, the kid does look scrawny, making TC wonder how he'll hold up.

"I'm the one that hired Laguin. Don't worry, he'll listen to me." TC claps Bunny on the shoulder, flinching at the feel of bone under his fingertips.

Inside the front door, two men in caps and dust-covered work boots lean against an L-shaped counter, talking to a lady on the other side. She looks bored, fanning her face with a notepad. The walls of the room are covered in pegboard displays of worm medicines, fly spray, and dehorn tools for sale. A swinging set of half doors separates the business space from the customer area. TC strides through the lobby and into the office division, motioning for Bunny to follow. Down a short hallway, he raps on a closed door. Not waiting for a response, TC pushes it open. A round man in a ball cap and black-framed glasses sits behind a desk with a phone to his ear. He smiles at TC, pointing to the empty chairs. When the call ends, he leans over, extending his hand. "TC, what's shaking, brother?"

"Brought you a worker for the trucks. This is Red Potts. He can help out the next few days."

"Red, huh?" Laguin smiles. "That works. I've got trucks waiting right now."

The three of them walk out the back and step down to a sizable concrete pad, their boots crunching against fine grains of ground corn and specks of red milo blown over the surface. Bunny notices a familiar sweet scent on the air and looks around for the source. "What's that smell?"

"Molasses," says Laguin. "That vat is full." He points to a dark metal tower.

"You just got that tanker delivery yesterday, right?" TC says.

Laguin nods, continuing his answer to Bunny's question. "We mix it with the cattle feed. Cows think it's lip-smacking good." The round man chuckles, his belly bouncing. The cone-shaped depression in the middle of the pad has a large auger positioned at the bottom. A pipe rises at a steep angle above the silos where it branches like spider legs to each of the silver bullets packed with grain. "Grab a shovel while I get this trucker to move up," Laguin says.

"Diggers over there." TC points to a group of shovels in varying sizes with handles propped against the wall. "Better put those gloves on." Bunny seems unsure but does as he's told without questions. It's so enjoyable being around a polite and appreciative teenager that TC makes a mental note to beat his own kids when he gets home.

The driver in the sleeper is jarred awake as Laguin raps on his door yelling, "Ready to unload."

"Looks like you're working solo, at least for now," says TC. "See that ladder on the trailer side? Soon as this driver gets the tarp off, you climb up with your shovel and push the corn down the center opening where the auger will take it to the bin."

Bunny gets busy shoveling, and TC drives away. He's in a hurry to get to Darleen's. Her husband is working in another county this week and should be gone until at least six o'clock. For the life of him, he can't imagine why such a bubbly, sexy girl agreed to marry that sour-faced guy. No matter. The cockeyed match had worked out well for TC. Wednesday is Darleen's day off from her job behind the counter at the feed mill. On most of her free days, she and TC do things together that their spouses would never approve.

The tiny house on the outskirts of town hides in the shade of a massive pecan tree. The trunk is so thick, two people can join hands and still not reach around it. TC knows. He and Darleen had tried once after finishing too many beers. But mostly, they stay inside and away from prying eyes. Careful to park in the back, TC makes sure his truck is hidden from the road.

"Well, hello there, good-looking." He smiles as Darleen opens the back door.

"Back at you, cowboy," she coos. The pretty dark-haired woman is a good ten years younger than TC. Today she wears a T-shirt that strains across a prominent set of breasts with noticeably erect nipples.

"My, my," he says, handing her the fragrant blooms. Darleen brings them to her nose before rolling her eyes up to make sure she has his full attention, then spins to flash a healthy, mostly exposed backside. She giggles and pulls away as TC charges after her.

Following her through the house, TC carefully checks the blinds on each window. "What took you so long?" Darleen asks, posing on the edge of the bed. She crosses her arms and pulls the T-shirt over her head.

"I had to help a neighbor kid."

"Since when are you a do-gooder, Mister Conway?"

"Well, since I realized this boy needs help, and I sorta feel obligated."

eight

"Hey, Red! Get your skinny keister on top of that milo wagon," Dale barks. The muscular guy and his buddy, Nolan, had showed up about halfway through the unloading of the corn that morning. When the first truck was empty, Bunny went inside. He's at the water fountain when Dale's demand about the second trailer floods in from the back door.

Laguin's head pops out of his office like a groundhog in February. "Let those guys handle it for a bit," he says. "You take fifteen."

When Bunny returns outside, an airborne shovel sails from the top of the trailer, just missing his head, bouncing at his feet. "Took you long enough. Better start shitting faster." Dale smirks down at him.

Bunny pulls on his work gloves and grabs the handle from the ground. He climbs the ladder, and Dale passes him at the top, bumping his shoulder to make a fast exit. "Guess we're gonna have to call you Slow Shit," he grins.

Watching Dale crab down the ladder, Bunny yells after him. "And I'll call you Late Shit." He chuckles, feeling satisfied. This isn't so bad. Unloading the trucks isn't difficult. He doesn't have to put any thought into the task of pushing grain to the middle of the trailer.

But the spot on top is hot and extremely dusty. The more grain unloaded with the level going lower, the hotter it gets, since no air blows down inside the four walls of the trailer. Bunny understands, since he's the new guy, Dale and Nolan are claiming the more desirable positions at the bottom near the auger where a cool breeze can make a big difference.

He works steadily through the morning and, as the last of the milo is scraped from the corners, he climbs down the ladder, finding himself alone. Dale and Nolan have abandoned their shovels on the grass, and grain is heaped into neglected piles around the auger. Bunny checks the cab, expecting to find a sleeping trucker, but it's vacant.

He wipes his brow on the back of his arm and squints up at the sun blazing straight overhead. Back inside, Bunny stops by the water fountain, and since the door is open, he looks in Laguin's office. It's dark and empty as well. Except for everything being unlocked, he's beginning to think the mill closed early and nobody told him. He walks to the front lobby where the counter lady sits comfortably in a chair. Eyes closed, her double chin rests against sizable breasts. She breathes slowly. Her lips pull in, then push out in a rhythm.

Besides the sleeping lady, there's no one around. The clock on the wall shows 12:15. Bunny checks out front, but when he pushes the door open, the bell jingles and the napping lady's head pops up just above the counter. "Good afternoon," she says with manufactured enthusiasm, then clears her throat.

"Oh, I'm sorry. Didn't mean to wake you," Bunny stutters.

"Wake me, what? How can I help you today?"

"It's me. B—uh, Red. I work here. Just started today."

"Well, why aren't you at lunch, like everybody else?"

"I didn't know. Maybe TC is coming to pick me up?"

"TC, you say?"

"Yes, ma'am. He brought me."

"Well, honey, you won't see that man until closing time, maybe five o'clock or so. Go on now and take your lunch break and stop bothering me." Bunny shuffles past her and starts down the hall, thinking he'll wait outside on the docks. "Wait a minute," she calls after him. "What's your name? Red? Come here, son."

Bunny turns back, taking a few steps toward her. "I'm Jean, but you can call me Momma J, like all these guys do. You bring anything to eat for lunch, baby?" He shakes his head, studying the floor. "That's what I thought. That damn TC." She shakes her head then groans, bending to retrieve her purse. Then she rummages inside for a minute and pulls out a clear bag she pushes toward him. "Here you go, baby. Egg salad sandwich and a couple of deviled eggs. My hens are busy these days." She smiles, revealing a dark gap on the bottom.

"Oh, but isn't this your lunch? TC will probably bring me something."

"Baby, TC didn't get that name for nothing. Tom Cat Conway is busy, probably trying to pollinate every flower in the garden, so you best eat the food." She takes his hand and closes it around the bag. "As you can see, I've not missed many meals in my lifetime." Her eyes crinkle. "Now do me a solid since I fed you. My little nap behind the counter, just between you and me, right?"

Bunny stares into her soft, brown eyes with his mouth open. It feels like he just took a sucker punch. "Oh, sorry," she says. "Did I pop your TC hero bubble? Well, never you mind what a silly old woman has to say, just idle chatter." She spins him by the shoulders and gives a gentle push toward the back. "Now, take your lunch, baby, 'cause I see another truck a-waiting."

Bunny eats outside on the loading dock. He's grateful for the sandwich but troubled by what Jean said. Bridget Conway deserves better, and maybe she already knows. She has those eyes, the kind that feel like she can see inside, straight into your soul. His thoughts drift to Raquel, and he longs for her to see him—*really* see him. From nowhere, the haunting memory of the last time with Raquel rushes back. The way she looked at him that day in the lunchroom. Her eyes were full of terror, like he was a monster.

When Dale and Nolan reappear, they go to work pushing the

neglected pile of milo down the auger. The next trucker revs his engine impatiently as Bunny climbs the ladder of the silo to attach the diverter feed pipe. When the tarp comes off the trailer, Bunny is unsure what he's looking at. "What's this stuff?" he shouts below.

"Ain't you never seen cottonseed, you stupid hayseed?" Dale smirks, his lip distorted with a wad of fresh snuff.

The dark kernels covered in bits of wispy white cling together in wads. When Bunny steps inside the trailer, the pointed ends jab through his jeans and find a way inside his pant legs and down his boots. The loose bits of white float skyward, tickling his nose, making him sneeze. Unloading the stuff is like shoveling heavy cotton balls. Bunny realizes he can use the shovel like a pan and, with his body weight, press down to force the seed through the opening at the bottom. Twice, clogs make them stop and disassemble the pipe to clear the obstruction.

The third time the motor seizes, Dale pushes the stop button beside the auger. "Get down here and help us, Red! I damn sure don't plan to be here all night!" he screams.

While Bunny climbs down the ladder, Nolan fetches tools and Dale goes inside for water. Bunny looks over his shoulder as Nolan backs out the screws to open the pipe and expose the blade. Since he's only watching, Bunny takes the opportunity to ease his foot pain. Dale steps back on the pad just as he empties half a boot of torturing kernels onto the concrete. "Hey, dumb shit! Don't—" Dale screams, charging across at Bunny. The leather sole of his boot sliding on the seed, Dale flies across the cement like a skater on ice. An Olympian on one leg, he sails, arms back, body rushing forward, a helpless rag doll jerked on a string. Headfirst he goes into the pit. Forehead cracking against the power button, Dale is knocked senseless. His right-hand jams inside the newly powered-on blade of the auger.

After the ambulance hauls Dale to the hospital, Nolan never says a word, just gets in his truck and drives away. The pit sits idle, and Bunny stands like a statue beside the hole, watching flies gather by the carload. The impatient trucker with half a load still on his trailer walks up, looking for answers. "What do you think, Red? Can we get this done?"

Staring into the concrete bowl of blood-swollen cottonseed, Bunny's voice sounds mechanical. "Reminds you of cherry pie, don't it?"

After the accident, Laguin makes calls for more help, and Red, now in charge, sends two young boys up the ladder to work inside the trailer. He almost steps on a mangled piece of finger before picking up the bloody digit that'd landed ten feet away. Bunny wraps it in wet paper and takes it to the break room refrigerator. When the truck is finally empty, Laguin meets Bunny at the water fountain. "You sure earned your money today, Red." He chuckles. Soaked in sweaty fuzz and covered in scratches, Bunny looks like he's been in a cage fight. "Boy, I appreciate you keeping after it today. Those other two guys..." He shakes his head. "Can I count on you for tomorrow?"

After collecting his gruesome discovery from the refrigerator, Bunny finds TC up front, talking to Jean. Amused by his jokes, she blots at laugh-tears, hanging on every word. You would think this guy is Captain America instead of just a cheating husband. "Hey, Red, getting the lowdown on all the excitement." TC smiles. Disgusted by how chummy the two are, Bunny only nods and follows TC out to the truck. "You wanna stop by the hospital, see your mom?" TC asks.

"Guess I better," Bunny says. "I can check on Dale, too. Got something belongs to him."

nine

Bunny is silent on the ride to the hospital. He downs two cups of cold water from TC's stash in the five-gallon cooler that claims space in floorboard, but never says a thing. Hard to tell if he's in shock about the accident or pissed about something. Those guys at the mill probably gave him a hard time, *pay your dues* sort of stuff. And that Dale who got his hand in the auger—that kid's always been a smartass.

They park at the hospital, and TC breaks the silence. "So, you want to come back to the mill tomorrow?"

Bunny nods. "Laguin asked me."

"That's great." TC smiles. "Means you did well, even with all the excitement today."

"Speaking of that..." Bunny pulls a small package from his shirt pocket. "I found this." He peels back layers of damp paper, revealing about two inches of what looks like a human finger. A stark white bone juts from the ragged, dark-purple flesh, the remainder of the skin, pale and looking plastic, almost like a prop from the Halloween bargain rack.

"Is that ... Dale's?" TC leans away, screwing up his face.

"Think they can use it?"

"Don't know. Let's get over to Emergency with that. Come on, I'll go with you," TC says and falls into a jog with Bunny across the street. When they reach the revolving door at the visitor entrance, he goes first while Bunny hesitates. Finding himself alone on the other side, TC looks back through the glass at a wide-eyed Bunny in a hypnotic trance. His head shifts from left to right as the door spins past his face like he's watching a tennis match. TC ducks out the traditional door to the side, leans around, and yells, "Hey, over here!"

They follow the signs and hurry down the hall toward Emergency. Boot heels thudding against the polished floor, Bunny interrupts the rhythm. "I hate the smell in here."

TC shrugs, "Normal hospital air. Makes you want to vomit."

The desk attendant tells them Dale is still in the operating room, but audibly gasps when Bunny presents the bloody nail with a couple of inches of meat still attached. They summon a nurse who takes the finger and hustles it inside.

Together, they watch as the doors swing closed before turning back toward the patient rooms. "Where did you find that?" says TC.

"Loading dock. You think they can sew it back on?"

"Maybe, hopefully, we'll see." Spying the gift shop on the way, TC stops and pulls several bills from his wallet, then extends them toward Bunny. "Here you go. Why don't you go in there and pick your mother out something." Bunny's face full of questions, his feet seem stalled in cement. "You know, like flowers or a balloon, something. Makes sick people feel better." TC smiles.

"Really?" Bunny looks stunned, just staring at the crumpled bills in his hand.

"Yeah, you know what she likes." TC pushes Bunny toward the shop. "Go look around."

"But?" Bunny waves the fist of money.

"Don't worry. You pay me back on Friday when you get paid."

TC takes a seat to wait outside the glass enclosure and smiles to himself, thinking about his day with Darleen. Eyeing the available phone on the wall, he uses the time to give her a call. Darleen's sweet voice flows like honey through the phone.

"Hey, you won't believe what happened," says TC. "Dale fell into the auger and messed up his hand."

"You're kidding? How bad?"

"Oh, it's bad, Dimples. Parts of that boy's fingers, they were picking 'em up like Easter eggs."

"Oh, my god!"

"I'm at the hospital now."

"TC, why do you call me Dimples? I don't have dimples."

"How do you know?" He laughs. "Did ya' have a good day?"

"Mmmm... I love my days off."

"I'd like to put in a request right now for a do-over."

"Keeping it warm, cowboy," she giggles.

TC cuts it short when Bunny emerges from the shop with something white and fluffy. A stuffed kitten wearing a red collar and bell seems very at home in his arms. "Nan will love this!" The boy's face is suddenly full of teeth. TC does a double take. "Thank you," Bunny's voice bubbles. He extends his hand, looking TC in the eye.

Touched by the display of sudden joy from Bunny being able to buy his mother a gift, TC pumps his hand and pats him on the back. "Sounds good. I need to run an errand while you visit your mom. Back in half an hour. Okay?"

Bunny's excitement disappears. He turns away, glaring at TC out of the corner of his eye. "Errand?" He smirks and shakes his head. "Is that what you're calling it?" Abruptly, he spins on his heel and strides down the corridor, leaving TC to wonder if it's just a case of teenage hormones. Old Jean at the mill had really lit into him about Red and lunch, or lack of, today. "That kid is so skinny, if you blew your nose, you might put him into next week," she had said. Maybe the boy has worms.

～

When TC returns to the hospital, he parks near the door so Bunny can see the truck. He listens to the last of a song on the radio and thinks about the weird run-in he'd just had with Cathy at the grocery store. It had been years since they'd enjoyed each other's company, and today she looked so different. TC couldn't recognize the happy young girl he'd once known. He looks out the window and mulls over the painful memory of the last time they were together. He'd grown tired of her possessiveness and made it clear she would not be in his future. Oh, she made threats, but TC had long ago insulated himself against that kind of thing. He and Bridget had had a talk the night before their wedding. He'd explained to Bridget that women would be jealous that she was Mrs. Conway, and a jealous woman might say anything. Through the years, he'd heard the rumors that circulated, but he'd made sure his wife knew just how to step over the bullshit.

TC peeks inside the brown bag on the seat next to him. Jars of peanut butter and jelly, a package of bologna, and a loaf of bread should hold Bunny at lunch for a few days. He's no cook like Bridget but figures the boy can throw a sandwich together. Growing impatient, TC retrieves his pocket watch to check the time. "Come on, Red." He exhales. "I'm ready to get home."

He clicks off the radio and drums his fingers against the wheel as a silent ambulance rolls into the lot. "All quiet. Jesus. Someone must have died," he says to his own image as he adjusts his hat in the rearview. He watches the attendants unload a covered stretcher and wheel it through the electric doors. "That's what that damn hospital smell is, death." TC climbs out, slamming the truck door. "I hate this place," he says. "Where is that kid?"

A young blond girl at the front desk rolls deep, chocolate eyes up to stare at the cowboy leaning against her desk. "Nan Potts' room, please," he says.

She directs her attention to a log book as TC's eyes travel to the bulging black lace peeking out of her low-cut neckline. "Room 109."

Her melodic voice is almost song-like. TC pushes his hat back and leans forward, balancing on elbows to glance over the edge of the desk. On the other side, a trim waist and short skirt look promising.

"So, you been here all day?" He flashes a smile.

"Yes." She sighs. "Almost time to get off."

"*Get off*... mmmm... promises, promises." TC chuckles, making the cute girl blush. "So, working girl? You, ever get a *day* off?"

Surprised, the smile dries on her lips. She clears her throat and holds up a finger to take a sip of water before answering. "Tuesdays... free every Tuesday."

"Tuesdays, huh?" TC grins and lifts a card from her desk, eyeing the name. "Might be worth moving some things around... Shelly." He slips the information into his shirt pocket before tipping his hat. "I'm TC." He smirks and strides away in search of room 109. He rounds the corner and confirms he's in the right place, seeing Nan Potts scrawled on the paper attached outside the room. The door's slightly ajar, so he pushes it halfway, hoping to motion Bunny it's time to go. There's the usual inside: a bed by the window, a cabinet, an empty chair. Nan's massive body fills the standard-issue hospital rack, but luckily her head is turned away, facing the window, and TC breathes a thankful sigh. The stuffed white cat rests beside her. On the floor curled in a fetal ball, Bunny is fast asleep.

TC creeps across the room and nudges Bunny with the side of his boot. "Hey, Red," he whispers, making Nan moan and shift. She turns her head on the pillow, her eyes fly open, and TC sucks in a breath, flinching under her deadly stare. The whites of her eyes strain from the sockets wedged above bloated, purple cheeks. A growl rolls from lips pulled taut as a slingshot. She lets fly a thunderous shriek that bounces off the wall, threatening to implode the room. Bunny jerks awake. His arms fly up, shielding his head. Wild-eyed, he gasps and cringes away from the excruciating rant. Scuttling on all fours, he huddles behind the nearest cover, TC's legs. Nan's screams come in bursts as she sails the TV remote, half a pitcher of water, and then the stuffed kitten across the room. With nothing left to throw, her body sags, one arm extended from the bed. She pants with exhaustion. The raspy breaths rattle inside her chest as she heaves, gathering strength for another round. A guttural moan starts small then winds with momentum as Nan's eyes laser focus on TC.

ten

TC DROPS Bunny off at his house, hands him the grocery bag, and says the first words he's uttered the entire trip. "Make lunch for tomorrow. See you at eight." Bunny takes the brown sack into the house and smiles, thinking about the opportunity to bring Momma J one of his sandwiches. He feels a little guilty that TC has to drive him back and forth and thinks about the blue car parked in the weeds out front. Nan's not here to squash his idea. Bunny finds the car keys in his mom's nightstand. Maybe he can get the old girl started.

Bunny is tinkering with the engine and doesn't see Jodie roll to a stop in front of the house. When she slams the car door, he jumps, banging his head against the hood.

She stands there, covered dish in her hand, as several feral cats clamber around her feet. Spurred by the sudden smell of food, the herd rushes toward the girl. Bunny rubs his head and peeks around the raised metal as Jodie kicks at the swarm clawing up her legs like the bark of a tree. "Hey, loser, get your mangy animals—off!" she screams.

Bending low, Bunny runs toward them, swinging a wrench. "Yaaaaal, yaaaal!" he bellows, and the cats jump and scatter.

"Wow, they're scared of you." Jodie grins. "Those little shits clawed my legs good." She rubs at her shins.

"Sorry, they're just hungry."

"Why don't you feed them?"

"Uh... trying to make them leave."

"What, so you just starve 'em, then?" Jodie makes a face.

Bunny nods and looks away, squirming in her disapproval. He nervously fiddles with the tool he's holding and wishes he'd taken the time to shower when he got home. Bunny tries not to look at the girl's tan legs in blue gym shorts or the way her shiny hair brushes against her shoulders. An awkward silence falls over the yard. Jodie stands her ground, insisting on an explanation. Her eyes shielded by dark shades provide an unfair advantage. She glares at Bunny, but he offers nothing. Bored with the standoff, she thrusts the covered dish forward. "Mom made me bring this." She drops her gaze to the ground, refusing to look at him now.

Bunny reaches for the food, watching Jodie flinch at the oily black under his nails. "Enchiladas," she snaps, filling in the unspoken question. "Mexican food Wednesday." She raises her hands, shaking her fingers. "Whoop... pee." She drags out the word, puffs her cheeks, and bugs her eyes. "Some type of weird Conway law." Her candor creates a smile he hides behind his hand.

"I... like enchiladas." Bunny struggles to fill the conversation, but it's a challenge to stand five feet from a girl that hates his guts. "Sometimes they have them in the lunchroom."

"Those nasty school things could never be called enchiladas. Those are more like Taco Bell rejects. Wait until you taste my mom's. You'll feel like slapping those lunch ladies for food abuse."

Bunny lifts the lid of the glass pan. Inside, six perfectly rolled enchiladas nestle side by side, bathed in red sauce and topped with cheese. The spicy smell rushes out, making his mouth water. He catches himself just before plunging in a hand to bring the intoxicating goodness to his lips. "Don't worry, I didn't spit in there." Jodie smirks.

"Wouldn't be surprised," he answers flatly, replacing the lid. "Your mom..." He shakes his head, his voice gone soft. He stops before making a fool of himself. With some of the cats still circling, Bunny puts the still-warm dish inside the Chevy and shuts the door.

"You fixing it?" Jodie points to the raised hood.

"Trying," he stammers. "Don't really know how."

"How long since you drove it?"

"A few weeks maybe. Nan wouldn't... she didn't..." Bunny shakes his head.

"Mmmm, just wondered. You were in my driver's ed class, right?"

"Never got to the DMV."

"That's sad. Worst part of that is standing in line."

"It costs, right?" Bunny says, anxious for an answer.

"Few bucks." She shrugs. "Mind if I look?" Jodie walks closer. "I've got Algebra II homework, so I'm in no hurry."

"Your family waiting dinner for you?"

"Nah, Dad's in a crabby mood. He'll shower and get a beer first." She moves to the front of the car and leans in to look. "Your battery, idiot. All this corrosion on the post." Bunny balances on elbows, watching Jodie wiggle the connections.

"So... how do you know cars?" Bunny asks slowly.

"Dad. He wanted a son, but guess I'm the next best thing." She looks up, stares across the yard, and seems to be deep in thought. "Hate to ask since you have a thing for pointed objects, but, you got a knife?" Bunny bends, rummaging in his collection of rusted odds and ends he'd brought from the house.

Eyeing the box on the ground with the metal handle attached to the front, Jodie taps the wood with her sneaker. "Is this a drawer?"

"Kitchen junk drawer," Bunny says. The scrutiny of her blank expression begs for more. "What? You don't have one?"

"Mom wouldn't allow that crap in her kitchen."

"Yeah, but she probably has cooking stuff."

"Don't you?"

"Not really."

"Screwdriver," she says, peeking into the mishmash. "Slot—got one of those in here?"

"Maybe." He locates the knife first and holds it out. "You going to stab me?"

"Hey, I'm not the one that got expelled."

Finding a screwdriver with a chipped edge, he pushes the handle to Jodie. "Afraid it's seen better days."

She waves him off. "No, no... your job, Potts. Loosen those brackets on the post. Don't get that white stuff on you. It'll burn."

Bunny struggles to position the tool into the slot.

"How's your mom? You see her today?"

The question takes him out of concentration, and Bunny stops working. "We saw her."

"We? Did Dad visit, too?"

"I fell asleep. He came to get me."

"Well, that explains it. Dad's shitty mood, that is."

Bunny shrugs. "She can't talk. Her legs don't work. And today, she was really mad."

"Why?"

"It's weird. She saw your dad and started screaming."

"Dad says she's crazy." Jodie widens her eyes and cocks her head, her intense stare boring into Bunny's brain.

"You afraid that'll rub off on me?" he says.

"Mmmmm... Speaking of crazy, I saw Raquel today." The tone of Jodie's voice is suddenly upbeat. Raquel, that's the name that gets his full attention. Bunny stops turning the screw, craving more. "So, what's the deal, Potts? You like her, right?"

Pretty obvious, he'd say, since the lunchroom thing, but Bunny honors the question with an affirmative nod. "Not sure she'll ever talk to me again," he stammers.

"One thing'd probably help—get this car running." She taps the fender with the folded knife. "Everybody hates the bus. Offer her a ride, bet she'll give you another chance." Jodie grins.

"Really?" Bunny asks. He suddenly feels light-headed, seduced by the small hope that Raquel might respond.

"Sure. But seriously, you need to hurry up there." Jodie points at the battery, twirling her finger. "I gotta get back."

He gets busy and loosens the clamps as Jodie snaps open the pocketknife blade. "We need to get the corrosion off." She leans in, scraping around the post to remove the white crust. "Okay, put those clamps back on and tighten the screws, just to snug." While Bunny works, she drives Bridget's station wagon close, opens the hood, and brings out a set of jumper cables.

Amazed, Bunny watches while Jodie clamps the red and black bites on the battery posts from her car to his. She starts her mother's car and lets it run for a moment. "Now try it," she yells over the noise and motions turning a key. The Chevy engine clicks, and when he tries it a second time, the starter catches and cranks. Jodie smiles and flashes him a thumbs up through the windshield. "Let it run a while," she instructs.

"Wow!" Bunny climbs out of the car, a big smile across his face. Unable to hide his amazement, he shouts, "Thank you!" and makes a theatrical bow.

"That's nothing." Jodie pushes her lips together. She glances up, then quickly looks away, color creeping into her cheeks. "You should think about a new battery—soon." She rolls the cables, returns them to the back of the wagon, and stops a few feet away. "Just do me a favor, Potts. Don't go blabbing about this."

Bunny's smile evaporates. He hooks thumbs in his pockets and looks at the ground. Her request is very clear. "Don't worry," he says, looking her in the eye. "You don't have to talk to me at school."

She climbs in and lowers the window. "See ya, Potts." Jodie gives a half-hearted wave in his direction.

"Tell your mom thanks," Bunny says. "And just so you know... my friends call me Red."

eleven

It's lunchtime and the two of them are the only souls left at the mill. Behind the counter, Momma J pats the stool beside her own chair. "Take a load off, Red."

The odd pair, more like grandmother and grandson, seem to have adopted each other as acceptable noon-time buddies. "Let all them other fools spend half-a-day's wage at the sandwich shop. You and me, Red, we're sacking our money back for the hard times," Momma J says, her watery eyes twinkling. Bunny can't imagine what Momma J thinks hard times are, but he knows where his life has been. Surely it can't get harder than that.

"You drive yourself in today?" Momma J says.

"TC's daughter, Jodie, helped me jump the car off last night."

"Your own wheels. That's good. Stay out of that mess. That TC is like a ticking bomb." She shakes her head and straightens her glasses. "Ready for some lunchtime poker?" She chuckles. "What's your opening bid? Show me what you got, Red."

"I'll open with one fresh, hand-crafted peanut butter and jelly sandwich," Bunny says, setting a plastic-wrapped package on the table between them.

"I'll see your PB&J and raise you two hard-boiled eggs." She cackles and holds up a clear bag, jiggling it like part of the male genitalia.

"I'll see your huevos." Bunny grins. "And raise with a package of oatmeal cream pies."

"Oooooh, I love those things. You know my soft spot. Okay kid, you got me. Take your pick."

Bunny snatches the eggs, happy to give Momma J the opportunity for the treat she enjoys. She tears the cellophane off the soft cookies, brings the package to her nose, and inhales deeply. "Brown sugar and molasses." She smacks her lips. "Been a long time, Red, long time." She leans back in her chair, chewing slowly. "Did I ever tell you about that fool possum that got caught in my crepe myrtle?"

"No, ma'am." Bunny smiles and bites into an egg.

"Those blame varmints love the blooms on my myrtle bush. They think they're some kind of candy."

The bell attached to the front door jingles. "Damn," Momma J says under her breath, rocking forward to stand.

"Jean, oh thank goodness." A familiar voice floats over the tall counter where Bunny is hidden from view. "I thought everyone was gone. Looking for Bunny. He's working today, right?" Bunny jumps up, making himself visible.

"I'm here." Eyes wide, he swallows, staring across at Bridget. Her face blotchy, her brows knitted, she rolls a tattered tissue between her fingers.

"Who the hell is Bunny?" Momma J blinks at him.

"Me," he says softly and touches her arm.

"You rode in with TC?" Bridget asks, gripping the edge of the counter so hard her knuckles are white.

"Well... no... today, I drove Nan's car."

Bridget releases her grip but, noticing the shake in her hands, she plants them flat against the counter. "I've got to find my husband. Jodie... my baby." Her voice cracks and she forces the words. "An accident..." She swipes at her eyes, sniffing. "I've been to the auction barn, the bank, and even Jerry's Burgers." She takes a breath, and the tears begin a freefall.

"Jodie? What?" The thin sound of Bunny's words is foreign even to his own ears.

"Street racing," she huffs before a gut-wrenching wail makes her face fold like a sock puppet.

Jean reaches across the counter, taking Bridget's arms. "Oh, baby girl," she coos, clutching her as Bunny races around the counter.

"Where is she?" he says. "Where is Jodie?"

Bridget comes up for air, blubbering, "Hospital, broken bones, maybe internal... sorry... sorry. I've got to get back. Please tell TC if he shows." She hurries out the door, taking the oxygen in the room with her. The vacuum of her sudden departure is so painful, Bunny charges for the door.

"Miss Bridget..." She looks over her shoulder. "Please let me go with you."

"No, no, Bunny. There's nothing you can do. Maybe TC will show and you or Jean can tell him. That'll be a big help." She sucks in a breath. "I need to get back." Bridget spins on her heel, running toward her vehicle. Helpless, Bunny squints into the sun overhead, painful and unforgiving. Her station wagon spins away, making the white dust of the lot billow, then spiral skyward, stinging his eyes and sifting in his teeth.

His appetite gone, Bunny walks back to the unloading dock. He doesn't feel like facing Momma J right now. No doubt she'll have plenty to say, but if he can't help Miss Bridget, then he'd rather be alone. His mind running ahead, a million questions scream at him. Street racing—Bunny knows those guys. A group of motor heads whose only reason for school is showing off to a ready audience. He thinks of Jodie. Tall and rail thin, she can look him in the eye, which is a little scary. What a great help she'd been with his car battery. He steadies himself, leaning against the cool brick of the building. Head foggy, his stomach churns, burning like it's full of hot peppers. And then there's TC. Bunny closes his eyes and grits his teeth. This guy doesn't deserve his family. The image of Bridget's tear-streaked face, full of pain and doubt, makes a painful stab behind his eyes. Bunny grips his fist and elevates a shovel with a harsh kick. The airborne tool flies and bounces with a clang to the loading dock. He steps down, grabs the innocent grain scoop, and frantically starts on the pile of corn by the auger.

After lunch, the day seems to drag on without end. All afternoon, Bunny shovels and sweats and works to keep his anger under control. During a water break, Bunny touches Momma J on the shoulder. "Did TC come by?" But she just takes off her glasses and shakes her head, cleaning the lenses on her shirttail.

Finished for the day, Bunny can't drive fast enough to the hospital to find out about Jodie. He avoids the revolving door at the entrance, and when he makes the turn to the lobby, there stands TC. Bunny jumps back, almost falling as he scrambles in reverse to the cover of the corner. He creeps forward, peering through the plastic branches of a massive decorative plant. TC leans against the reception desk, talking to someone behind it. His loud voice bounces about the cavernous room. Although the words are unrecognizable, Bunny can make out the highs and lows of a pleasant conversation. The second voice is soft, definitely female. A wheel-chaired man circles wide around Bunny's lookout nest behind the Ficus. The old guy glares as he rolls past, pumping his arms frantically to distance himself.

Bunny resumes his recon position, convinced TC is not just asking for information. His eyes locked on the target, he holds his breath, watching as TC hands a long-stemmed flower over the counter.

"I've got to do something," Bunny whispers. He straightens and starts around the corner to approach. TC, waist deep in his performance, is only a few feet away before he breaks eye contact and looks to his right.

"Well, hey there, Red. Long day at the mill?"

"You could say that," Bunny answers softly. "How long you been here?"

"Few minutes. On the way to check on Dale."

A pretty girl on the other side of the counter busies herself with the white lily. She fills a small vase with water from her drinking her glass and positions the elegant stem in a prominent location on the desk. But TC's cocky stance—his smile, and the casual way his hat is pushed back—says everything. He doesn't know about the accident. He hasn't heard about his daughter.

Miss Bridget can't find him here, not like this. "Hey, mind if I walk down the hall with you to see Dale?" says Bunny.

"Yeah. Okay, I guess. Why don't you head that way? I'll join you in a few."

"Uh..." Bunny stumbles, looking for words. "I... need to talk about something." He focuses on TC's face, hoping to send an urgent message.

"Well, okay," TC says slowly and gives Bunny a sideways look before turning back to the girl. "Don't go anywhere." He pulls out his pocket watch. "I'll be back before you leave."

The two walk several feet away, then Bunny stops to face TC. "I need to tell you, Miss Bridget is here in the hospital." TC's mouth forms an O and his eyes squint at Bunny. "It's Jodie. There was an accident."

TC suddenly snaps to attention. "What do you mean?"

"Miss Bridget came to the mill today, upset, looking for you. She said Jodie was in the hospital." Suddenly pale, TC's face looks like he just brushed against a live wire. Beads of sweat pop across his forehead, and he reaches out, placing a hand on Bunny's shoulder before turning to run toward the Emergency room. Bunny wants to follow, craving information on Jodie, but TC and Miss Bridget need their moment. Oh, he's a snake alright, but his wife needs him, and she shouldn't have to face that... at least... not today.

twelve

THE KNOCK at the door echoes through the house, causing Bunny to almost fall from his perch on the chair in the bathroom. He's struggling to look in the mirror at his new aloha shirt. He peeks around the corner from the hall. Bridget is out front. On the way to the door, all he can see are things in the house left undone—dishes in the sink, a pile of dirty clothes, over-flowing trash. Bunny opens the screen a few inches. "Good morning." She smiles, stifling a giggle behind her hand. "Nice shirt."

He hopes to make the visit short before it gets weird with her standing on the porch. "You think?"

"You're going back to school today?"

He nods. "My sentence is up."

"Can I ask you to collect homework and assignments Jodie has missed? That girl is giving me a hard time. She's miserable and fussy from her injuries, and I'm afraid to take time away searching out all her teachers."

"Sure." Bunny exhales, the small request not at all as challenging as the dragon he was prepared to slay. "We're in the same classes, except for Phys Ed and homeroom."

"That makes me feel so much better." She sighs. "Thank you!"

Bridget makes a step to leave before she remembers something. "Oh, Bunny, come to dinner tonight, unless, you already have plans."

"Plans? What are those?"

Nervous about his clothes, Bunny returns to the mirror. He was swayed at the store with the help of a young girl who told him the blue tones complemented his hair. But he's skeptical, never having owned anything like this—especially something with palm trees and sky-blue water. But the sales clerk had convinced him, saying, "Everyone deserves to own at least one fun garment." When Bunny climbs up to see himself in the bathroom mirror, the surprise reveal makes him boomerang for a second look. The colors of the shirt are happy and fun. Perhaps Raquel will see him the same way.

Excited about his return, Bunny checks his appearance in the rearview again on the drive to school. It's too bad he can't help Laguin today, but suspension days up, it's time for him to get back to class. With all that's happened in the past week—his new job at the mill, the car, and his new nickname—Bunny feels like a changed person. "Make way for the new and improved Red Potts," he shouts into the highway breeze of his open window.

He'd spent all evening cleaning the Chevy for today. His hopes are soaring. Perhaps Raquel will allow him to give her a ride home. He couldn't sleep last night, thinking about seeing her again. The car might be old, but today Bunny has her clean, smelling sweet, and ready for his girl to sit beside him. He glances down at the fluffy white kitten wearing the red collar curled on the seat. Nan didn't want his gift. She made that plain when she hurled it across the room. But the cute stuffed animal just might make Raquel smile.

Bunny arrives at school and rushes to take the last available parking spot in front. His brakes squeal and send an irritating screech across the front yard. Mean Man Watson is there, along with other students, waiting for the second bell. The big man's hand still wrapped in a white bandage, he appears to be holding court among a circle of admirers. The grating sound of the old car hijacks the group's attention, and Watson directs his focus to the blue Chevy.

Bunny slams his door just as Watson yells across the yard, "What do we have here?" Conversations stop, heads turn, the audience is primed and ready. "Hey, loser, where'd you score that piece of shit?"

After only a slight nod in Watson's direction, Bunny walks toward the school.

Less than satisfied, Watson steps over, blocking his path, and with his good hand shoves Bunny's shoulder. "What're you wearing? Hey, look everybody. Bunny Boy thinks he's Jimmy Buffett." Side-stepping Watson, Bunny hurries his walk to the building. But before he can reach the door, Watson yells, "Who said you could leave that pile of crap in front of the school? Littering is against the law, shithead."

Bunny keeps moving. He sees Raquel's bus, the 209, drive up, and he's anxious to catch her before class. Students in the hall glance as he passes and quickly turn their backs to huddle and whisper. But Bunny doesn't care about that. He's looking for Raquel.

Just ahead, Principal Pemberton steps from his office, shoulders back, arms crossed, his imposing silhouette prominent against the high shine of the floor. He glares down the hall like a gunfighter squaring for a fast draw. "Potts, my office. Now." He smirks, seeming to enjoy his authority. Just beyond the human road block is the door Raquel will come through.

"I'll be there, but can I just say hi to a friend? Take a sec?" Bunny says, attempting to slide past Pemberton.

"Now, Potts." He raises his voice and grabs Bunny by the arm. Bunny cranes his neck and stands on tiptoe, searching faces among the sea of bodies. "There she is!" he exclaims, sucking in a breath as Raquel glides through the door, even more beautiful than he'd remembered. The hall is packed with students, but she's the only person Bunny sees. Her attention elsewhere, she hugs books, chatting with someone as fellow bus riders fill the space.

"Please... my friend is right there." Bunny pulls against the principal's grip, struggling to follow Raquel's face in the crowd.

"Not a request, Potts—a requirement." The bold voice makes

heads turn, and Pemberton tugs Bunny, upsetting his balance. He stumbles and almost goes down, catching himself by one hand on the floor. The slow wave of students grinds to a stop from the commotion and stalls to an impasse of rubberneckers. Bunny rights himself and looks up just as Raquel's eyes find his. Happiness pulsing, he can't stop his impulsive smile and small wave in her direction. But Raquel's stagnant expression gives him nothing, and Bunny is hauled away to the principal's office.

"Empty your pockets, Potts," Pemberton demands, pushing Bunny toward a table in the corner. "Book bag, too."

"Just books, a couple of pens, spiral notebook," Bunny says and pours out the contents.

"Pockets," Pemberton demands, the last bell sounding.

Lastly, Bunny pulls out a small roll of cash, and a smooth, speckled rock he likes to carry. "What's with the shirt?" The principal steps closer, eyeing Bunny's palm trees and scrunching up his face. "What kind of garment is this, Potts? This *thing* is out of dress code."

"But... why?"

"No collar, not allowed."

"What about... T-shirts?"

"Is this a T-shirt, smart guy?" He pokes at the items on the table from Bunny's pockets. "Where did this money come from?"

"I got a job."

"Doing what?" Pemberton snorts and snatches the pens and rock from the pile. "No weapons allowed."

"How am I going to take notes in class?"

"Mmmmm... now that's a problem. You should have thought about that before stabbing a football player. Go! Get out of my office!" Done with the shakedown, Pemberton slings open the door. "And, Potts, don't let me catch you wearing that thing again."

Bunny slides the rest of his stuff off the table and into his open bag before slumping down the empty hallway to his first period. He'll have to wait now and hope to catch Raquel at lunch. The math class door is closed. He paces outside, trying to decide what to do.

The consequences for entering late would mean he'll be sent back to the principal's office for a tardy slip. Hardly worthwhile.

Instead, Bunny enters the gym across the hall to wait for class to be over. The empty, cavernous area of hard surfaces and high ceilings reverberates with his steps, and he lazily wanders onto the gleaming wood of the basketball court. With no one to object, he chuckles, enjoying the sin of being on the hallowed game floor in street shoes, and expertly backslides around the center court circle. From the open side door, the grunts and shouts of early practice filter in from the football field. Bunny slips past unnoticed and finds the locker room open. *Ahhhhh, the golden ticket to the in crowd—the football team.*

He pushes the door. He's entering sacred ground. The walls are painted in garish school colors of black and red. Showers to the left, urinals to the right, and, front and center, benches by the athletes' cubbies. Each space is personalized with a shiny number accompanied by a glossy poster of the uniformed player. Most of the images smile, but a few of the faces have menacing looks. Book bags dangle from hooks inside the lockers. Bunny takes a seat on a bench to soak in the naughty feel of his off-limits visit. Spinning around, he fixes his eyes on the space that belongs to number 64, the smirking face of none other than Mean Man Watson.

Bunny paws through Watson's possessions. Unzipping the pouch in his loose leaf, he finds pens, pencils and... what's this? A knife? That's clearly not allowed, right, Mr. Pemberton? He considers the weight and balance of the weapon, bouncing it slightly in his palm, then opens the blade. Eyes on a suitable surface, he digs into the smooth center of wood in the locker box. In a few minutes, Bunny sits back, eying his work. "My gift." He smiles, snaps the pearl handle closed, and slides it into his own pocket along with the needed writing instruments. Time to disappear. He takes a last look from the door. The pale, splintered wood now a gaping scar, it almost glows against the dark back panel of Watson's locker where crude, three-inch letters spell out R-E-D.

thirteen

Bunny collects the math assignments after class and waits calmly through the tongue-lashing from his teacher. "You have lots of catching up. Do you plan on passing, or not?" His teacher's ire is slightly amusing. Bunny is an excellent student, and until Nan went to the hospital, he had never missed even one day. Ten years and Bunny had been there each time the school doors opened.

He thinks back to the time his mom dressed him in long sleeves and tied a scarf around his neck. She had been trying to hide the red blisters that spotted his arms and neck and told him the teachers were just looking for a reason to send kids home instead of doing their job. It wouldn't have been so bad except the weather had been very warm, and he remembers feeling faint. Several times he'd had to ask to leave class for a drink and had been able to cool his burning face with water from the fountain. Chickenpox had seemed to be everywhere that spring.

Bunny leaves the classroom and spots Raquel at her locker. "Hey, Raquel," he calls, waves, and starts a jog in her direction. The hallway, alive with voices and slamming lockers, is a maze of activity. A girl balancing on crutches limps along in front of him. As Bunny sidesteps around, he bumps her, and books slip from under her arm.

He rushes to retrieve the notebook, which pops open to send papers flying. "Sorry, sorry," Bunny says, handing her the books. She seems embarrassed, ducking her head to hide a smile and manages a weak, "Thank you." When Bunny looks up, Raquel's backside is disappearing into the ladies' room.

The rest of the morning, Bunny sits in one class or another, but his only thoughts are of Raquel. If he can just talk to her, she'll see nothing has changed. The last period before lunch, Bunny watches the clock, ready to bolt from the door to the lunchroom and spend time with Raquel. But when his science teacher dismisses the class, she says, "Bunny, I need to see you." He hurries to her, hoping to resolve whatever it is quickly. Ms. Campbell taps a fist full of homework papers against her desk, aligning them into a neat pile before securing them with a large clip. "Bunny, I'm not going to lie to you. Your disciplinary problem from last week may present an issue with getting you into the archery club." She rolls her eyes up to his. "Violence is something this group does not tolerate."

Ms. Campbell was the one that had recommended Bunny for the Bull's-Eye Club. She first saw his interest when she told him about Sagittarius, The Archer, being his zodiac sign. Since then, Bunny has watched the night sky, feeling a kinship with his celestial brother. "But... why?" he stammers.

"I believe it's because the items used in this sport can be, and often are, actual weapons. The sponsors for this club are very particular and cautious. They demand students of the highest character."

Bunny's head sags from his shoulders. The archery group was one thing he'd been looking forward to. The most accurate members are awarded their own fancy bow with precision arrows and invited to represent the club at state-wide competitions. He'd even bragged to Raquel about what a sure shot he was, even with his homemade equipment. He'd told her he couldn't wait to be a member so he could bring home the trophy. Bunny had never belonged to a club or played a sport. Practices and meetings took place after or before school and relying on the bus for transportation prevented that. "But... I got a car now... I can do the meetings," he protests.

"Sorry. I'll try to put in a good word." Ms. Campbell pats his shoulder, her eyes growing large, staring at his chest. "New shirt, Bunny?"

By the time Bunny gets there, the lunch line is all the way to the door. Through the glass wall separating them from those eating, he spies Raquel. She is sitting at a table with several girls. He waves, hoping to catch her eye, but she doesn't see him. She looks happy, chatting with new friends. Bunny taps the glass but only raises the attention of everyone in line, including a teacher just ahead of him. "Hands off the glass," she barks.

All the while he stands in the slow-moving train of hungry students, Bunny watches Raquel. Occasionally, he tries the wave again, but she doesn't look his way. When the food queue turns into the serving area, the separating wall blocks his view. Today of all days, the ladies behind the glass want to talk. He points, they scoop. "Where you been, Bunny?" "How's your mom?"

Finally emerging on the other end, he stops, tray in hand, not able to believe his eyes. The table of girls is still there, but Raquel is not. Her half-eaten tray of food sits at her place. "Where did she go?" Bunny asks, standing behind the vacant chair.

"Who?" says the girl in the next seat with a smirk. She tosses a mane of dark hair over her shoulder, eyes him, and pulls a loud slurp through a straw off the bottom of her chocolate milk.

"Raquel," Bunny says, trying to tamp down his annoyance with this game. But the table mates seem to know nothing and the response is noncommittal. "She was here. I saw her. Look," Bunny points. "Her tray. She coming back?"

"Oh, that girl." The table giggles. "She left."

Bunny shakes his head. "Left her tray?"

"She was in a hurry. I think she had a problem."

"Is something wrong?"

The high school princesses trade looks before their mouthpiece delivers the final blow. "Girl thing, you know." The table erupts in giggles, and Bunny's face heats. He jerks away as if hit by an electric current. "Her period... psycho!" she screams across the room.

On cue, the girls all throw their chairs back and stand. Fists raised, they pump the air. "Psycho, psycho, psycho." Their voices grow louder. Bunny backs away, stumbles, and almost falls, dropping to one knee. His tray going sideways, food slides to the floor. Other tables join in the fray, and the volume quickly multiplies to the fervor of a mob. Bunny spins around, surrounded by his tormentors like a trapped animal. Ms. Campbell at the next table jumps up, frantic for help with the out-of-control room. Every student is now on their feet, shouting, punching the air. "Psycho, psycho, psycho!"

Bunny bolts from the lunchroom, desperate for a place to hide. Taunting voices in his ears, he runs across the deserted front lawn toward his car. Unlocking it, he pushes the stuffed kitten into the floor, flops across the front seat, rolls into a ball, and sobs.

After the tears stop, he takes some deep breaths and rubs his face dry against the car seat. Why are they so mean? He just wanted to talk to Raquel, to show her he's the same guy. The same guy that let her paint his nails, listened to stories about her big family, and enjoyed her mom's delicious burritos. Her green eyes had sparkled when he'd told her he'd been recommended for the archery team. She got excited, said her little brother would be interested in the Bull's-Eye Club. They had connected. He felt it... and knew Raquel did, too.

The bell sounds in the distance, marking the end of lunch. Bunny groans, thinking about afternoon classes. Three more hours. What if... he stays here... takes a long nap... waits for it to end. He can wait for Raquel after school. Surely he can see her for a few seconds. He's already missed a week of class. What difference could one more half day make? When the second bell sounds, Bunny breathes a sigh, relaxes, and closes his eyes.

Later, when the roar of engines wakes him, Bunny rubs his face awake, watching as the buses speed past, one after the other. Black diesel clouds explode from exhaust pipes that seem too small for the big boxes on wheels. The welcome parade of black and yellow is always a happy reminder the school day is almost done.

The drivers, mostly veterans, have developed a humorous and casual acceptance of irregularities. But the driver of the 209, Raquel's bus, is the junior high coach. Johnny Jones, standing maybe five feet two, is in charge of the basketball team. A super athlete, he earns the respect of his students with his ability to kick to a stance from a prone position. The coach has only been driving since his wife gave birth recently. Coach Jones still believes in bus rules.

Knowing this, Bunny feels his best chance will be boarding just as though he's a passenger. He rode that route once before and Coach allowed it, but that's when he was with Raquel. Maybe he'll remember. Bunny grabs the stuffed kitten, stuffs it under his arm and strides over to bus row.

"Hey there, bell hasn't rung." Coach Jones rolls his wrist, checking the time.

"Uh... got out early. Finished a test," Bunny lies, hurrying to the open door.

"Hold up there. Nobody on before the bell." Coach throws out an arm, blocking the way. He narrows his eyes and moves his head, looking Bunny up and down. "You don't live on my route, do you?"

"I... ride with a friend and walk from her house."

"Yeah, I've seen you." Coach squints. "Tell me, does that girl want you riding with her?" Certain by now all the teachers have heard about the pencil incident, Bunny tries again.

"We're friends." He nods aggressively.

"I'll ask her," Coach says, crossing his arms. "Wait over there." He points to the side of the school, fifteen feet away. Bunny slumps off to lean against the building. His stomach twisting with worry, he has to stay positive. He pulls the fluffy animal from under his arm, hoping to get a few seconds with Raquel when she comes out the door. One on one, he knows he can make a difference. That is, before the coach cross-examines her.

In a few minutes, the sound of the last bell makes Bunny jump to attention, and students begin filing outside. A few of them look surprised when they see Bunny lurking on the other side by the door. Coach Jones goes back inside the school while kids board. "Come ooooon, Raquel," Bunny mutters, his hands squeezing a chokehold on the stuffed cat. Minutes tick by and the steady stream of students slows until the last stragglers wander out. Still no Raquel. Rubber door seals on the first bus slap closed as it roars away, leaving behind a foul haze of exhaust. Coach Jones dashes from the school, hurrying to his own bus parked second in line. Just before he jumps aboard, he turns and yells back at Bunny. "Oh, hey, your friend isn't coming today. She got another ride."

fourteen

THE CONSTANT WHINE from the floor is really annoying TC. He drives on, eager to get home and rest his ears. While his truck bounces over the caliche roads, he talks to the box on the floor. "Your family sure lives out here in the sticks." In the distance, wavy heat patterns rise from the rooftop of the school. When he turns onto the blacktop that runs behind the building, its lifeless flag hugs the pole like it's afraid of heights. "Hot one today," he chuckles.

Up ahead, he spots someone on foot. Getting closer, he sees it's a girl and one he doesn't know. TC rolls to a stop just ahead of her and lowers his window. "Kind of warm for a stroll." He smiles, leaning across the steering wheel. She glances up but walks past his truck.

The girl is red-faced, her cheeks streaked with trails of sweat. He creeps his truck forward beside her. Dark, shiny hair bounces on her shoulders while her arms are tightly wrapped around several books. Cute little thing, but she won't slow down or even look up. "You've got a load there. Would you like a ride?" TC says just as the sound from the box on his floor intensifies to an urgent cry.

The girl stops and twists her head. "What is... that?" she says, drawing out the words, her eyebrows peaking.

"Oh, let me show you." TC lifts a black-and-white ball of fur from the open box.

"Ooooooh, a puppy!" she squeals, her face turns into a delightful smile.

"Yes, just picked her up."

"Can I hold her?"

"Sure, just open that door right there," TC says, bringing the fur-baby close to his own face. "I bet this little lady will like your lap better than mine."

The girl shifts her load, manages the door, and plants the books on the seat. Her hands free, she cradles the puppy, holding her close. She laughs when the cold nose touches her cheek, then a pink tongue shoots out, licking her face. "I love puppies and the way they smell." She buries her nose in the fur.

"My cow dog, Rowdy, is getting old. One day, this little lady will have that job," says TC.

"Wish I had a dog. But my dad says we already have too many mouths to feed."

"Big family?"

She nods. "Three brothers, three sisters and me, the oldest."

"I don't know any houses on this stretch of road. You coming from school?"

"We haven't lived here that long. My father works the Bosque Ranch."

"That right? You realize, that's east of the school and you're going west?"

"Really? Guess I'm a bit lost. Left in a hurry."

"Bosque Ranch is a few miles from here. I could take you, that is, if you want to arrive any time before dark."

"I'm not supposed to accept rides from people I don't know."

"Good advice," he says, tossing his shades onto the dash. He offers his hand. "I'm TC Conway, in case you want to identify your abductor." He flashes a broad smile. Full disclosure works every time. "Say, what grade you in?"

"Tenth. I'm sixteen."

"'Bout what I thought. I have a daughter in your class. Jodie. Know her?"

The girl's face opens with the mention of a daughter. She seems to think a dad would be immune to the charms of a young girl, but that really depends on the girl. Temporarily hypnotized, TC stares at her white, perfectly aligned teeth surrounded by heart-shaped lips. "I know Jodie." She grins, her voice sounding more relaxed. "Sure you don't mind taking me?" She hands him the puppy and moves her books aside. "Can I hold her on the way?"

"Yep. First time old gal's been quiet the whole trip."

TC drives on, winding his truck first this way, then that, over the country roads. Spending his entire life in the community, he knows all the farms and ranches and where everyone lives. The girl is content to nuzzle the puppy and giggles when the tiny, wrinkled mouth mistakes her finger for a chew toy. "So, did you miss your bus?" TC says slowly.

"No, I went out the back. Avoiding someone."

"A creep, huh?"

"Sort of, I guess." When they reach the entrance to the Bosque Ranch, she points to the right at the fork. "Our house is up there."

The rolling green terrain of the land is dotted with clumps of cedar and live oaks where large numbers of cattle are drawn like magnets, the shade underneath a place for them to cool, swat flies, and socialize. On the next hill, a modest, white frame home snuggles under a similar canopy by the road. The home looks tidy, but questionable for a sizable family. A tire swing hangs from a branch and sways on the breeze. Several chairs, some overturned, surround homemade tables of plywood and sawhorses in the shade. His tires crunching over acorns, TC glides to a stop in front. "Looks like y'all had a party."

"Sundays after mass. Dad's friends." There's sadness in her voice, and she turns her head away, looking out the window. Her voice going soft, she speaks to the wind. "He's allowed friends..."

"Barbecue?"

"No, just beer. Lots of beer..." Her voice tapers off. "Mother prepares food, but the yard party is just for *los vaqueros*."

"Damn. Missed my invite." TC grins as the girl gives him a sideways glance. "Nice up here, more breeze. Is that your swing?"

"The little ones use it. Hope they're not worried about me."

"They on the bus?" She nods. With windows down, the warm wind huffs across the hilltop and through the truck. Hair blow blowing away from her face, her skin bathed in the afternoon light glows like expensive silk. "Anyone home?" he asks, draping an arm over the seat, unable to look away.

She shakes her head, then gasps and quickly covers her mouth with a hand. "I shouldn't have said that."

"Mmmmm, probably shouldn't," TC mutters, staring into her bottomless green eyes. "But that figures, no car, no truck." She does a double take, not sure what to make of his observation. "Look—" He takes her notebook and, finding a clean page, scribbles his name and office number in the barn. "Now then," he says, smiling, "you'll have somebody you can call when you're trying to disappear." Her body stiffens, and she returns the puppy to the box. Almost immediately, the serenade from the floor begins anew. Reaching a hand inside, she quiets the cries. "Hey, I haven't named her yet," TC says, drawing out the moment. "Would you like to?"

"Really?" She smiles and picks up the pup again, bringing her nose to nose to stare into the tiny face. "How about... Sugar, cause you're so sweet. Do you like that?"

"Good name," says TC. "Tell you what, since you named her, she can belong to both of us. I'll keep her at my place, but that's only a couple of miles from here," he says and jerks a thumb over his left shoulder. "You're welcome to see Sugar or me, anytime."

She lowers the dog to the box and scoops up her books from the seat. "Thank you for the ride." Her cheeks burning, she hurries out the door.

"Hey," TC leans down, looking out the window. "You never did tell me your name."

"Oh, sorry." Her laugh easy now, more confident being just steps away from her own door. "Raquel." She smiles and gives a small wave.

fifteen

BUNNY ISN'T HUNGRY. He hasn't eaten all day, but his insides feel heavy, like he's swallowed cement. But he promised Ms. Bridget. She'd asked him for supper. If he didn't have plans, she said. Unless plans meant crawling under his house to hide, guess he didn't have any. That's where he's been for the past hour, keeping company with spiders and probably snakes. The cool darkness is always a welcome retreat for Bunny. And today, after school, it feels especially right.

His mind will not stop with thoughts of Raquel, so troubling he's exhausted. All day he'd tried to see her, talk with her, but everything was against him. The idea of her riding home with someone else is more painful than Bunny can bear. Surely she wouldn't get in the car with Mean Man Watson. But the way Watson leered at her that day at lunch, that guy would try it, just to show Bunny he could.

Once he's talked himself into it, Bunny climbs out of his protective cave and dusts himself off. He plans to make an appearance at dinner as promised. When he coasts the Chevy to a stop on the Conway hilltop, he's so spent, he wonders if he can get through the evening. He groans getting out of the car, grabs the small stack of school books, and slumps toward the back door. Rowdy, sprawled across the side porch in the late-day sun, raises his head, watching

Bunny walk through the grass. The dog gives a half-hearted bark of acknowledgment before returning to his nap.

"Hey, loser." The unexpected sound makes him jump. Camouflaged in the shade, Jodie gives a little wave. He walks to the glider where she sits, her crutches parked within reach. "What am I supposed to call you now?" She smirks. "Red?"

Bunny takes a seat, careful not to disturb the bulky bandaged foot propped there. "Only if we're friends." He blinks into the dim light under the tree, his eyes adjusting.

"Well, Red, I wouldn't go in there, if I were you." She points to the house.

"What?"

"Mom's mad."

"But... she's always happy."

"Yeah, well, not when she gets a phone call."

"A call... from?"

"Some nosy gossip who can't mind their own bizzz-ness."

"So... Ms. Bridget knows?"

"Knows what?" Jodie snaps, her voice growing stronger. "That dad's a great-looking guy with an outgoing personality? Everybody knows that."

"So, your mom can deal with gossip?"

She nods. "Yes, but it upsets her. So, she's making chili." Jodie nods, bugging her eyes. "Yeah, hot as it is and that's what she's making for supper. Mom's chili is Dad's favorite. He likes his extra hot and spicy."

"Okay," Bunny says and leans forward on elbows balanced on knees.

"Mom says if the food has enough peppers, taste buds stop working." Jodie fights back a smile, forcing her lips into a hard line. She bends, getting close like she's got a secret. "Let's just say, Rowdy may not be the only one eating a can of Alpo tonight."

"Sounds like I need to go home." Bunny rises from the seat.

"No, stay, please." Jodie puts a hand on his leg. "Mom likes you, don't worry."

But he does worry. He wonders if Bridget's small, private retaliation somehow makes up for her suspicions. Once planted, the nagging thought would be impossible to ignore and, more than that, especially hurtful as she goes about being a caring wife.

"So, how was your first day back at school?" Jodie asks, seeming anxious for news outside of family.

"Got your assignments." Bunny nods toward the books at his feet.

"Oh, joy. Did you take Raquel home in your car?"

"No," he says, making a face. "She left with someone else."

"You're kidding. Who?"

Bunny shrugs and pushes back, rocking both of them gently. They sit together in silence as the sun slides down the edge of the sky, painting cloud snowdrifts a delicious shade of creamsicle. A damp freshness hangs in the air, and the smell of moisture is clean and refreshing. "Bet it rains tonight," he says.

Rowdy comes into view from the side of the house. The dog's off-center gait reminds Bunny of a scolded child. The slow trot, head down, tail between his legs—the poor animal looks as worn down as Bunny feels. Jodie pats the seat and Rowdy hops up, collapses beside her, and drops a furry head into her lap. She rubs his ears, making his eyes drift closed as he lets out a pitiful whine.

"Poor Rowdy. He feels rejected," Jodie says. "Dad brought home a puppy. He says Rowdy's getting old, and he expects him to train her."

"Ugh… that's cold," says Bunny. He looks down, surveying the wrapped foot on the seat beside him. The just-visible, pink-polished toes are a nice surprise. "So, how's the ankle? And the ribs?"

"Hurts, but I got drugs. Probably need plastic surgery." She points to the long bandage on her face. "But not sure Dad will swing for that."

"What, why?"

"If I had looks, that'd be different. Worth it, I guess."

"He doesn't think your face... is worth it?"

She shrugs. "A nasty scar on me is not a real loss."

"Did he say that?"

Jodie shakes her head, looks down, concentrating on Rowdy, and draws a perfect part with a nail to expose a strip of light skin. "I know what he thinks."

"So why did you get in the car with that motor head at school?"

"Pretty girls do. Guess I wanted to prove I could, too." Jodie stops fussing with the dog to look up. The flattened mix of black-and-white hair across the dog's head reminds Bunny of an old man's comb-over. "God sure taught me a lesson about trying to be something I'm not," Jodie sighs.

Not believing what he hears, Bunny's head spins, taking in the plush green of the hilltop setting. Beyond that, the Conway land rolls out before them as far as he can see. He narrows his gaze, eyeing the impressive rock work of the sprawling home that rises out of the ground behind her. "Don't do that," he says. Jodie's hand stops in midair above Rowdy's head. "You know, the feel-sorry-for-me dance. Doesn't fit."

A smile tries to escape and makes her lip quiver, but she manages to control it and sticks out her tongue instead, curling it into a perfect horseshoe.

Without hesitation, Bunny rolls his own tongue, pushing it through puckered lips, forming a stark U-shape pointed back at Jodie.

"How crazy!" Jodie laughs. "That's an inherited trait, you know. I'm the only one in my family besides Dad who can do it."

"Nan can't." Bunny shakes his head. "It always irritated her that I could."

"What a team of losers," Jodie says and ruffs up Rowdy's new do. "Rejected and banged-up bunch of tongue curlers."

"Speak for yourself. I'm not giving up. Just need... to talk to her." Bunny almost spits the words, surprised by the sound of his own defiance.

"Please tell me you didn't try to impress Raquel wearing, uh... that."

"My shirt?" Bunny sits up, smoothing the front. Jodie cocks her head, letting her eyes roll back. "Doesn't it look good with my hair?" He smiles.

"Oh, girlfriend, we gotta go shop."

Their laughter, interrupted by a sudden boom of thunder, makes them jump as Rowdy howls, then whines. "Here it comes." Bunny just gets the words out as a blinding flash cracks not far down the hill. The jagged lightning jolt fires up a tree branch that flames bright against the dim light.

"Hey," screams Amy from the open door of the house. "Mom says to get inside."

Jodie struggles to stand on one leg and surprises Bunny by taking his arm for balance. "Okay, Rat," she yells over her shoulder at the little sister eyeing them from the doorway. "We're bringing Rowdy."

Bunny hands the crutches to Jodie and helps as she gets in position to move. "Now remember, don't eat anything from dad's spicy pot," she says. He hangs back, watching. Her injured leg bent at the knee, she squeezes the padded hand grips on the crutches, pushing forward. The deliberate effort makes him think of a street scooter he'd received one Christmas. He was so excited that he drove Nan crazy flying through the house. That is until she got fed up and burned it in the trash heap.

A family secret shared, and he's been included. The heaviness gone now, his insides feel better... light. Bunny breathes deep, filling his lungs with the swirl of damp air and faint wood smoke. Jodie looks over her shoulder, waiting, and motions for him to follow. "Don't worry, Red." She smiles. "Mom really does make the best chili ever."

sixteen

BUNNY HAS DREAMED up a plan that kept him awake all night. He's not going to try to seek out Raquel at school, look for her between classes or at lunch, or wait for her by the bus. Instead, he will simply watch from a distance to see what happens.

As the school day progresses, Bunny pays attention in class, turns in school work, takes notes, and smiles at his teachers. In short, he strives to be a model student, but he speaks to no one. He observes Raquel from across the room, eating lunch with friends, but Bunny is content to sit alone.

As soon as the last bell rings, signaling the end of the school day, Bunny gets in his car and drives straight to Raquel's. He parks behind her house and watches from the corner where he can see the flash of yellow approaching over the next hill. It's quiet outside the ranch hand's place, and after several sleepless nights, Bunny nods off and bangs his forehead against the steering wheel. But remembering he has snacks from Nan's secret collection, he grabs one for the much-needed jolt to stay awake.

About an hour after he arrives, Bunny sees what he came for. The school bus is headed toward him. He hears the squeal of brakes as it stops in front of the house and watches the cloud of dust puff over the rooftop from the caliche road. Then the sound of young voices as the Martinez clan unloads. From his corner lookout, Bunny sees the younger children run toward the house. Last to climb down is Raquel, and as usual, she balances a pile of books. The doors slap closed, and the bus roars away. Bunny hurries from the back toward Raquel, who freezes mid-yard, her face losing its color. "Raquel, please don't be mad. I have to talk to you." He rushes forward.

"Bunny?" she stammers, putting up a hand to stop him. "Why are you here?"

"I tried to see you at school yesterday but... couldn't. I thought maybe you didn't want to be friends any longer."

"You shouldn't be here, Bunny. I'm going to get in trouble."

"Why would you?"

"My dad. The kids told him what happened at school with Watson. He said I couldn't be around you. He thinks you're *loco*."

"That what he thinks?"

"How... how did you get here?"

"I'm not crazy. You know that."

"My dad." Her face contorts, and arms full, she stamps her feet. "My dad's going to beat me for this."

"He beats you? Please tell me that's not true." She looks away and shrugs. "I want to show you something." Bunny takes her elbow and pulls her to the backyard. "See, I have a car now. I can bring you home. You don't have to ride the bus."

"My dad will never allow that."

She turns on her heel and walks toward the house. "You should go. I'm sure my little brothers and sisters have already called him. Dad's probably on the way here now."

"Then I'll stay. I'd like to talk to him."

"Nooooo, Bunny, Dad has a gun—a rifle in his truck."

"If I can't see you, then... then I'd just as soon be dead."

"What's wrong with you? Maybe you are *loco*."

"I'll leave if you promise to sit in the car and talk first. Please?" A feeling that he's being watched makes Bunny turn toward the house.

A group of small heads and twice as many curious eyes stare from the window.

"There you go." Raquel points toward the faces.

"Please..." Bunny gestures toward his car, then opens the passenger side. "How about if you bring them out?"

"The kids?"

"Sure, big car, four doors." Bunny smiles. "I might have a little something for everybody in here."

Raquel drops her shoulders, looking defeated, and beckons to the eyes fastened on her like paint to a wall. The back door slams against the side of the house, and six smiling kids push each other as they battle to be the first outside. Bunny races around, opening the car. "Anybody hungry?" He smiles. "I've got some goodies." He reaches in and pulls out a box overflowing with packages of chips, cookies, and candy.

"Bunny!" Raquel scolds and turns away to hide a smile. "Where did you get all that?"

"My mom," he says, smiling. "Found her stash."

The stair-step heights of the children reflect ages so close that hand-me-downs would wear out before making the circuit. But these kids are not wearing secondhand clothes. All are neatly dressed, the boys with fresh haircuts, girls with braids and ribbons. These children clearly hold a place of importance in the family. Respectful of Raquel, they hang back, waiting for her direction. "Is this the guy?" the tallest boy says.

"The pencil stabber?" a small girl blurts, then scurries behind her sister.

"Dad says you're crazy," the tall kid says, crossing his arms. The band of small to tall stands motionless, as if fused together, their dark eyes, big as baseballs, locked on Bunny.

Still holding the box of treats, Bunny walks to the front of the car to lean against the hood. "Can I share something with you guys?" Six heads nod. "You know about bullies at school?" More nodding. "The guy I hurt is a bully. He said some terrible things in front of your beautiful sister, Raquel. That's why it happened."

A collective "Ooooooooh" circulates through the young jury, followed by an almost religious silence. Bunny hangs his head, praying for forgiveness.

"Raquel, is that right?" says tall boy.

"Yes," she replies. "That's what happened."

The smallest girl, still peeking from behind her sister's skirt, calls out in a tiny voice, "Can we have a treat now?"

Raquel walks close to Bunny and sets her books on the hood. She cranes her neck, looking inside the box at the vast assortment of snacks. "Got any Twinkies?" She smiles, prompting the hungry group to rush forward to make their own selections. "Since y'all are having a picnic—we don't need crumbs in the car—so how about we sit at the tables under the tree?" she directs. The kids run to the front of the house, and Bunny touches Raquel on the shoulder.

"Want me to talk with your father? I don't want there to be a problem between us... ever."

"At least now the kids are on your side. Very clever. But I don't know about bribing Dad with sweets." She tics her tongue.

"I've got the car now, a job. I'm making some money, so I can take you out, if you'll let me." She looks at the ground, but Bunny can see her cheeks darken. His insides are so unsteady, he's afraid he'll throw up.

"You mean like a—date?" She rolls her eyes up to his. Bunny nods his head so fast you'd think it's attached to a spring. "Never been allowed to go out with a boy."

"All the more reason to talk with your dad."

"First, let's see how he reacts to you," says Raquel.

Bunny smiles, choking back his nervousness as they walk around the house to join the rest. Raquel introduces the tallest boy as Rafael. "Call me Raff," he says.

"I'm Bunny, but my friends call me Red. I've seen you in school." Raff nods his approval. Raquel's brother is probably fifteen at the most, but he already has an impressive set of sideburns and dark shading across his top lip. The oldest son, he seems eager to be the man in the absence of his father. "I bet you're the brother that's interested in archery," Bunny says, hoping to connect.

Raquel makes the rounds, introducing Bunny to everyone. The youngest girl, Teresa, with pink ribbons woven in her braids, rushes away to the swing. Raquel takes requests for orange soda while Bunny walks to the limb of the giant oak where the rope is secured. Teresa climbs into the suspended tire. Her bare legs draped over the side, she modestly covers her lap with her skirt.

"Would you like me to push?" asks Bunny. She smiles and nods as he hugs the hard edge of the rubber, draws it back, then shoves it forward.

The laughing girl flies, kicks her feet, and screams, "Higher... higher!"

Raquel returns with double fists of drippy glass bottles. Bunny rushes to assist, but not before another girl—Eva, he remembers—rescues the opener from her sister's pocket. She expertly pops the metal lids and flicks them to the grass below, where drink caps collect in mounds. Bunny soaks in the circle of activity, marveling at the feel of family. It must be nice to have brothers and sisters, a mom and dad. And they care, ready to take on the world to protect each other. He wants this for himself and Raquel. He wants them to have their own home and be married for about a hundred years. Unlike his own father, Bunny will consider the role of dad an honor.

Everyone fed and refreshed, Raff takes a seat across the table, sizing up Bunny. "You know, Red, the best thing would be to let me speak to my father about this first."

"You mean before I surprise him," Bunny says, hoping the strange crack in his voice doesn't give away his instant relief. "Probably right." He stands to leave. "Raquel, can we have lunch together tomorrow?" She looks down. Her nervous fingers lace then unlace. She glances up, feeling the intense stare from her brother.

"We'll see," she says quietly, her lips pushed together, sealing emotion.

"I'll walk you to your car," says Raff. Once the two clear the corner to the backyard, Raff stops. When Bunny turns, Raff leans close and places a hand on Bunny's back. "Next time, *amigo*, instead of a pencil," he says and makes a slashing motion across his neck, "you should use a *machete*."

seventeen

BRIDGET STARES around the small office, feeling disappointment. After all these years, still the same monochromatic-grey driftwood sculpture thing on the wall, the same dust-collecting ball-bearing clacker on the table. Not one item has changed, and Bridget would know. She visits her therapist most Wednesdays, as she has for the past five years.

At first, it'd bothered Bridget that the office had no personality. She knows Victoria, Tory for short, is married. A vulgar-sized ring adorns her third finger. Pretty girl. Bet her husband is a looker. And Bridget tricked Tory into acknowledging that she has a son. But where are the heart-warming photos of the smiling kidlet? Where is the elaborate, gold-framed wedding portrait? Where is the plate of fresh-baked peanut butter cookies and the coffee pot? If she only had an afternoon, Bridget could make this room inviting.

"You know that's not how it works," sighs Tory.

"But just this once, can't you tell me, as a friend?" Bridget insists.

"I ask the questions. I don't advise you what to do." The leggy female sitting across the desk takes a sip from her water before looking off into space, her dark eyes fixed on nothing, corner of the ceiling, maybe. The flame of a candle dances inside the jar behind the desk. Lavender. It's always lavender. When Bridget asked about the ever-present scent, she was told lavender was a calming fragrance. But she thought cinnamon or vanilla would work better—at least it would for her. The therapist seems distracted today. In fact, something has felt off about Tory this entire session, starting with when she first opened her notebook.

"But Tory, maybe after the session?" Bridget checks the time, only about ten minutes left. "Could you be a friend afterward and give advice?"

Ignoring the latest plea, Tory pushes on. "So about the call. How did it make you feel, Bridget?"

"Are you serious? How would you feel if an anonymous caller described your husband's privates?"

"Bridget." Another heavy sigh as Tory twirls a silver ear hoop. "This is not about me."

"I'm aware."

Years before, when Bridget first walked into the county mental health facility, she was introduced to Tory. They sat together, the therapist asking questions. Bridget thought the entire process could not have been more uncomfortable if she'd been naked in front of the woman. The idea of exposing herself to this beautiful young professional felt inhuman. She had allowed no one, especially anyone so different from herself, to know what she suspected. And when Bridget left the first day, with her feelings ruffled up like a chicken molting, she had breathed a sigh of relief, knowing she'd never return. But as the week wore on, she thought back on the conversation, replaying the questions over and over like a favorite song. Somehow, the answers coaxed from her felt empowering.

When Bridget had returned the following week, she'd planned to ask if there was another therapist. Someone perhaps with saggy breasts and an ample middle. But Tory had greeted her that day in the lobby with a lovely smile. Not wanting to hurt the other woman's feelings, she couldn't get the words out.

That was five years before and, over time, Bridget had become very attached to her therapist. After all, this woman is the only person who knows the depth of her pain. The weekly visits have proven such a release, Bridget can almost feel her pent-up anger deflate like a spent balloon. The Conways certainly can afford better than the county facility, but the low rate and close location allow Bridget to book weekly and in secret.

"Let's look at this another way. What response do you suppose the caller intended to elicit?"

"To upset me, send me to the moon with anger." Bridget squeezes her fists, pounding the chair arms. "Make me so mad I'd file for divorce."

Instead of yelling Bingo, Helen crosses a heeled pump over a knee and waves her foot as the gleam of satisfaction lights her face. The corners of her mouth twitch so she hurries more questions. "And, what happened then?"

"I, ugh, made chili," says Bridget. Tory scowls. Apparently, she remembers the chili.

"And did that help?"

"Well, yeah, for a minute anyway." Bridget chews her lip, hoping for at least a smile. Tory has on the favorite shoes today, the red patent heels that Bridget loves. She'd considered trying to find a pair just like them, but then logic got in the way. She'd laughed at the mental picture of herself puffing around her kitchen in those or sinking into the earth out in the garden.

"So, why do you think you got that call?"

"So, they, whoever *they* are, would win."

"Describe that."

"Someone else would have TC." Bridget's voice cracks as she reaches for a tissue.

"Does this upset you?"

"Of course. He's my husband." Bridget dabs at her eyes. Helen lowers her glasses, looking over the top, eye to eye with Bridget. Her pen poised in the air, she waits, playing a game of chicken. "My husband is the one prize I've ever had. I know you know. Just look at me!" Bridget thrusts her hands out, palms up. "I'm no show-winning specimen."

"But didn't you say you were aware of your husband's roving eye?"

"Yes, but I thought I could fix him. I guess."

The honest words make Tory direct her attention back to her page, scribbling away, her red-lacquered manicure flashing brightly. Bridget fans her own fingers, considering her short nails. Ridiculous. Her gardening gloves would never fit with those spikes. When she stops writing, Tory glances at the wall clock. "Looks like that's about all for today, but I have one more thing we need to discuss."

Bridget sniffs and tosses a crumpled tissue into the basket, amazed that Tory has something more to say. She sits up straight, ready to give her full attention, but the pretty young woman looks unhappy, the corners of her mouth droop. Perhaps it's finally something she wants to share about herself. A tragedy for her would be awful, but Bridget is anxious and ready to help. Tory retrieves a single page from her desk, concentrating on the words. "Our county finance coordinators have raised this issue, I'm afraid." She shakes her head. "We offer our services at a severely reduced rate to area people who can't afford more. I don't know why this is just now coming up, but I feel like the new director is flexing his muscles." She glances up from the letter. "I'm afraid they have directed me that, given your financial status, Bridget, we can no longer provide you with counseling." She tosses the paper away like a dirty napkin and drums her nails against the wood surface.

"But... but who am I going to talk to?" Bridget stutters, feeling like the floor has fallen away. "I need this. Can't you tell them... something?"

"Actually, Bridget, you should be happy." Tory tries to smile, but her shiny lips look crooked, forced. "You can afford better, and counseling with a doctor, that's a good thing." Her voice strains to sound upbeat, but that's the last Bridget hears. Her brain turns off, and a roar in her head drowns out everything. Tory's mouth is moving, and she hands Bridget a business card. It's some psychiatrist in a big town an hour away, and Bridget knows she'll never make the trip. She has just lost the only person who knows her secrets. Her only ally.

eighteen

Bunny is floating with excitement on the drive home from Raquel's. So sure that Raff will put in a good word for him with the dad, he can't wait to see her again. If she says yes to lunch at school, then he better be prepared. Maybe she likes the crust cut off her sandwich. Bunny smiles, making plans as he thinks of what he can pack for the two of them. Life might be worth living after all.

He slows his car, turning onto the road to home. Driving closer, he sees something ahead, and three rail-thin feral cats dart away. Dread filling him, he finds one of Nan's prized Dominicker hens. Just a pair of useless feet and wings, flattened, and matted black-and-white feathers clinging to bits of flesh. Rib bones curve skyward like the praying hands of the carcass, exposed and still. "Murdering assholes," Bunny yells, side-arming rocks at the trio who watch from the ditch. His fault, really. His mind so full of Raquel, Bunny realizes now, he'd left the chickens out for the past two days.

The short quarter-mile drive to the house is littered with carnage. A group of cats hunch over something in the field and there's another headless hen, two-thirds gone on the road. "They've killed them all," Bunny whispers.

When he steps onto the porch, he hears the telephone ringing inside. Pushing open the front door, he almost falls, then jumps back and gasps. The living room is a moving sea of cats. They huddle in swarms on the kitchen counters, tear at the sofa, and curl together on the bed pillows.

"Awwwwww!" Bunny runs in, scattering animals, who dart away. Rushing to answer the phone, his shoes crunch glass before he realizes Nan's happy-girl photo has also been knocked to the floor.

Paralyzed by shock, his mind thick as glue, Bunny babbles into the phone, "They're in the house."

"Excuse me?"

"They broke in... so many."

"Is this the Potts' residence?"

"I've got to... do... something."

"This is Alice Becker from the administration office at the hospital. Who am I speaking with?"

"Bunny Potts... please, I've got to... go."

"Don't you hang up! I've been calling this number for two days."

"You... don't understand... please!" Bunny sputters, so upset he can't move. With no clue what to do next, he clings to the phone, the voice like a lifeline of sanity among the horror unfolding before him. The starving animals swarm over a bag of potato chips and a chocolate bar on the counter. Bunny's precious loaf of lunch bread, devoured. The jars of jelly and peanut butter shattered. Shards of glass point up like land mines from sticky splatters where thousands of purple kitty prints track away through the house.

"Is Nan Potts your... mother?" The words hit like a slap, demanding his attention.

"Yes, is she ... okay?"

"We are transferring your mother to the rehab center."

"Rehab? Is she better?"

"She is stable and will be cared for at the Willow Creek Rehab Center. And, young man, it is important that we have a valid number for a contact. Is this the best number, or is there someone else we should call?"

When he disconnects, his anger boiling, he wakes from the helpless stupor. Bunny throws open the front door, grabs cats, and sails them by the tail like loaded slingshots. He pulls them, hissing and fighting, from under the bed, chases them out of the bathtub with a broom, and gathers the hostile fur balls by the armful to heave them outside. His arms and chest bleeding from claw marks, he can't feel a thing.

He finds a screen torn open at a window behind his bed. It had been just a small hole, but sharp claws have shredded the material, providing a freeway for the desperate animals. The jagged edges, coated with strings of matted hair, wave like fingers on the breeze. Slamming the window closed, he gags on the inside air of the house, thick with the sharp stench of feces, vomit, and tobacco-brown tomcat spray. There are more cats in the hamper, the closets, and the cabinets. After forcefully ejecting what he hopes is the last, Bunny retrieves his bow and arrows from the barn. It's a task he should have taken care of days ago. But when he'd considered it, his feelings got in the way. With no money to feed them, he'd hoped they'd just leave—move on, as they say, to greener pastures. But this... this is how the ungrateful little shits repay his kindness—by killing Nan's hens and wrecking the house. It's time to be a man now.

Luckily, the bounty of secret sweets left by Nan is safe inside the refrigerator. Bunny selects Pop Tarts and graham crackers and brings them outside. He steps off a distance, in one-yard strides to twenty feet from the porch, and positions his chair. Basket of arrows handy on his right, he breaks a pastry in two, tossing one piece on the porch. Taking up his bow, he aims and draws back.

Bunny lets his first arrow fly. His aim perfect, he impales a striped tabby, the first one to the bait. The noisy death rattle of the animal thrashing on the porch does nothing to stop the second from coming or the third. Pull, set, draw, pull, set, draw. The actions mechanical, he marvels at his own accuracy. Soon, Bunny must retrieve arrows and pull them out, slick with blood, to continue the eradication. When the hungry cats stop coming, the porch and surrounding area is littered with the dead and the dying.

Bunny fetches the wheelbarrow from the barn, rolling it to the front porch. He tosses in the limp corpses like water-soaked towels filling it to almost overflowing. It's a struggle to push the load the quarter mile to the main road, but Bunny needs the fence line for his project. One by one, he hangs the feral cat bodies, winding one leg through the wire. He's meticulous, lining each at the same height, inches apart, like wood picket slats. When done, he stands in the middle of the road to admire the line of death. "A warning, just in case I missed any," he whispers, wiping sweat with a sleeve.

The tunnel of trees on either side of the road funnels the sound of a distant engine. Bunny jumps into the ditch and flattens, hiding until the car passes. Spread-eagle on the ground, his chest pumping hard, he tries to slow his breaths. His face only inches from his own blood-covered hands, the metallic smell makes him gag, then dry heave into the dirt. For the first time, now he can feel his arms and chest on fire, oozing red with ragged claw marks and tooth punctures. Bunny clenches his fist, denying the pain to remain still. The engine slows, then comes the grab of rubber and the faint uneven squeak of a window being rolled down. For a few seconds, Bunny listens to the engine idle, then suddenly tires spin, gravel flying, as the car roars away.

nineteen

THE NEXT DAY, as Bunny drives home from school, the sun streams through the windshield and covers him. The welcome warmth seems to penetrate all the way to the bone. He feels light and satisfied, pleased with himself. Bunny sat with Raquel without incident at lunch today, even though the hard looks from the other students had the feel of a silent attack. He hadn't been able to bring her a special lunch prepared by his own hand as he'd planned, but they ate the cafeteria food. Well, some of it, anyway.

The assignments for Jodie are in the seat beside him, and he drives straight to the Conway house to deliver. When he passes his macabre fence display, the sickening smell causes Bunny to hold his breath as he stops to retrieve mail from the box. Recognizing the red fur of one of the cat corpses touches a memory of how Bunny could always find that one hiding in the laundry hamper. He shakes aside the sad thought threatening his good mood and drives on to the Conways'.

When Bunny arrives at the big house on the hill, he notices TC's truck parked out back. He knocks on the door, and Bridget's smiling face appears. "Hey there, Bunny."

"School stuff for Jodie," he says, waving a handful of papers.

"Hungry? I've got cookies. Just took 'em out."

"Smells great!" He grins, hooked by the addictive chocolate aroma wafting from the door.

"Big glass of milk sound good?"

The Conway house is so welcoming, Bunny can only imagine how it must feel to come home to this. His mouth waters from the intoxicating smell, and he's certain whatever Bridget is making, it's delicious. The floors are so clean they shine, the windows framed by drapes, and the walls decorated with oil paintings framed in gold. Bridget pours a tall glass of milk and slides a dish down the counter with three perfectly shaped, golden cookies dotted with bits of gleaming chocolate still soft from the oven.

"What do you have there?" she asks, pointing with a spatula at the stack of envelopes he places on the counter.

"Nan's mail I've been collecting."

She fans the stack of envelopes and casually looks at the return addresses. "Bunny, some of these are bills. That's something you need to take care of."

"That's why I brought them. I need your help."

"Help?"

He nods, chewing a cookie. "Nan gets money in her account, but not sure how I can use it."

"Oh, I see. That's a TC question, for sure." She walks to the kitchen window and looks outside. "I'd have thought he'd be back by now." She cranes her neck, stretching on tiptoe to see.

"His truck is outside," Bunny jerks a thumb.

"I know, but he went across the road with Anna-Marie. The Belchers, the old couple that live in that little blue house down the way—they've both had health issues and really can't do much, so TC helps sometimes. The daughter, Anna-Marie, is home from college on fall break. She came over to ask if he could help with a horse that turned up lame. He rode over with her to see what he could do."

"Where's everybody else?"

"Meredith is at basketball practice and Amy at a 4-H Club meeting. Oh, and Jodie, poor thing, she has cabin fever so bad she begged to go with her dad. I think he was a little put out with her, but you know Jodie, she persisted. TC just picked her up in his arms and carried her to the truck." Bridget rolls her eyes. "At least with her tagging along, he'll be on good behavior."

Bunny almost chokes at her comment, struggling not to spit a mouthful of milk. She must know about her husband. Dumb for words, Bunny finishes the cookies and drains the last sip. "Best cookies I ever ate," he grins.

"Oh, hush. You always say that." Bridget swats at him, unsuccessful at stopping her smile.

"It's true."

"Then how come you hardly ate your chili the other night?"

"Wasn't... really hungry."

"Be glad you didn't try that hot stuff TC likes." She smiles. "All that pepper tastes like dog food to me."

Bunny stares into Bridget's eyes, unsure how to react. Is she just teasing, or does she want to talk? Her eyes sparkling, a smile plays on her lips. "Well," she adds. "I only make that version for him. Everyone else gets regular chili," she says and directs her attention to cleaning the already gleaming counters. "More cookies?"

"Ahh... no, better get home."

"That reminds me, Bunny. What is that mess in the fence in front of you house?"

"Trying to keep people from unloading their stray cats."

She shakes her head, frowns, and gives him a look before directing her attention to the inside of the oven. He realizes Bridget is disappointed. Bunny picks up his empty dishes and carries them to the sink. "Guess... I should've... I don't know..." He stammers. With his back to her, he stares out the kitchen window, making the confession easier. "My anger... just..." He throws up his hands and turns to her. "They ruined the house, killed all Nan's chickens."

"Oh, Bunny, the cats got inside?" She touches his shoulder. "You need help? Cleaning up, I mean?"

He shrugs. "I slept outside last night."

"Oh, honey, we can't let you be run out of your house." Her soft, grey eyes bore into his, waiting for permission, but his silence gives way for her decision. "Leave your door unlocked. I'll come by tomorrow."

He grins and tugs at his cap brim, amazed by Bridget's generous heart.

"You can stop over and see TC at Belcher's about this," Bridget says, tapping the stack of mail. "The big red barn up near the road. Jodie is there. She'll be glad to see you. That girl is such a little socialite. missing her friends and all."

The turn-in for the barn is between Bunny's house and Conway's hilltop on the opposite side of the road. When he pulls into the driveway, a white truck he doesn't recognize is parked out front. The radio blasting, it's cranked so loud it puts Bunny's teeth on edge. He raps on the open door, making lost-in-the-music Jodie jump. "Think you got that loud enough?" he yells.

"Hey, lame-o," she says, turning it down. "I'm stuck here." She throws her hands up. "Dad didn't even get my crutches."

"So, waiting in the truck makes you want to be deaf?"

"I'm protesting, you ass. Somebody screws with ya, make it known." Funny. Maybe Jodie should share that advice with her mom. "Anna-Marie has this killer sound system in this truck, twelve speakers, even vibrates your butt. I'm just giving it a ride. You come by to be annoying?"

"Yes," he nods. "How is the class cripple?"

"Screw you, Red." She holds up her middle finger.

"Your dad... seen him?"

"Inside, working on a horse."

Bunny gives a thumbs-up, grins, and pushes the truck door closed. Almost immediately, the volume rockets back to ear-bleed level, and he turns away to follow the short trail to the barn. When he reaches the door and pushes, the sun spills inside, making dust particles sparkle and dance between the bright and dim light. Bunny blinks into the dark, cavernous space, getting his bearings. A center aisle stretches before him and looks to continue the length of the long barn. Stalls of wood slats border either side, occasionally interrupted by random snags of mane or tail or the divot from a horse nibble.

Gates are all open, the facility seems vacant, with mounds of fresh sand, dry water bowls, and feed buckets turned upside down. Bunny considers calling out but decides instead to look around. Walking slowly down the path, he squints into the dimness, first to the right stall, then left. Except for the annoying bass thump from the truck outside, it's peaceful here. Aware of the massive space surrounding him, Bunny fills his lungs with a deep breath of damp, animal-rich air. He feels small, exploring in the big dark place, like a mouse scurrying about undetected at night. From the far end of the barn comes a sudden snort and Bunny stops, listening. Then another snort from the dark. Bunny moves cautiously toward the sound and, in the last stall, discovers a chestnut-colored mare. She hangs her head over the top rail, offering a dark speckled nose. He allows her to smell his hand, then strokes the jet-black forelock that drapes her forehead. The confined horse stands perfectly still, her front leg bent, the angled hoof cocked off the ground. Stooping down, he sees the injury, expertly wrapped to the knee in a white bandage soaked through with purple medicine.

A solid wall of wood marks the end of the stalls. But in the wall, Bunny notices a sliver of light. It looks like a crack in the wood at first, but getting closer, he sees it's a vertical cut through a portion of the wall. A secret door so near to being closed, the act of shutting it was probably done in haste. He intends to turn off the forgotten light inside, thinking of saving the barn owner a bit of electricity. But a sound from the other side curtails his reach to the door in midair. A giggle, then a moan, and Bunny stops breathing. A sudden chill makes his heart jump so hard he can see it thumping under his shirt. But the erotic sounds from inside continue, giving assurance his presence is unknown.

He thinks of running. He should leave this place. But seconds tick by as Bunny struggles with doing the right thing and doing the thing he can't help but do. The guilt is overwhelming, but... he can't stop himself. Silently, he leans close to the small line of light, aiming an eye inside the secret room. The inside glow flickers erratically, like the light of a burning candle, but, his eye locked onto a vision, he can see nothing else—a woman's body, bare-breasted and bathed in the golden hue. She lies back, supported in the curve of a leather saddle. Enchanted by her generous breasts, the gentle curve of her hip, he can't take his eyes from her. As his own desire quickly grows, her face contorts with pleasure. She moans, allowing her head to loll back on her shoulders. Her hands drawn down, she seems to guide something there. And in the dim, he can just make out the silhouetted curve of something dark between the spread of her thighs.

His mind lost in the forbidden, Bunny's hands fly on autopilot, hurrying with his own zipper. The woman writhes and moans. Her mouth open, she pants. Faster now, faster, she reaches forward, squeezing out yelps of delight timed to the rapid beat from the music outside. Bunny pants as well, his heightened senses rushing headlong like a mustang charging off a cliff. Suddenly, with a loud gasp, she arches her back and cries out, falling limp with exhaustion. Bunny wipes his hand on his pants and rights himself, immediately feeling wracked with guilt and shame. Still, he can't resist a last look inside, hoping for another performance. This time, his eye lands on something he hadn't noticed. Hanging on the wall next to the girl is the signature Stetson hat belonging to TC Conway.

twenty

BUNNY EASILY FINDS the Willow Creek Rehab Center. It's only a few blocks away from the feed mill where he'd spent the first half of his Saturday. He's happy to get back to the physical work, and he and two new hires have already unloaded two semi-trucks this morning. Since it's lunchtime, this is Bunny's best opportunity to see Nan.

He finds a place in front of the cream-colored brick on the main street of town. Bunny parks and stares at the faded Willow Creek Rehab sign leaning haphazardly against the trunk of a massive tree. He must have passed this vanilla building plenty of times, but with the nondescript structure hidden behind an overgrowth of greenery, he can't remember ever seeing it before.

Bunny pushes open the door to the long, screened-in porch and a strong disinfectant-over-nicotine odor rushes at him. A full line of rocking chairs wearing a paint box of tired colors sits idle. A stack of magazines and folded newspapers waits on a nearby table. The room is so dim in the shade of surrounding trees it could be called anything but a sun porch. And unless the residents strap on a miner's hard hat equipped with light, no reading goes on here. Anyway, it smells more like the employee break room.

Entering the lobby, Bunny sees a small desk lamp burning. In the glow, a pair of illuminated glasses magnify a round, red-cheeked face. When Bunny approaches, the lady behind the desk, engrossed in a novel, doesn't notice him. The cover of the book in her hand features a muscled man, naked from the waist up, carrying a young woman partly covered in a torn, red ball gown. "Excuse me," Bunny says and prompts the lady to point one finger skyward, her milky eyes gliding across the page. She finds a place to stop and looks up, creasing a corner. "Nan Potts. Can you tell me where she is?" Bunny asks.

"Where's my lunch?" She blinks behind thick lenses.

"Lunch? Uh, no... I was... looking for someone."

She shrugs and reopens her novel.

"Ma'am," Bunny interrupts.

"Piss off, kid." She glances up, her dark pupils like islands in a sea of bloodshot white.

"Excuse me? Please... my mother, Nan Potts, was transferred here yesterday." His voice growing stronger, Bunny leans in to put a hand on the desk. That's when he notices her bath robe.

"You people need to bring me my damn lunch," she snaps, droplets spraying from a limp scowl. Across the room, Bunny can see light and hears voices from an opening. Side-stepping the romance enthusiast, he hurries to the noisy area filled with tables and chairs.

No food is visible yet, but a sharp, savory aroma floats on the air. Garlic. Smells like Italian lunch day in the school cafeteria, making his mouth water for a scoop of noodles with sweet tomato sauce.

"Get the hell outta my place," screams a shrunken man in a bow tie and vest. Hunched over, he's supported by a cane. The fancy dresser hovers at a full table where four women stare up at him. A head taller, Bunny can't help but notice the meticulous grooming of his snow-white hair, the side part perfect, the front lifted and flipped just so. The old guy smells like he just gargled Old Spice.

"Now, Jerry," says a sizable lady wearing a baby-blue nurse's uniform that probably fit twenty pounds ago. "You can sit over here with your buddy, Ned." She pats his shoulder and points to the next

THE FORGOTTEN SON

table where one vacant spot remains among two wide-eyed ladies and gape-mouthed Ned.

"Sheeez in my chair," Jerry spits, his face turning as red as his tie. He points and glares at a tiny woman feeding cheese doodles into her mouth. She responds with an orange-crusted smile. Other residents shuffle and roll into the room to claim territories, making Bunny think it's unlikely Nan could join them here. Bunny turns to the lady in blue.

"Nan Potts. Would you know where I could find her?"

"Name doesn't ring a bell." The woman shakes her head, monitoring Jerry, who curses and pumps a fist in the air.

"She's new, yesterday. I—" His words are interrupted as he's bumped backward by blue-uniform lady. She lunges across the table, intercepting the downward swing od Jerry's cane aimed at the head of the tiny, orange-crusted woman.

She waves for help, and two workers appear to escort the now sorrowful Jerry from the room. He blubbers as he's led away to time out.

"I'm so glad you get to stay with us girls," a tablemate giggles. "Jerry thinks we're all gaga for him, but really, his farts smell like rancid chicken." She pinches her nose and clutches the stained fingers of the lady who just missed out on having her head dented.

"Sorry," says the blue lady. "New transfers are all on Hall One. I'm afraid we're short-handed, so peek in the rooms and see if you can find her." She smiles and glides away to police other lunch infractions.

With the help of a sign, Bunny locates Hall One. There are doors, both to the right and left, down a long corridor. Most have names of occupants scribbled in black marker on white boards on the wall. The array of sound bleeding from the rooms collides in a jumble of noise in the common hallway. A desperate man's voice calls from several doors down. "Help me! Help meeee." A squeaky wheelchair rolls past, and a TV plays music for a soap opera program Nan faithfully watches.

Led by the familiar melody, Bunny checks the board outside the room for a name, but it's blank. The door partly closed, he pushes it slowly. And there she is, just a lump creating an uneventful rise in the bed, the covers pulled tight to her chin. Nan seems smaller than he'd remembered, curled under the faded blue spread as if she's trying to disappear. The TV blares while her untouched lunch congeals on the tray. Eyes fixed on the giant hourglass on the screen, she doesn't seem to notice Bunny.

"Nan, I've been trying to find you." He walks to the set and lowers the offensive volume. He takes a seat on the edge of the bed and pats her foot through the covers. No response. Nan's eyes set and unblinking, drool streams from the pulled corner of her mouth. The awkward vacuum of conversation prods Bunny to lean forward and touch her tray. "Your lunch. Like me to help?" He retrieves the knife and fork and cuts the slab of cold meat loaf. He guides a forkful toward Nan's face, but she doesn't notice. "Come on, Nan, you've got to eat to get better." After a few attempts, his only success is smearing a streak of mashed potatoes onto her pale lips.

Helpless, Bunny stands to cool his face against the concrete block wall, allowing his gaze to travel outside. The window looks out to the back of the lot. There's a patch of green with another long hall jutting out like a mirrored twin. Between the two arms of the building is a leaning shepherd's hook. It hovers just above the grass, bowed under the weight of a birdhouse. The once-yellow wooden box sways on the wind from the crook of the rod by a rusty wire loop. No self-respecting bird would live there. But like the residents of this place, maybe a down-on-his-luck feathered friend would have no choice.

"Nan," he says and turns back to her. "Don't give up." He kneels beside the bed and strokes her hair. When he finger-combs the dark strands away from her face, a shocking line of white makes him gasp. Unbelievable. Nan's turning grey. "You're all I've got," he whispers and pulls her hand up, cradling it between his. Measuring her palm to his own, Bunny turns it over. Long and tapered, such pretty hands;

his eyes lock on her vacant ring finger, stirring a sadness in him. The crushing guilt of his own existence is nothing new, but today, with all that makes Nan reduced to this sad place... it feels almost unbearable. Her life without Bunny, Nan's regretful mistake, could have been so much better. His mind goes to the smiling girl in her bedside photo at home. "You got the baby, Nan." He shakes his head and holds a breath with the rush of his emotion. "But the baby scared your man away."

Bunny waits until the music comes, ending the program, before he stands to go. "I've got to get back to work. I've got a job, just on weekends, but... it's great. TC helped me." This entire visit, Bunny thought Nan couldn't hear or maybe just refused to listen. But now she groans and two-finger-pulls the blue spread over her head.

"You can hear me!" he almost shouts. Bunny carefully rolls the cover down, unveiling her face. She delivers a hard look before turning away. "Talk to me... at least look at me, Nan." But there's no response.

Bunny pulls the door to his mother's room closed and leans against the wall outside in the hall. His eyesight fuzzy, tiny flicks of light flash in his vision. Faint, his legs wobbly, he slides down to sit on the floor. The lady in blue scrubs he'd befriended earlier appears from the corner, pushing a squeaky cart down hall number one.

"Well, hello again. Guess you found her?"

He stands, feeling awkward, and jams hands in his pockets, never sure what to do with them. "She finished with her tray?" Blue Scrubs smiles, stopping her wheeled collection at Nan's door.

"Can I ask you something?" Bunny says, staring into her warm brown eyes. She nods and looks back, giving her full attention. Yes, this lady will give straight answers. "How many of the people that are here..." He takes a breath. "How many... get better and go home?"

Lines crease her forehead. His question is a surprise. She makes her lips into a hard line, considering the answer. "Willow Creek... is more like a last stop." She touches Bunny's arm. "We try to make them comfortable."

twenty-one

HALF OF THE MORNING GONE, and TC is just now getting his first cup of coffee. It's not like Bridget to leave him sleeping. She's probably pissed because he was gone most of the night. It seems someone needed his attention again for a late-night call to the big red barn. Bridget is usually understanding when the neighbors need him, but lately she's been sending signals that say otherwise.

TC is dragging this morning. After last night, he's figured out that Anna-Marie must be more than a little disappointed in the available men at the university. That girl's like a leaky faucet. Once turned on, it's hard to turn her off.

Twenty birthdays difference between their ages, and this morning, TC feels every bit his larger number. He and Anna-Marie have enjoyed each other's company for years. He watched her grow up, being neighbors and all. But their relationship started when she gave him the eye at a high school basketball game. When she handed him a steaming paper cup in the concession stand, their fingers touched and their eyes locked. Anna-Marie did not look away.

Over the next two years, there was always something that needed his attention at Anna-Marie's place. And anyway, showing young girls how to enjoy sex was a gift. TC regarded himself as a master teacher and was happy to contribute. But then the day came when she was to leave for college. TC remembers well the night before she was to board the plane going east. She had never shown him her tender side, but with his arms around her, the silent tears against his chest were something new. But it was time. Time for Anna-Marie to get a different kind of education and maybe find love along the way. TC was surprised when she called that first fall, saying she'd be home for Thanksgiving break. He scratches his chin stubble, grinning at the memory of last night. That girl's a wildcat.

"When are you going back to school?" TC says, as Jodie crutches into the kitchen. Annoyed by the absence of Bridget's made-from-scratch biscuits and gravy, he makes do with a second cup.

"Few more weeks, doctor says. Don't worry. I'm keeping up in school."

"Wasn't worried." He grins and tips his hat brim back. "Just tired of looking at you."

"Yeah, yeah," Jodie says, taking notice of the work gloves laid out on the table. "You just miss my help. I'm a better hand than most guys."

"Sounds right. Where's your mom?"

"Potts' house. Something about… a cat invasion." Jodie shrugs and goes back to pouring orange juice.

"Your momma." TC shakes his head. "Too much love, too much caring."

"Kinda makes up for you, then." Jodie grins, looking back as she double-times it on her crutches out of the kitchen.

Even tired as he is today, TC knows he has to oversee the operation of separating the yearlings from the momma cows in the high pasture. He's been running a bull with the group for the past few months and is sure by now all the ladies are knocked-up. Time to get the babies off and allow the cows to dry up and get ready to do it all over again. TC employs the best ranch hands he can find, but he has to keep an eye on those punchers. If they can take a shortcut, they will. With no real stake in the ranch, the most important thing for the cowboy is enough coin to throw back a few on Saturday night. It's no big deal to them if the number is short. But even a few head of missing cattle cost him money, and TC always counts carefully.

TC can feel Bridget's anger, even though her comments are always silent. The fact she didn't wake him with a cup of coffee, saying breakfast is almost ready, screams displeasure. He needs to stop by the Potts' place and see if he can mend fences.

Sure enough, her station wagon is out front. His eyes scan over the weathered wood of the old place, stirring a sadness inside him. The front door hangs wide open. Waist-high weeds and grass in thick clumps stand across the lawn and hug the side of the house. When TC reaches the porch, he steps over ominous dark splotches of stained wood. "Is that blood?" he mutters under his breath, kicking away house flies that seem to love it. The boards under his boots groan and make him wonder if the sorry-looking stuff is going to break from his weight. The entire place feels like a sad, slow-motion rewind. Last time he had been inside was when he lifetime-deeded it to Nan. That was before Bunny was born. It's much worse than he'd remembered.

One step inside the open door and the nauseating smell makes TC grab his nose. "Oh, my god, Bridget?" Her head wrapped in a bandanna, she appears from the door of the bathroom. "How can you stand this?" TC says. "This is like a port-a-john times fifty."

Bridget rubs her chin with the back of a yellow gloved hand. "Guess I'm desensitized." She smiles. "Dirty diapers, cleaning bathrooms, sleeping alone. I try to get past the bad things."

Yep, she's pissed. "This place needs a match," TC says, looking around.

"Well, it's Bunny's home, and right now, he can't even stay inside. Glad you're here. You can judge for yourself. We've got to help."

"We? Looks like you're already working up a sweat."

"I want you to look around. Open the refrigerator, the cupboards, go look in the closet."

Refusing to let go of his nose, TC roams through the house obediently and peeks into cabinets and closets.

After a minute or two, he finds her with a dustpan mounded full. "Did you see? Nothing to eat except trashy snacks. No clothes or towels. Pitiful." Bridget vocalizes her disgust, but her positive action is throttled down. Fulfilled by her calling to save the world, she's happy as a child on a swing.

"All this?" TC taps his boot against a half-full, thirty-gallon trash can. "All this just happen?"

Bridget bugs her eyes and shakes her head. "A lot of this has been here for a long time. See, it's all dried out. I've been sweeping it from under the beds, the table, the closets."

"She really is crazy, then," he says, looking off into space.

"Nan?" Bridget nods. "I heard she's not doing well, either. Massive damage."

"Okay, momma." TC smiles at Bridget and tips his hat. "I'm headed over to work the high pasture. Probably be dark before I get home, late start and all." He gives Bridget a sad look, hoping to stroke her loving heart.

"Maybe one day you can teach Bunny. Get him comfortable on a horse, learn the ranch."

"Mmmmm, don't think so. Babysitter, that's outside my pay grade."

"But, you always help the neighbors," Bridget says, taking him off guard. "Even when it pulls you from our bed."

Stunned, he couldn't believe this. This skinny woman is calling his bluff.

"Did you see that front fence?" Bridget points toward the road. "He needs a role model, work with a man, have something he cares about."

"Pretty hard to miss," TC grins, admiring her grit. "Hope crazy isn't passed from mother to son. Horses and cattle are big enough to do some damage."

"Poor kid has no idea. Just look at this place."

TC shakes his head, marveling at how satisfied he'd felt just minutes before with the memories of last night. Now, standing here, it's like the walls are closing in. Role model? Not so sure about that. He can almost feel the rope tightening around his neck. "Well, I'm gone, Mrs. Conway," he says, using her favorite pet name. He turns for the door, feeling an urgent need for fresh air. "You'll work your magic. Looks like you don't need me."

"Not today, but think about getting Bunny involved with the ranch," Bridget says, doubling down on the request. "Oh, TC, see that broken glass there by the bed?" She points. "I haven't made it there yet. Can you get that?"

When TC stoops to collect the jagged pile, his boot happens to kick the loose photo, sending it under the bed. "Well, shit," he whispers. He gathers a palm full of shards, trashes them, and inspects the splintered wood frame. "I don't think this is salvageable," he says, tossing it into the can. Next, he gets on hands and knees, feeling blind under the bed for the runaway photo. As his fingers sweep the floor, he knocks it even further out of reach. TC bends lower to see where it's landed but jumps up with a sharp pain. Turning his palm over reveals an oozing cut, a piece of glass he'd missed sticking out. "Oh, for the love of god."

This time when he hunkers down to look, he removes his hat, leaning forward on his elbows. His face only inches off the floor, the smell he's stirred is so intense he turns his head and holds his breath. TC reaches as far as possible, and with the bed frame digging into his shoulder, his fingertips can just touch the corner. After several tries, he manages to drag the photo out.

When TC looks at the picture, he's dumbstruck. His mind warps backward with the weight of the past. "Oh, I remember..." he whispers and glances over his shoulder, making sure he's alone. The pretty girl in the photo is laughing, head thrown back, her smile wide, eyes squeezed tight with happiness. The paper edge is thick, and he flips it over to discover more of the image folded underneath. It's something he'd dismissed long ago. A memory so forgotten his mind screams—*was this real?* It's a young Nan. Her sandy hair shining in the light, her carefree posture saying, "not a care in the world." And to her right, hidden behind the fold and inside the frame, is the image of a tall, young cowboy with a shiny watch chain hanging from his pocket.

twenty-two

PREOCCUPIED WITH NAN'S SITUATION, Bunny is surprised when he finds himself pulling up in front of their ramshackle home. He sits in the car for a moment, staring at the weathered wood and sagging roof. He imagines Nan on the porch with one of her beloved cats draped across her lap. She hums as she rocks, stopping occasionally to sweet-talk the fur-baby. It's a scene he'd witnessed many times walking up the road from the school bus. Nan lavishing her love on the animals, a tender but hurtful memory. His nagging need for a mother's touch has faded over the years, but the painful thought still wounds his heart.

As he walks close to the door, the place feels different. Nan may never return. The thought of being on his own has Bunny off balance. It feels like walking up a hill with one short leg. His perpetual loneliness at a low point, he stops on the porch. It's clean. The sticky blood has been scrubbed away, and with it, the congregating flies. He opens the door, ready for the smelly assault, but the sweet richness of vanilla waits inside. The floors are shiny, the counters clean, the room bright with twenty years of grime erased from the window glass. Bunny marvels at the color of the porcelain, the gleam of the faucet, the glow of the wood. "Oh... how... how?" he mumbles, his eyes straining to take it all in.

The sound of an engine outside demands his attention, and Bunny looks out to see Bridget. She pulls a casserole dish out of her car.

"I had to run home for this," she says, balancing a glass pan with hot pads. "Jodie put this together so... don't blame me if she didn't do it right. Just goulash, but it smells pretty good." Bridget plants the heavy, foil-covered dish on the stovetop with a thud. The smell of garlic, tomatoes, and beef marry into a mouth-watering aroma, stirring Bunny's hunger. Hands on hips, she takes in the room. Satisfaction radiates from her, and she beams. "What do you think?"

Embarrassed by a sudden wave of emotion, Bunny turns his head away. He takes a breath, hoping to steady his voice. "I wish... Nan could see this."

Admiring her work, Bridget acts distracted. She glides through the rooms and seems to check off items from a mental list. "Still want to stock your refrigerator with healthy foods. Can you cook, Bunny?"

He shrugs. "Sandwiches, eggs... when we had chickens." His voice going soft, he studies the floor.

Bridget cocks her head, blinking at him. "That's a hard no, then. Mmmmm, perhaps I can show you a few simple dishes." Her eyes sparkle with the sound of her own words. "Dishes?" she repeats, her eyebrows shooting up. "I didn't find many."

Bunny points to the small stack of blue metal plates and cups on the counter. Having swept up plenty of their mismatched thrift store pottery and glass over the years, Bunny was secretly glad when Nan ran out of ammunition.

"Clothes," she announces and snaps her fingers. "Are there more? I took what I found to launder, but there must be more."

Suffering in the spotlight, Bunny pockets his hands and mumbles, "My trunk."

Bridget's face goes pale, and she bobs her head toward the

wooden box against the wall. "That... that is your trunk?" It wasn't a trunk really, only the lower portion remained. Nan had taken a hammer to it years before. Bunny had been hiding slutty magazines, so she'd pried off the hinges and burned the top. The remaining open wood box was Bunny's only storage. "Well, never mind." She touches his arm. "I'm afraid the cats had their way in there. Now, sizes? Definitely slim fit." Bridget circles, looking Bunny over like a steak in a butcher's shop. Seeing his confusion, she adds. "I'll pick up things for you to try." She stops directly in front of him and squares his shoulders with her hands, giving him no choice but to look into her face. "There must be somebody you'd like to dress nicely for. Maybe a girl? I found the washing machine on the back porch." Bridget gestures. "Can you show me how to turn it on?"

"Been broken a while."

"How do you do laundry then?" Bridget says, her eyes so big they're ready to pop from her face. Bunny points toward the bathroom. "The *tub*? You're kidding." She makes a face, exhaling air like a flat tire.

With this last news, Bridget seems tired, her energy spent. Her face droops, shoulders sag, and her smile fades. "Well, I'll let you get some supper in you," she says, turning for the door.

"How..." Bunny stammers. "How did you do all this?"

"Oh!" Bridget spins about, suddenly energized with recognition. Her face overflowing with eagerness, she looks like she might lead a cheer. "Do you like it? I hope so. Vanilla, the fragrance, is my favorite. So much better than what we were smelling." She smiles and takes a breath, seeming to want more praise but happy with Bunny's expression of wonder.

Still trying to accept this new and improved version of home, the same place where he's lived his entire life, Bunny's head rotates like an owl. "I never thought it could look... like this."

"Now, I know it's a little bare," Bridget says, fanning her long fingers. "Some furniture wasn't salvageable. Broken or soiled. But we'll collect a few things. Maybe some paint on the walls. What's your favorite color, Bunny?"

"Don't know." He shrugs. "Purple?" Bunny remembers a fuzzy sweater he'd seen Raquel once wear.

"Mmmmm, well, we'll talk about that," Bridget says, pressing her lips tight. "Oh, one more thing. The phone." She points to the nightstand where it sits on the cradle.

"I believe it's important you get messages when you're not here, you know, for your mom. I'll get you an answering machine. I wrote my number down here so you can reach us." She grins, waving a small note pad in the air.

For the first time, Bunny notices the vacant space on the nightstand. It takes just a second for him to remember what's missing. "The photo, Nan's picture..." His voice sounds frantic, even to his own ears. He touches the worn space on the table. The framed photo had sat there as long as he could remember.

"Oh, yes," says Bridget, her eyes crinkled with thought. "It was shattered, the glass and frame. I asked TC to clean that up. Wonder where the photo went?" She bends down, looking under the bed. "Don't see it. I'll have to ask TC."

"It's just... I need that. It's the only picture of her." As Bunny gets the words out, his vision is cloudy, his eyes overflow.

"Oh, Bunny," Bridget says and throws her arms around him. "Your mom? You see her today?"

He buries his face against her shoulder and heaves, letting go of a lifetime of suck-it-up. His raw pain jars Bridget into mommy mode. She pats his back and whispers. "It'll be alright, Bunny. It'll be alright." His gut-twisting cries are so powerful, he can hear her sniffing back her own tears.

The two of them stand together as Bunny empties his sadness. When it tapers to silence, she takes his shoulders, holds him at arm's length, and stares into his eyes. "Now listen to me. I want you to eat, then take a nice, long bath. You're an obedient son, Bunny, and that's why you care. Tomorrow, there's more to do, and don't you worry. I'll find your photo."

He wipes at his face and nods as Bridget kisses his cheek. *Is this what a mom is supposed to be like?* When Bridget turns to leave, Bunny watches at his door as this angel of a lady drives away. Very confused, he has no way of understanding her bottomless well of kindness. He has nothing to offer, so why is she doing this? It's not like she doesn't have better things to do. Miss Bridget has her own family, husband, and a big house. What does she care if his floors are clean or what he has for supper?

twenty-three

BRIDGET WOULD GIVE anything to have seen the look on TC's face when he saw that photo. For her, there had been something cleansing about the painful discovery. When Bridget pulled back the concealed portion of the picture, her long-time suspicions were confirmed. She is not, as she feared, losing her mind.

Staring at the image of her handsome young husband with his arm around that woman, something snapped inside her. Bridget is the one who bore his children, cooked their meals, washed the clothes. She's the one that kept the house and made it a home. Just like that, the anxiety she had always felt around TC just dried up and blew away. Bridget had always been terrified of making a wrong step, saying the wrong thing, upsetting TC. Her married years were like walking on hot coals, afraid of giving him a reason to find another woman. All this time, she had been a loving wife, and for what? TC had been carrying on from their wedding night—probably even before.

Bridget knew TC had done something with Bunny's photo. He probably hid it or, please God, don't let him have thrown it away. "I've got to get that back," Bridget says, thinking of the grieving boy worried about his mom. Her mind on fire, her back aches. What a sack of snakes that image opens, like the question of Bunny's mystery father. Had TC's seemingly generous gift of the little house and land been a bribe to keep Nan quiet? Bunny is a victim in this carnage, just like she is. Amazing how TC just swaggers through life, ruining people, then spitting them out like chewed gum.

When Bridget tops the hill, there's a white truck parked at the back of her house. "Ugh, company. What now?" She huffs in frustration. Her tired muscles dragging from her brutal marathon day, her mind is foggy and confused by her painful TC discovery. Nerves standing on end, all Bridget wants to do is fall into her comfortable chair and stare at a blank wall.

"Hello, Anna-Marie," Bridget says, knocking on the window. The girl sleeping across the seat jumps awake.

Eyes blinking, Anna-Marie lowers the glass. "Oh, Bridget, sorry to bother you. I was looking for advice from TC." The sweet smell of honeysuckle drifts from inside the truck. Standing close, Bridget can see the girl is wearing a pink spaghetti-strap lace blouse with a good half of her breasts exposed by the plunging neckline.

The almost-gone sun has packed up and taken the warmth of the day with it. The night air blowing across Conway hilltop is strong and cold. "Girl, you're gonna catch a chest-cold dressed like that." Bridget manages to laugh, making Anna-Marie blush and reach for her sweater in the seat. "Afraid TC hasn't made it home yet. He got a late start today, after last night." The sound of her words seems harsh, and Bridget reminds herself to be cool.

"Guilty, sorry," Anna-Marie apologizes. "It's just that my poor mare, Lady, is in a bad way. I'm worried about her. She's my best saddle horse."

The low simmer of Bridget's anger boils. This girl is not fooling anyone, looking for TC dressed like a hooker. She's probably wanting a giddy-up replay of last night when she had TC out until almost sunrise. Intrigued, Bridget plays along, giving her best wide-eyed expression. "Maybe you should have a vet take a look?"

"Well, yes." Anna-Marie looks down, talking into her lap. "It's just, I haven't been able to pay for the last time Doc was out, so I can't call him back—not while I'm still in his debt. Me in school and mom and dad with their health, we always seem to run out of money before we run out of things that need to be paid."

Automatically, Bridget experiences a pang of sympathy for the girl. She's known the Belcher family her whole life, and they have had a bad run of it. First, Anna-Marie's daddy was diagnosed with lung cancer, and then her momma needed a hip replacement. But then Bridget pats the window edge of the fancy new truck and remembers the whopping price tag these beauties come with. "Nice truck," Bridget says, taking note of the crossed American flag decal on the door. "Is this the limited bi-centennial edition?"

"Yes, got it last year."

Bridget takes another look at her visitor's almost naked breasts, now covered in goose flesh even though she's hugging her sweater with a pretense of modesty. Trusting her eyes more than the girl's words, she recognizes the smell of bullshit. Her aching back cracks as she tells her heart to get out of her head. "I see, but I'm not sure what TC can offer."

"I know, but he has a real touch. My Lady responds to him."

"Oh, I bet she does. I know mine always has."

"Oh, you have a Lady, too?"

"Don't we all?" Bridget smirks. Tired of role-playing the gullible victim, she changes things up. "Have you had your supper yet?" she asks. "Come inside to wait. I've got a casserole and salad all ready." Bridget attempts a smile. "Come on now, it's getting chilly. No use waiting out here in the dark and cold."

"Oh no, I couldn't."

"Sure you can," Bridget says and quickly opens the truck door. The reveal of the rest of Anna-Marie's outfit makes Bridget gasp. Two shapely, long, and naked legs disappear into a pair of plaid men's boxers. Before Bridget can edit herself, words fly. "TC has a pair just like that." Her face suddenly flushed with anger, Bridget struggles for control. She recognizes the boxers immediately, being such an unusual pattern and one that she had special-ordered all the way from Ireland. It's the distinctive plaid of the Conway clan. TC would never wear a kilt, even to please her, but she had ordered the drawers, thinking he would enjoy the next best thing.

Reaching for the open truck door, Anna-Marie seems embarrassed and surprised. "Not really dressed to get out," she stammers, pulling it closed.

"I see," says Bridget, certain now of the only thing Anna-Marie has in mind for TC. The conversation feels like a frantic ping-pong game. The white ball smacks the table on her side, and Bridget backhands a return. "No worries. Let me run inside and make you a plate. If you hang on, I'm sure TC will be here soon." She spins on her heel, hoping she's done a good job of convincing the girl, and hurries inside the house.

Jodie meets her mom at the kitchen door. It's obvious she's been spying out the window. "What's going on, Mom? Why do you look so… crazy?"

Bridget glances in the mirror beside the door, flinching at her own image. Her hair pokes out at angles from the wrapped bandana, and dirty sweat trails line her cheeks. Shot full of adrenalin, her eyes bulge from their sockets.

"Can you make me a plate?" Bridget's request sounding more like a demand. Jodie stares at her mom like she's deaf. "Please," Bridget says, trying to reassure her confused daughter. "I'm going to take it outside to Anna-Marie." She turns her back on the open-mouthed Jodie and rushes up the stairs to her bedroom.

Bridget runs to her side of the bed, lifts the mattress, and reaches underneath. The smooth hardness of the cool steel against her fingers is gratifying as she pulls the Remington .38 into the light. Funny, she thinks, staring at the weapon. *Our marriage bed is where I've always stored the gun. What a foretelling bit of irony. The symbol of our shot-to-hell union.* TC had given Bridget the pink-handled revolver several years earlier at Christmas. She turns the gun to check the safety, then secures it in her waistband and covers it with her blouse.

Glancing out the second-story window, she sees the white truck still in the driveway. "Stupid girl," she whispers. She races down the stairs just as Jodie turns from the stove with a loaded plate. "You want sweet tea with this?" But Bridget ignores the question, snatches the food, and heads for the door.

In the almost dark of the outside, Bridget pauses, pulling the door closed behind her. She takes a deep, healing breath and feels, for the first time in years, strong and in control. "My house, my family," she reassures herself. Balancing the hot plate of food in her left hand, she casually approaches the driver's side of the truck. The hum of the window going down feeds her energy, and she realizes there's no turning back.

"Oh, Bridget, really, you didn't need to do this," Anna-Marie gushes, smelling the food.

"Afraid I did," Bridget says through gritted teeth. She pulls her weapon and points it at Anna-Marie. "Now, you shimmy out of those boxers and hand 'em over." She holds the pistol on the wide-eyed girl as she bumps around inside the truck like a woodpecker on speed. Anna-Marie keeps her mouth shut as she shucks off the underwear. In short order, the newly freed shorts fly out the window. "Don't forget your supper," Bridget says and dumps the plate of hot food into the girl's bare lap. Her cruelty is rewarded with a yelp. With two now-steady hands, she taps the steel barrel against the open window, demanding full attention. Bridget's voice strong, she delivers her warning. "TC is *my* husband. And before you come sniffing around here again like some bitch in heat, you better ask yourself, 'Is getting laid worth getting dead?'"

twenty-four

TC SHOUTS, "OH, MY GOD," as Anna-Marie's truck goes up on two wheels. Speeding through the ninety-degree turn to the highway, she almost rolls, but bounces down on four, her white truck racing toward TC, who's headed in the opposite direction. He flashes his lights and pulls to the side. But she zips past, driving with something besides her hands because both of them are out the open window shooting TC the double-barrel bird. "What the hell is she doing?" he mutters, watching her truck disappear in the side mirror.

Clearly, the girl is upset about god knows what, and his instinct is to turn around and chase her down. But he's pulling a loaded trailer, so that won't work. TC feels good about the deal he made, swapping the cow and calf pair for the filly in the trailer. Still, there's the question of how Red will react. Bridget's big idea that the boy should learn the ranch might not pan out. He might not have any interest. If he wants to learn, TC has decided to show him a few things. But if it's a halfhearted effort, he'll cut the lessons and save the sweat.

When Bridget first pushed the idea, TC had walked away, positive he would never do it. But then he reasoned it'd be good to have someone besides himself who could look after things. Someone reliable that he could count on. If he was in the middle of an afternoon meeting, say with Darleen, and something went sideways, no longer would he need to cut things short. If cattle bust through a fence, a horse gets hurt, or any of the screw-ups that happen, TC could rely on his new hand. Red working the ranch might be a good thing.

Eager to show off what he's done toward Bridget's request, TC stops at the house before heading to the barn. "She's one of the prettiest little fillies I've ever seen." TC smiles at Jodie. "Get you mother and come take a look."

"Mom's asleep, I think. She came home looking all crazy, said she was tired, and went upstairs. Meredith made sure Amy got her bath and brushed her teeth."

TC walks back to the truck and horse trailer as Jodie crutches along behind, in the precious illumination from the light pole. TC slides the upper window open, pats the edge, and makes a clicking sound. "Come on, pretty," he calls softly. "Come on."

A heavy clomp sounds against the wood floor. First one, then another, then three, four... until out of the darkness, a slender muzzle appears. A blaze running the length of the head is brilliant against the blackness. The light streak is flanked by auburn so shiny it gleams like fire. The filly's dark eyes, with a fingernail of white, flutter inside the jerk of her head. "There now, it's okay, pretty girl." TC holds his hand flat as flared nostrils move over his palm. Soon, he's able to stroke the soft, pink-speckled nose. Accepting now, one more step bumps a hoof against the metal side, and the full head emerges from the trailer window.

"Oh, so beautiful," says Jodie.

"Told ya."

"Early birthday present for me?"

"Afraid not. Got her for Red."

"What? Why?"

"Request from your mom." He puts up his hands, shaking his head. "That big heart."

"Dad... Ronald McDonald doesn't know horses. Maybe get you an order of fries."

TC frowns at his daughter. "Okay, smart mouth. Teaching him'll be a good job for you."

"Me? I can't even walk, much less break a horse."

"She's not ready. Got some growing to do. Be right about the time you're mended."

"Whatever," Jodie snaps and crutches to the passenger side.

They drive the trailer to the barn, and TC leads the filly into a stall. The other horses, curious about the newcomer, murmur a course of throaty sounds and stamp impatiently as they strain against their stalls to get a look. He puts the young horse into the space next to Mae, his oldest mare. The gentle old lady will calm the baby. He gives the new girl a ration of oats, shows her the water bowl, and adds a block of hay to her rack. As TC walks away, he hears Mae already talking to her new neighbor.

The wind howling through the dark barn is a reminder of the nights he'd followed his father when he was a boy. With six children in their tiny house, the Preacher would often seek a quiet place to compose his sermons. About a quarter of a mile behind his boyhood home was an ancient log barn. When Preacher Conway would escape, armed with pencil, paper, and the Good Book, TC would sneak out and trail behind at a safe distance.

Shivering outside the barn in the darkness, TC had peeked between the logs where the mud had fallen away. Preacher would set up the lantern and settle into the hay where he would scribble notes. TC remembers once nodding off during the watch, his face tucked inside his jacket, warmed by his own breath. When he woke, the disturbing image seared into his brain like a brand. Preacher with his arms around a woman, her hair long and loose, flowing across their entwined naked bodies, the Good Book discarded in the hay.

TC knew his father had remorse for his indiscretions. He'd felt the misdirected anger in every strong lash from Preacher's belt. Beating TC was his father's personal atonement. And afterward,

Preacher would seem happy, kiss his wife, and sit by the fire, studying God's word. That is, until the next time. That's when TC first became fond of old barns. They felt sacred, like church, but a lot more fun.

Fingers to his ears, TC scowls at Jodie to kill the loud music pumping from the 8-track as he hops back into the truck. "Surprised Anna-Marie hasn't shown up," he says. "That mare of hers is still healing."

"Oh, she did."

"Really? When?"

"You just missed her... actually."

"She ask for me?"

Jodie shrugs. "Mom took her a plate of food, then, she left."

"She hungry?"

"Guess. Ask Mom."

TC drops Jodie off at the house. He wants to check on the mare anyway and hopes Anna-Marie will turn up at the barn. TC drives to the Big Red Barn and walks the long corridor where he's greeted by the chestnut mare. Her head over the top rail, she gives TC a soft whinny. "How you doing, Lady? How's the leg?" The horse waits patiently as TC unwraps the injury and examines it by lantern light. "Little bit better." He pats her chest, soaks the wound again in the purple antibiotic, and skillfully rewraps it. "Wonder where your owner is?" he asks, giving the mare a neck rub.

On the way home, TC remembers the disturbing photo he'd seen at Nan's today. When he stops at the house, he glances inside his truck glove compartment where her youthful face stares at him, an irritating memory he'd left behind long ago. Who knows why she'd kept that? He slams the door and vows to find a new frame for it tomorrow.

After he eats a cold supper left on the stove, there's still no word from Anna-Marie, so he calls it a night. He opens the bedroom door, and as he steps into the dark room, the reading lamp snaps on. Bridget glares at him from the chair under the light. Startled, TC realizes she's been waiting in the pitch blackness. Across the end of their bed, smooth and flat as if on display, are his Conway clan plaid boxers. The sight sends a coldness to his stomach as a rush of heat makes sweat pop across his brow.

"TC, you son of a bitch!" Bridget screams, leaping from the chair. Her arms swinging like a windmill, she rushes at him. One of her balled fists catches the side of his head before he's able to wrap her in a self-defense bear hug. Shaking with anger, she sobs into his shoulder. Their bodies pressed together, Bridget empties her tears, soaking his shirt. After a time, she quiets. Sagging from his grip, she pushes away to face him. There's nothing he can say. He can't deny Anna-Marie. Hell, the evidence is on the bed. The only thing worse would be for Bridget to catch them in the act. It's painful to see the bottomless hurt in Bridget's soft, grey eyes and now he must deal with the elephant in the room. But TC's magic hands might make that disappear. He knows his wife is overdue for some lovemaking, as she calls it. He closes his eyes and imagines being with the girl who'd taken the boxers off him last night. If he does a good enough job, Bridget might forget why she's angry. TC cradles her slender face between his large hands. "She's gone," he whispers, and pulls Bridget in for a hungry kiss.

twenty-five

BUNNY'S HANDS tremble as he pulls his door closed. He'd just jogged around the back of the blue Chevy after opening the door for Raquel, but with his stomach in knots, his lungs feel like they've stopped working. He buries his fingers under his thighs, hoping she didn't notice he had the shakes. "All set?" He smiles across the front seat, thinking Raquel looks especially beautiful in her red jacket today. The striking contrast with her long, dark hair makes Bunny's heart flutter. Just like a powerful drug, he can stand only brief glimpses of her smooth skin and red lips before feeling faint and looking away.

"Yes..." she answers, ducking to look under the sun visor. "What do you think those guys are up to?"

Bunny had noticed them, too. Mean Man Watson and his posse were out front of the school and watching them. "They probably just wish it was them with you—instead of me."

"No chance of that." She flutters her long, dark lashes. And even though he tries to make light of the situation, experience tells Bunny something is up, making his already nervous stomach churn like a hamster on a wheel. He smiles and transfers his hands to the safe driving positions of ten and two. Nothing is going to screw up his trip with Raquel.

"So glad you can take me home."

"What did you say to make your dad change his mind?"

"Actually, it was Mother. She told him I could start dinner so everyone could eat earlier."

Bunny backs the car from the space at the wall and points it toward Raquel's house. A quick glance in the mirror confirms Watson is still standing in the schoolyard. The big man glares after them, his outline rising out of the group like a photo Bunny had seen of the Empire State Building.

"I'm so happy." Raquel smiles. "I hate riding the bus."

"Better make your dad something special for dinner. What are you making? Enchiladas? Tacos? Burritos?" Raquel laughs wildly, blushes, and covers her mouth with her hand. "So quick to assume that's all we eat," she scolds.

"Sorry… I just thought…"

"Exactly." She tries to hide a smile. "We're having hamburgers and fries." Bunny does a double take, unsure about her answer, but Raquel only nods, looking back with happy green eyes. They drive past the impressive sign near the highway touting the success of the football team. Over the summer, last year's win had been added to the list—1976 State Champs. "The stupid football team is the only claim to fame in the entire school," she scoffs.

"Yep, that's why those guys get away with everything." Bunny guides the car up the hill and notices a small vibration in the steering wheel. He looks back, wondering if he'd hit a rock or a small animal. Nothing behind him.

"I meant to tell you—I like your new clothes." Raquel grins.

"My neighbor lady picked these," Bunny says and smooths the front of the blue plaid shirt. "I never had one with these things."

"Oh, silly, that's a pearl snap."

"That what cowboys wear?" says Bunny. "Maybe she thinks I should be one."

"Well, I like it," Raquel laughs, then reaches out, touching his hair. "Now, if we could just do something with this."

Bunny flinches and jerks his head away. "My... hair?" he stammers as his hands fly off the wheel, making sure his ears are covered before grabbing the wheel again.

His reaction throwing her off, Raquel nibbles her thumb then answers softly, "Yes... so much of it."

Bunny glances in the mirror at the mass of red curls pushing below his cap. The shudder in his hands again, stronger this time, is followed by a sudden grinding squeal.

"What's that?"

"Something is wrong," Bunny shouts. The squeal becomes an unbearable hammering just before the engine dies. The car continues to roll with its own momentum as thick smoke trails around the hood, dousing the windshield black.

Raquel plasters herself against the opposite door. "What's happening?" she shouts, her voice shaky, her face gone white. "Are we on fire?"

Steering off the highway, he cranks down his window and pushes halfway outside to see. The car slows, and Bunny gets off the road, hoping for a flat spot. Gliding to a stop, he gets out and tries to lift the hood... like he knows what he's doing. The metal is so hot it burns his fingers, and he yelps in pain. He goes to the trunk for a rag and tries again. Now he's able to pull the release, and when he pushes the hood open, black smoke covers him in a greasy, grey residue. Bunny wipes his eyes with the rag and watches helplessly as a dark cloud boils off the engine. Out of the car, Raquel shrinks back. She stares up as the wind swirls the dense burst skyward like smoke signals. The acrid stink of burned oil coats the air, and she grabs her nose.

With boyish hope, Bunny tries the ignition again. This time, the pitiful click-click of the starter says *we give up*. "Looks like we're stuck." Bunny backs away from the heat. He takes a few steps closer to Raquel. "I'm sorry. Never had nothing like this happen before. Don't understand." He shakes his head and kicks a rock into the ditch. "The car was fine." His mind churns. What happened? All he wanted to do was give Raquel a ride home. Now this! When he looks up, Raquel's eyes crinkle as she bites her lip. "What? What's... funny?" says Bunny.

"It's just that... your face," she manages before erupting in laughter. "Go look."

Checking in the side mirror, Bunny sees his face speckled in grey soot, his eyes streaked where he wiped at them. "We're stuck, and you're laughing?"

"Maybe someone will see the smoke and rescue us," she says, pointing to the sky. "At least, I hope. I have to make good on my promise to start dinner or dad won't trust me." No sooner had the words been spoken than a red convertible appears, topping the hill behind them. "Look, Bunny, there's someone."

Not ready to ask for help, Bunny says, "We could walk... I'll carry your books. Only a few miles." But when he notices the flowery wedge-heel sandals on Raquel's feet, he adds, "Maybe?" But she doesn't seem to hear his idea. She watches as the red car crunches gravel, pulling off the road, and coasts to stop behind them.

The driver makes Raquel gasp. "Well, well, what do we have here?" smirks Mean Man Watson as he strides to the front of his car. He parks his butt against the hood and crosses his arms with a satisfied expression. "Looks like a little car trouble." He smiles. "Hey, loser," he says, pointing at Bunny, hooting loudly, and slapping his leg. "Your face looks worse than normal."

"We've got it under control... so, we're good." Bunny tries to sound confident but is pretty sure he's about to throw up.

"Good?" Watson bugs his eyes. "She doesn't look so good." He gestures toward Raquel. "Out here in the ditch, watching your sorry excuse of a car simmer on the side of the road."

Bunny steps closer to Raquel. "We don't need your help."

"Well," Watson snorts, "I couldn't do anything with... with... *that*, anyway." He pushes off his own hood and strides to the front of the blue Chevy. Shaking his head, he laughs. "Looks like a bigger piece of shit than it was." Watson does a slow saunter, circling Bunny to get closer to Raquel. "What I could do is take the little lady home." He flashes a nasty grin and reaches for her arm. "Come on, let me take you home in style."

Raquel jerks away, stepping close to Bunny. Her footing twists on the angle of the ditch and she stumbles. Bunny and Watson dive from each side to keep her from falling.

"Look—" Watson points to her sleeve where Bunny has left a black print. "Now he's ruined your clothes. Can't you keep those greasy loser paws to yourself?"

"You—keep your hands off her," Bunny shouts and steps forward.

"You've got some gall, you skinny shit. I'm trying to help, and you're too stupid to realize that." Watson grabs Raquel around the waist, snugs her under his arm, and carries her like a football headed to the end zone.

"Get off me you... you baboon! Auuuuuggghhh! Put me down." Raquel kicks wildly and pounds him with her fist. Watson strolls with his prey toward the convertible.

Bunny rushes at the backside of the man mountain. He clutches his hands together, doubling them into one giant fist, raises it high above his head, and crashes it home at the base of Watson's neck. The big man turns in his tracks, pissed off for sure.

"Are you kidding me?" he asks, giving Raquel her feet. She draws back and lands a solid slap across Watson's meaty face. His silly grin evaporates as he blinks for a second, touching the red outline on his cheek. He charges Bunny, wraps him in a headlock, dragging him by the neck to the open trunk of the blue Chevy where Watson tosses Bunny inside like a paper wad and slams the lid down. "You know what? You two deserve each other," Watson shouts.

When Bunny hears Raquel's voice pleading, "No... no," his breathing stops. He strains to listen. *Please God no. What is...*

"Good luck finding them," Watson laughs. Then a door slams and an engine roars as rocks pepper the side of Bunny's car.

Bunny pounds against the lid from inside the trunk. "Raquel, can you hear me?"

"I'm here, Bunny," she says close to the keyhole.

"Get the key and open the trunk." Bunny screams.

"He threw the key away, out in the pasture."

"You're kidding?"

She sounds on the verge of tears. "Bunny, I don't know what to do. I'm going to be in trouble with Dad."

"If you could get a screwdriver or tire tool, maybe you could pry the lid open." Bunny's muffled voice floats out.

"Do you have any of those things?"

"Yep. In here… with me. Raquel, you think you could find the key?" he asks, trying to keep his voice from sounding desperate.

"Bunny," she answers, her voice suddenly upbeat, "someone… someone is here."

"What? Who?" Bunny yells from the trunk. "No, wait," he pleads. "Not your dad. He'll think I'm an idiot."

"A friend. He gave me a ride once."

Bunny can only hear Raquel's muffled voice talking as he pounds against the lid.

"Raquel!" His shouts only slam back inside the darkness. "Raquel!"

twenty-six

TC CAN SEE smoke rising off the horizon. He's already driving in that direction, so he races ahead to see what's going on. The smoke is beginning to wane by the time he's topped the second hill. Now just ahead he sees the blue car still smoldering on the side of the road. "Is that... Red's?" TC says out loud.

When he pulls off the highway, it looks like the girl he gave a ride the other day. She is sitting on the back bumper.

"Not wise to sit on a burning car," TC says, walking up.

"My friend... Bunny is in there!"

"Sure enough? Red, you okay?" He calls, rapping against the metal.

"TC?"

"I'm here. Probably a dumb question." TC gives her the palms up gesture. "But... key?"

"Mean Man threw it away." She points to a freshly plowed field. "Out there."

TC tugs at the brim of his hat, groans, and walks to his truck. He bangs inside the toolbox and returns with a crowbar he wedges under the lip of the trunk lid and heaves toward the ground with a grunt. The metal whines and bends, and the lock pops free. Raquel claps and surprises TC with a gentle touch on the shoulder. Bunny, cocooned in a fetal position, raises his head and squints into the light.

"Red," says TC and extends a hand. "You okay?" Refusing the help or to even look at TC, Bunny nods and stretches his long legs over the side.

"Wanna tell me what the hell went on here?"

"Just giving her a ride and my car..." Bunny nods at the dead vehicle, then shoots Raquel a look and snaps, "How do you know him?"

Stunned by his hostile tone, Raquel looks like she just got soaked with cold water. "She's a friend of Jodie's," says TC. Bunny doesn't respond, and there's no sign that he buys the explanation. The kid is staring her down. TC walks to the front of the car, close to the popping, still-hot metal. "Smells like burned oil." He shouts, "When's the last time you put oil in her?"

"I'm in a hurry to get home," Raquel blurts, switching her attention to TC. Her voice suddenly pleasant, she produces a smile and asks sweetly, "Could you help me, please?" Her actions seem to feed Bunny's sour mood.

"Yes, ma'am." TC does a two-finger salute off his brim. "Load up." He retrieves the crowbar from the ground and waltzes to his truck door. "There's a friend of yours inside." He chuckles and opens the passenger side, unleashing a fluff ball on short legs that charges across the seat.

"Sugar, my baby girl," Raquel squeals and lifts the puppy, burying her nose in the fur.

Bunny shoves his hands in his pockets and mutters, "You two sure got a lot in common—friends, dogs, rides..." He glares at Raquel, but she doesn't react, being knee deep in puppy kisses.

TC notices that Bunny's clothes, face, and arms are covered in oily black. "Awww... Red, you're a mess. I don't want my truck interior stained or smelly. If you want to ride with us, I'll have to ask you to sit in the back with Rowdy. Nice shirt, by the way." TC turns away. "At least, it was."

Bunny doesn't say a word, but obediently steps on the bumper and swings a leg over the tailgate. The black-and-white dog in back slinks away, leery about sharing his space. Bunny slumps to the front of the pickup bed, folds his legs, and takes a cold seat on the metal. He offers his hand to Rowdy, but the animal crouches at the opposite end, refusing to budge. "Just you and me, pal," Bunny sighs.

Raquel waves a puppy paw in Bunny's direction just before she and TC hop inside the cab. As TC brings the truck up to speed, Raquel gives a quick look out the rear glass and gets a face full of the back of Bunny's head and hair pressed against the window. "He's acting weird," she says softly.

"Is he your boyfriend?"

"Not really, just friends."

"Maybe to you... but something tells me he feels differently." TC raises his eyebrows. Raquel makes a face and sets the puppy on the seat between them. She rummages in her bag, brings out lipstick, and creates a show smoothing it on just so. Then she smacks red, pouty lips in the mirror, blots a kiss print on a tissue, and casually drops it on the seat next to TC. Next, her attention turns to arranging windblown hair.

TC pretends not to notice the beauty routine but can't help but think about those lips pressed against his own. She's not dumb. She knows what she's doing. It's hard to believe this is the same big-eyed girl he'd driven before. But now she feels safe enough, with Red sitting in the back, to push the boundaries. And it's like she wants to punish the kid for caring too much. Is this tease aimed at TC, or is it only to make Red blind with envy? "So," TC says as he tries to think of something besides what color panties she might be wearing. "Is all that primping for me?"

She stops looking in the mirror long enough to cut her eyes at him. "Hadn't planned on hitchhiking when I left school."

"If I saw you on the side of the road, I'd pick you up. Oh, wait." He chuckles. "Already did that." She controls a smile, pressing shiny lips together, and turns away to look out the side window. "Last time, when you were avoiding some creep?" says TC. Suddenly interested, Raquel's head spins around. "Was that Red?"

"He can be... possessive."

"So, how did Red end up in the trunk and the car keys in the field?"

"This bully at school, Watson, on the football team."

"I know him. The guy has pro written all over his future."

"Well, he's a horrible person."

"That strong oil smell..." TC's voice drifts off. "Did Watson just show up there, out of the blue?"

She nods. "Tried to take me home. Bunny got mad."

"Don't blame him. I'd bet money that guy doctored the gas tank."

"He and his little posse of admirers were watching us when we left the school." Raquel adjusts herself in the seat, and crossing her legs, she turns toward TC. "Lucky for me you rescued us." He glances over as she delivers a big smile. "You really are saving me. My dad only let me ride home with Bunny because I promised to be early."

"I take it your dad doesn't like Red?"

She shrugs and pets the puppy, now played out and napping beside her. "Doesn't know him, but he heard he got expelled. How is it you know Bunny?"

"He's my neighbor," TC says, marveling that she's making it so obvious—all but telling him she's not that interested in Red. But this girl is too young, and he's too old, and that's that. After Anna-Marie, he'd decided seasoned women with neglectful husbands were a much sounder choice. Except when TC looks at Raquel again, that smile almost makes him forget about the age thing.

"Pretty girl like you—it probably eats at a star athlete like Watson, seeing you with Red."

"Why do you call him Red?"

"Doesn't everybody?"

"I call him Bunny. It sounds sweeter."

"Exactly."

They ride on without words, take a right at the fork, and follow the gravel road, climbing the hill to Raquel's. When the house comes into view, she exclaims, "Dad's not home yet." The relief in her words is almost musical. She gathers her books and plants a ready hand on the door handle. As soon as TC slows to a stop, Raquel bolts out. Halfway across the yard, she remembers and turns back to wave and blow TC a kiss.

The forgotten young man in the back of the truck has already suffered a major blow to his girl game, and now he's forced to witness this parting insult. "A simple 'thank you' would've been great," TC says out loud. Not happy being used for revenge, he gets out to check on Red and finds him slumped down, almost hidden in the pickup bed. Bunny's eyes just visible above the side, he scans Raquel's house like an alligator breaking the surface of a pond. TC taps against the metal. "Hey, Red, I figure this Watson character doctored your gas with motor oil. You and Rowdy okay back here?" There's a soft whine and the dog creeps to TC.

In slow motion, Bunny's head makes an unnatural rotation. "I'm figuring it out," he murmurs in a deadpan voice. His harsh look demands attention, and TC straightens from his casual lean against the truck. Bunny's face is like stone, his glassy stare uncomfortable. His sudden calm seems false, like camouflage hiding an explosive. Bunny pulls himself to his feet and climbs to the ground. Face to face, he stands almost as tall as TC. His voice is clear and controlled. "I had to make sure Raquel got home safe, but I'll walk from here."

He watches Red stride away without one word to stop him. When the boy reaches the top of the hill, TC retrieves the souvenir tissue from his shirt pocket, holds it to his nose, and breathes in Raquel's youthful smell. "Bunny Boy, I'm not your competition," he mutters into the wind. "At least, I keep telling myself that."

twenty-seven

It's easy enough to find Mean Man Watson's house. Bunny has dreamed about his plan all week. All he needs to do is follow the string of cars after the Friday night game. If the football team has their way with the scoreboard, then Doc Watson always hosts a party following the win.

Reduced to traveling on foot since the sabotage of Old Blue, Bunny keeps to the side of the road and hides in the shadows. About three miles in, he recognizes the lights of an approaching big rig and puts out a thumb for a ride. The driver probably feels sorry for him, standing in the dark with a big pack across his shoulder, and picks him up. The guy behind the wheel even knows about the famous after-game blowouts at the doctor's mansion. "Have fun, but don't get caught," the trucker says, laughing as he drops Bunny at the turnoff.

"Don't get caught," Bunny repeats. "That's the plan."

Careful to stay away from the headlights of late arrivers, Bunny creeps fifty yards to the Watson house. He crouches behind a large tree, watching to get the lay of the land. "I have to get closer," Bunny says through gritted teeth. Although he had handpicked his truest arrows and fine-tuned the bow, at this distance, his homemade equipment will never hit the target.

Long strings of lights drape in crisscross lines across the massive circle drive, creating enough brightness in the distance to rival a sunrise. A thumping bass dominates the music that floats into the night to welcome guests. Bunny is amazed at the number of people. He recognizes most of them as they climb from cars and trucks. Then guys in white shirts drive the vehicles to an open area, parking them in neat lines. Their host, the good doctor, greets the distant voices, full of excitement. These are Bunny's classmates, teachers, and neighbors, but they are not like him—not like Nan. He's an outsider, and this a hostile environment.

The front is where guests arrive, but watching cars is not why he's here. Bunny adjusts the awkward pack across his shoulder, realizing his position must improve. Mean Man shouldn't be hard to spot, not with his hulking size. Careful to stay away from the broad drape of light, Bunny circles the estate, pausing behind shrubs to stay undercover. Near the backyard, the music intensifies to an obnoxious level. Smoke billows from a large, custom grill on wheels as a man Bunny recognizes as the coach in a long apron flips sizzling burgers and dogs. And lights, so many lights—they're everywhere. Lights in the trees, on the walkway, and on the deck where the cheerleaders perform a synchronized routine while players and friends whistle and hoot approval.

Enchanted by the leggy-girl dance and loud music, Bunny doesn't hear the footsteps behind him. "Whatcha doing?" asks a muddled voice from a dark silhouette just feet away.

Bunny jumps from his crouched position and stands to face the intimidating figure. The sudden scare makes him so nauseous he almost doubles over. "I, uh…" Bunny bends, holding his stomach. "Gas—sorry… trying to get away from everyone." And right on cue, he expels a loud and smelly poof of flatulence, a talent he's possessed as long as he can remember.

"Oh, lordy," says the dark figure as he fans the air and turns away.

"Yeah... sorry," Bunny says, clenching his stomach.

"What's in the sack?"

"Just came from practice. Afraid to leave my equipment."

"Practice?"

"Uh... baseball... I'm on the school team."

"What's your name?"

"Jaaa-mie?" Happy with his answer, Bunny silently congratulates himself. Jamie Burns is the first baseman.

"Well, Jaaa-mie, I'm Big Mo," he slurs. "I live back there." He points to the dark outline of a roof almost visible through the trees. "I help Doc. You and Clarence friends?"

"Who?"

"Clarence. You know, Doc's football star."

"We go to school together." Bunny smiles, amused at learning Mean Man's given name.

"Don't remember you."

"I... I'm new... to the school."

"Oh, so your first after-party?"

"Yes."

"You got food yet? Burgers smell tasty."

"No, no." Bunny bends again, demonstrating his stomach problem. "Better to stay away from everybody."

"I get the farts, too, but looks strange, you being out here. I gotta keep an eye on things."

"Sorry just... you know," Bunny stammers.

"You can hang out with me till it passes." Big Mo takes a couple of unsteady steps, more or less toward the woods. "I was just going to, uh..." He stops, scratches chin stubble, and licks his lips. "Uh, take a break. Want to walk with me?"

Bunny nods and follows. They wind through the thick growth of trees, their shoes crunching over dry leaves as frogs deliver a serenade of passage. Trailing behind, Bunny watches as Big Mo stumbles on the dark path then rights himself with the help of a nearby sapling. Glimpses of an angled roof flash into view along with open patches of sky until the small cabin seems to rise out of the blackness before them. At the door, Mo points toward a bench near the walkway. "Have a seat," he says, then bumps face first into his own door before he's able to grasp the handle.

The trees provide a buffer, so the music is now reduced to a background rhythm. Bunny takes a seat on the bench and stores his sack under his feet. He spins about, straining to see into the darkness. Moonlight gleaming off a building in the near distance holds his attention until Mo reappears. "Now, where were we?" He groans, bending to the bench, and raises a bottle of amber liquid to his lips then wipes his mouth on the back of his hand.

"What's over there?" Bunny points.

"That? Equipment building. Mowers, tractor, even cars during the party. Keeps 'em out of the way so nobody jacks with 'em."

"I guess Clarence wouldn't like that."

"You're funny, Jaaa-mie." His words slow, Mo shakes his head and laughs. "That big boy would go full-on gangster if somebody touched that red bullet," he slurs. "Guess you missed the birthday. Clarence almost lost it when Doc drove the car out with the big red bow across the hood." Mo raises the bottle again. "Never seen a smile that big."

Mo's words have Bunny rethinking his plan. Revenge might better be served without use of the arrows at his feet. To destroy something Mean Man loves would be a personal assault. The pain of the unknown would drive him insane. Watson fancies himself a hero, so the nagging question of who did this at his celebratory event would deliver a blow much worse than physical pain.

The distant laughter of the crowd filters through and prompts Mo to ask, "You feeling better? Want to join your friends?" But Bunny is sure the group roughhousing around the pool does not include anyone he could call a friend.

"You tired of me?" Bunny asks, thinking Mo might want to be alone and drink himself into tomorrow.

"Didn't want you to waste your time hanging with an old drunk." Mo chuckles. He two-finger-fishes a package from his shirt pocket and, lighting up, takes a drag. He blows the smoke skyward before his dry mouth begs for another drink. Well, at least Mo knows who he is.

"Guess you're right," Bunny says and palms Mo's lighter off the bench. "Thanks for the company."

Mo tips the container toward him, delivering a glassy-eyed toast. "Anytime, Jaaa-mie."

Bunny disappears into the trees but watches as Mo, still clutching his bottle, lies across the bench and begins to snore. Keeping to the shadows, Bunny creeps past, headed toward the equipment barn.

The full moon guides him to the massive metal building, where he thankfully finds the door unlocked. Bunny scans in wide-eyed wonder at the number of cars, trucks, and boats inside. He could drive a different one every day of the week. But there's only one that really interests him, and it's parked conveniently near the door. Bunny's hand trembles as he touches the flashy red paint on the hood. He tries the door, but it's locked, so he shines his flashlight through the glass to the buckskin interior and gleaming wood of the steering wheel. "What a shame," Bunny whispers. "Shame that such an asshole owns it."

He locates a half-full gas can by the lawn equipment. "Bingo." Bunny pulls the cover off a ski boat, drags it over, and pushes it under the red car, then pours the gas, allowing it to pond on the canvas. He flips Mo's lighter, tosses it in, and giggles as the fire huffs, licking the undercarriage. Ecstatic, he rushes outside to enjoy the show. Within seconds, the flames are jumping as high as the windows and then—the jarring explosion.

Ready to run, Bunny does a full spin, searching, before realization fills him with dread. His sack—it's in the building. He rushes back to rescue his equipment, but shouting voices growing louder make him stop. Through the window, he can see the car now consumed inside a raging inferno. It's too late.

twenty-eight

SATURDAY MORNING, Bridget is so wired up, it's like she's a different person. She can't bring herself to sit across the table and look at TC over breakfast, so after hours of sleepless torture and before anyone else is up, she drives away from her house. No destination in mind, just an aimless search for what to do now.

Finding herself in town at such an early hour, most shops and businesses have yet to unlock their doors for the day. The exception is the local donut shop. Bridget heads home with a dozen chocolate-covered and a large coffee. Caffeine and sugar she doesn't need, but she can do nothing but mindlessly eat as she replays the image of that girl wearing TC's boxer shorts.

When Bridget approaches Bunny's house on her way home, she makes a snap decision to turn into the Potts' place. In desperate need of an available pair of ears, she wants someone to listen. Without the welcome release her therapist once provided, her nerves are so frayed they feel like hot coals under her skin. And now this latest shock, which confirms what she'd long suspected, has left her hollow and lost. Bunny's not family, and that's a good thing. And he's not some other woman waiting in the wings to swoop in on her man who can't keep it in his pants. Besides, Bunny has to know she cares, and after all, she's helped him. Bridget believes she's due a favor. Maybe he'll be willing to listen.

She can see the dirt flying even before she reaches the house. Getting closer, she can see Bunny outside and deep enough that just his head and shoulders are visible. Bridget parks, retrieves a lawn chair from the back of her station wagon and takes it close to where Bunny is working. He looks different, bandanna tied over his head, no cap today. He works shirtless. "Mind if I sit here and watch?" She waits for approval before opening the chair. Bunny nods, leaning an arm against his shovel. The skin of his scrawny chest is so transparent Bridget does a double take; certain she can see the pounding of his heart.

She fetches her coffee and the box of donuts, offers one to Bunny, and holds her tongue about the boy getting a sunburn. He shakes his head at the donuts but hops out of the hole to get a drink of water, then goes back to moving dirt. Bridget starts, "I've been driving and hope you don't mind, but I really just need to get something off my chest." She selects a chocolate treat and closes the box. "I found out," she says, "that TC has been diddling that Anna-Marie girl."

Bunny glances out, his head still visible, his expression unchanged. He continues to work as she goes on. "I mean, I thought so many times, but this…" She takes a bite and, still chewing, looks across the meadow to her own house. She's always been proud of her hilltop home, but today the place looks sad and feels disappointing. "I'm probably the last one to find out." Bridget shoves the rest of the donut in, talking around the mouthful. "Mind if I ask, did you know about this?" Her words are sharp with distrust, and she narrows her eyes like a heat-seeking missile. Just as quickly, her face morphs to confusion. "Don't answer, don't answer," she says, putting up a hand defensively. "Not fair for me to ask." Bunny hasn't said a word, but she takes his lack of denial as a yes. "Guess I'm the laughingstock of the county, thanks to my husband." Bridget's lips tremble as she maneuvers the coffee to her mouth.

Bunny stops work again. Blinking sweat, he swipes an arm across his forehead.

"I've read about women getting breast implants. Do you think big boobs would make a difference?" she fires at him. "Would he love me then?"

Shocked at herself, and before he can make a sound, she shakes her head. "Sorry, sorry, what a thing to say." She can feel heat rushing to her cheeks, so she keeps her head down. "Didn't mean to say that, but do you think that would work?" Bridget drops her elbows from her knees, letting her shoulders sag, then slowly looks up. "I know, I know. I'm not much to look at." She can't make her mouth stop, even though the words sound embarrassing to her own ears. "Even my own father said that. Little girls are supposed to be the apple of their father's eye." She smirks. "But I never was. Never was Daddy's little girl. Too tall, too thin, they said." She cocks her head, looking straight at Bunny. "As if we can change what we're born with."

Standing inside the dig, Bunny's face suddenly twists with pain. He sinks down, fingers clawing the edge of the open earth, and rests his chin against the ground so all that's visible is his head. He fixes eyes on her.

"You okay?" she asks, sure she'd hit a nerve. Bridget knew the stories. How rough Bunny had it as a child. "Guess we all want to be special to our moms and dads." She tries to smile. "I see you're busy. Don't let me slow your work. It's just that I'm so tight in my mind, I can't think of anything but TC and that girl. Wish I had a hole to dig or a job or something away from everything that flies in my face and reminds me of him. You sure you don't want one of these?" Bridget pushes the box toward Bunny. This time he dusts his hands and, careful not to touch the rest, selects one, nodding a thanks as Bridget continues. "It's impossible to get the two of them out of my head. The two of them... eerrrrrr! And she's just a kid, a couple of years older than my Meredith. And TC didn't even try to deny it." She shrugs. "Well, how could he?"

She's curious about the hole in the ground, but hesitant to ask. She's witnessed a few unusual things on her visits to the Potts' house, and this looks suspect. "You digging to China?" She laughs softly. "Can I come, too? Sometimes I think about just running away, you know?" But he probably doesn't. Suddenly, she feels ridiculous and small, complaining while this boy who has nothing shows up each day and goes forward. Is it his grit or courage, or maybe just a lack of intelligence? No, Bunny is naïve, not stupid. She silently scolds herself for unkind thoughts.

The sun is already hot this morning, and Bridget squints up, locating the source as though she has the power to turn down the heat. A small breeze pushes past, and she watches as Bunny closes his eyes, allowing the cool to wash over him. She notices the chocolate has formed a pool in the box and looks up just in time to see Bunny suck the melted goo from his fingers. "It's a hot one today, and you're really working up a sweat," she says, giving a weak laugh. Finished with the donut, Bunny drinks deeply, then peels off the bandanna and pours the rest of his water over his head.

"Your... hair," she stutters. "What did you do?"

Bunny tosses the glass to the side, then rubs a hand across the shiny, bare skin now shaved clean of his signature red curls. Bridget struggles to compose her face, but looking at his head, she can only think of a taxi with wide-open doors. "Nan doesn't like me with long hair," he mumbles.

"So... you did that for... her?" He nods and replaces the bandana, careful to include the free flying tops of his ears.

"Well, that's so sweet. You need a ride to see her?" Bridget says, eager for something to occupy her mind.

"She'll be here soon."

"Here? Nan's coming home? My goodness. Well... hallelujah!" Bridget manages to smile, feeling a bit deflated. With Nan back, guess she'll have to give up her pet challenge of improving Bunny's life. She shivers, remembering the animal infestation Nan had allowed in their home.

Bunny goes back to work and pounds furiously with the blade, then scoops yet more loose soil from the hole. She watches in silence, mulling over a stab of jealousy at the boy's deep devotion. Devotion, even to an abusive parent. Bridget thinks about her own daughters. She would sacrifice anything for them, yet they would probably choose to walk naked down the middle of the street before they'd agree to cut their hair to please her. "Mmmm, just like TC," she whispers under her breath. "My family thinks I'm a doormat. So, your project here?" Bridget points. "Something for Nan?"

"Yes."

"Really?" Bridget smiles, glad to have a riddle to solve. "Let's see." She narrows her eyes, studying the location. "Right off the porch there... Maybe a beautiful koi pond?" No reaction, so she tries again. "I know, I know—a hot tub, right? You're going to sink it, build a deck around." But there's only a grunt from Bunny, who's muscling a shovelful. "Err, mud pit." Bridget snaps her fingers. "Little competitive mud wrestling?"

Bunny stops and grips the long handle, breathing hard. "She's coming home," he says. Walking to the hole's edge, he reaches out and takes Bridget's hand and pulls her close. His unexpected touch, coupled with his awkwardness, is unnerving. It tilts her comfort level off balance, him standing so close. His appearance without the comical red locks is disturbing, and his face with dark shadows and puffiness... He's aged overnight. The icy-blue eyes, now inches from her own, are glassy, like a feverish child. She tries to pull away, but Bunny's fingers cinch tighter, demanding attention as he leans in and whispers, "She's gone."

twenty-nine

THIS IS the second day in a row TC leaves his house without a proper breakfast. Bridget is upset, he gets that, but didn't he smooth it over last night? For half the night, they'd made love like teenagers and fell asleep, exhausted, in each other's arms in the early morning hours. And for his macho efforts, he thought surely his wife would have a pan of her signature buttermilk biscuits on the stove and maybe some fried ham and creamy sawmill gravy. His mouth watered just thinking about it. Instead, when he pulled on his jeans this morning, her side of the bed was cold, and when he looked out the window, her station wagon was gone.

Just as he's getting into his truck, TC spies a black hearse headed up the lane to the Potts' place. He can see Bridget's ride is also parked down there. "What the actual hell?" he says out loud. Pissed off, hungry, and now confused, TC races down the hill to investigate.

When he arrives at the Potts' house, Bridget and some bald-headed beanpole are standing out front. They shout directions and wave to the driver, who's doing a botched job of backing the stretch vehicle. As he gets closer, TC can see the Rambo wannabe holding a shovel is actually Red. Guess that explains the sizable hole in the ground. "What's going on?" TC shouts, jumping out of his truck.

When Bridget turns, she's so pale she looks ill. Old girl must have put her clothes on in the dark because the inside white neck tag of her blouse flips on the wind. "Bunny's mother passed away last night." She gestures to the long black car. "Bunny is going to bury her." She sniffles, catching a breath.

"What?" TC bugs his eyes. "Here? Beside the house?" Bridget's face is full of the wide-eyed *'why not'* of a child, but without a shred of understanding. "Hold on there, hoss." TC waves to the driver, striding to the front of the car. "You can't do this. That's what cemeteries are for."

"You the next of kin?" the man behind the wheel asks. "I was told this was the deceased's wish."

"Well, yeah... but it was a life estate. When she passed, the land came back to me."

The driver gets out to see where this is going. "Just told to deliver a body." He points to a paper in hand. "To this address."

"Hold on a minute." TC puts up a finger and goes back to the huddle of Bunny and Bridget. "Red, real sorry about your mom, but we should bury her proper, in a cemetery."

"She wanted to come home." Bunny's red eyes glare at TC. "This is our home."

"But is this even legal? Pretty sure there are regulations."

"Actually, in Texas you can bury someone at home," the driver says. "Not common. Only second time I've delivered to a residence."

"As I've explained—" TC's voice grows loud, his temper boiling. "The land came back to me when Nan died, and no way my ranch is becoming a graveyard."

With this declaration, the alien version of Red starts to snivel, and mother-hen Bridget rushes to comfort him. "Oh, lord," TC shouts and turns away.

"Hey, man, I'm on the clock here," the driver persists. "I've got another pick-up waiting." TC's patience is wearing thin with this little guy. Head to toe in a black three-piece suit, he wants to appear in charge, but the shine of the cheap fabric and gleam on the buttons tell TC who he's dealing with. "Additionally, there'll soon be a problem with the remains." The driver leans close, directing his words at TC. "The body hasn't been prepared, so it's *au natural*, if you know what I mean. And the TOD plus heat of the day..." He cocks his head, eyebrows shooting up.

"TOD?"

"Time of Death." The driver produces a handkerchief and mops his brow. "Yes, sir, hot one today," he says. "Getting hotter all the time."

Red sinks to the ground. Knees doubled, he squats, rocking back and forth on his heels, his whimpers growing louder. Bridget kneels beside him. The driver paces, his eyes darting with a nervous twitch as he frowns at the crude opening in the ground. Arm around Red, Bridget guides him away. TC's truck is close, and in his hurry, he's left the engine running.

"I'm going to let Bunny sit in your truck while we talk." Bridget says. TC throws up his hands, feeling outnumbered, and watches without protest as she opens the cab. "Bunny, sit inside where it's nice and cool. Dry your face. I'm sure there're some fast-food napkins in the glove box. Let us sort this out." She lets the boy crawl in and shuts the door.

Spinning around to TC, Bridget shakes a finger in his face. "How can you deny Bunny this?"

"I'm going to bulldoze this place."

"Bunny lives here."

"All this low area is now going to be a lake. Already got plans. Great run-off from our hilltop."

"But if Nan hadn't died, that would've been years down the road."

"Who'd have thought she'd kick the bucket before the kid left home?"

"People rarely die on schedule."

"Ain't gonna happen." TC shakes his head and kicks a fist-sized dirt clod into the open hole. "I've got plans for this little corner, and they don't include a body floating up in the middle of my lake."

Bridget flexes her fingers, squeezing them into fists, then does it again and again. He sees the anger behind her eyes. "TC," she says slowly and looks at the ground before lifting her chin. "Don't you owe Bunny? Don't you owe him this at least?"

"If this is about money, then I'd rather pay it myself than be okay with weirdness."

"That's not what she wanted. Bunny promised his mother."

TC turns away, muttering under his breath. "Evil bitch knew this would be her final jab at me."

The antsy driver reappears, shuffling toward them with another interruption. "Sorry folks, but..." He looks at his watch. "I've got another body call. I really need to complete this delivery."

"People just dropping everywhere, I guess." TC smirks. "Give us a minute, son." When he walks away, TC turns to Bridget. "I don't owe anybody. Years ago, I did a good deed of giving that whacko woman a place to live. Turning the property into a burial ground for crazies was not part of the deal."

"TC, I never ask for anything. You run wild and free with other women—yeah, you can't deny it—and I... I just give and give some more. If you don't owe Bunny, well then, you owe me. TC, you *owe* me!" Her eyes big as horseshoes, Bridget stands before him, defiant as a corner fence post. *Well, well, the old girl has grit after all. She's become a real champion for the underdog.* TC takes off his hat and runs a hand through his hair, wondering what's happened to his sweet wife. That fire in her, that's something new.

TC looks across the meadow, admiring his impressive rock home on the hill. He's proud of the place and didn't build Conway Ranch by letting unreasonable people get in his way. Then he glances back at the ramshackle place Red calls home. The boy will soon be out of school and move on and, anyway, TC can't very well put an orphan on the street. His plans for the picturesque lake can hold for now. "I guess... it's always possible to transfer it after the kid moves away."

"It?" Bridget says.

"Yeah, the body."

"Fine. Now please tell Bunny, so he can bury his mother."

Already regretting giving in on this stupidness, TC does as he's told and walks to his truck. When he pulls open the door, spread across Bunny's lap is the photo of laughing Nan and her young cowboy. The kid's disturbing appearance only seems to have matured while he sat in the truck. His parchment-colored skin is streaked with trails of sweat and tears. The up-close starkness of the shaved head and red-rimmed eyes almost makes TC gasp.

"This," Bunny says, his finger resting on the photo. "This... is you!"

thirty

A FULL WEEK passes before Bunny is ready to go back to school. He'd spent the time beside his mother's grave singing the familiar rock and roll songs she loved. Creedence Clearwater and Rolling Stones. He croons to himself, the lyrics of "Fortunate Son," his forehead pressed against the bus window as the blur of fence posts fly past.

The kids at school show how glad they are that Bunny is back by keeping their distance. It's like he's a stranger. He'd worn a knitted skull cap today, and the few faces Bunny matches eyes with look right through him. He searches for Raquel minutes before the last morning bell rings, hoping by now she's over the botched car ride home. But he doesn't see her in the hall, so he takes a seat in first period class and answers roll call before he's directed to see the principal.

Alone inside the office, Bunny looks around for something to occupy him. He breathes deep, filling his nose with the sharp smell of sawdust, and notices the pyramid of freshly sharpened pencils on the desk. He considers pocketing one but dismisses the idea, remembering what happened before. Hard to figure why the school principal would have an entire stack of what he'd labeled as weapons.

Beside the pencils is a photo. A couple hovers over a small girl and a three-candle cake that reads *Happy Birthday, Tanya*. Only the face of the principal is familiar to Bunny. As he studies the image, Bunny notices Pemberton had significantly more hair then, but something else is odd. They're all smiling, even the principal, and he doesn't even like kids.

"Don't touch that," Pemberton snaps, rushing into the office.

Bunny jumps, distancing himself from the photograph. "Sorry. Didn't know you had a daughter."

Pemberton painstakingly returns the photo to its rightful place. "I don't. I mean, I did... This visit is about you, Potts, not me." He sinks into his chair opposite Bunny. "Glad you graced us with your presence today." Pemberton glares across the desk.

Bunny hangs his head and mumbles into the carpet. "Sorry, I... I just didn't feel like being here."

"What's that? You didn't feel like it? I haven't 'felt like' being here for years." Pemberton makes air quotes. "And I shouldn't have to remind you, Potts, no caps or head coverings allowed at school."

Bunny one-handedly grabs the skull cap off, exposing the pale skin of his newly bald head. "Sorry, just trying to keep from shocking everyone," he says. Pemberton flinches. The familiar deep line reappears between his eyes, and he stares for several seconds. Uncomfortable with the awkward silence, Bunny says, "Guess you didn't know?"

Pemberton's voice is now only a whisper. "I... didn't know."

"Not the kind of news you want." Bunny nods.

"You seem to be... taking it well. What did the doctor say?"

"Uh... death."

"You're serious?"

"Yes."

"When did you find out?"

"Few days ago."

"Oh my God, Potts. I'm sorry to hear this." Weird, thinks Bunny, Pemberton has never even met Nan. "Well, glad you're back." The principal looks uncomfortable and stands, apparently done with him. Then he points to the beanie wadded in Bunny's hand. "You go ahead and wear that, son," he says and pats Bunny on the back. "We'll just not worry about the dress code violation for now."

Morning classes pass without a single word from another student. Bunny even does a quick look in the bathroom mirror to make sure he hasn't somehow become invisible. At lunch, when he enters the line, he notices Raquel at a table and gives a small wave. She looks away without a response. Yep, she's mad, but it's not his fault the car broke down. Bunny makes his way through the line, forced to walk right past Raquel.

As he gets close, her face lights with recognition. "Bunny, I didn't know it was you." She smiles and grabs her own tray, following him to a table. "I heard," she whispers and touches his arm. "I'm so sorry. Is that why you have a beanie?"

"My mom died."

"Oh, no, Bunny. You okay?"

"I cut my hair off. Said you didn't like it."

"I said there was too much of it. You look so different. How are you... by yourself?"

"I'm learning."

"So... you're not sick, Bunny?" Now Bunny smiles and shakes his head.

"While you were gone, you missed the excitement. Did you hear what happened at the Watson's house?" Bunny fakes a dumb look. "At the party after the game, his red car got burned up."

"Really?"

"Police came to school, questioning everybody. Some kid named Jamie, on the baseball team, they took him in for a line-up."

"Line-up? Why?"

"A guy who works for the Watsons said he thought Jamie did it."

"What happened?"

"Nothing. Jamie wasn't even there, and the old guy couldn't pick him out."

"Sorry I missed that."

"Just as well. Watson's been sniffing around ever since. Heads up." She nods, her face suddenly serious. "Look who's coming this way."

Mean Man strolls toward them. His hands hidden in the front pocket of a team hoodie, a permanent smirk across his face, he's flanked by half a dozen teammates who walk in lockstep behind the big man. Watson stops beside Bunny and Raquel to deliver a menacing stare. Yep, there it is. Funny, the only other person who recognizes Bunny is Mean Man.

"Say, Potts, looks like you and I both lost our rides. But, I've got another one ordered and headed this way. The new little beauty is midnight black. You like it dark, don't you, girl?" He grins at Raquel, and his pack of rude minions snicker, right on cue.

"Sweet," Bunny manages with all the sarcasm he can muster. "When my truck gets here, guess we'll both be happy."

"Bullshit!" Watson bellows. "Truck, my ass. In your loser dreams, maybe."

"You getting a truck, Bunny?" Raquel perks up with fresh interest.

"My dad and I are picking it up. Be ready in a few days," Bunny says.

"Your dad?" Raquel says, her face coming alive with curiosity.

"This guy," laughs Watson, pointing to Bunny with a toothpick. He waves it like a tiny magic wand. "You don't even have a dad. Must be part of your little fantasy."

"Pretty sure everyone has a dad."

"You know, you're not out of the woods yet, Potts. Arson is a felony. That'll make your butthole pucker, don't it?" Watson clenches the toothpick between his teeth, flashing a shark smile.

Bunny pushes to his feet, steels his stance, and squares his shoulders at Watson. "If you had anything to pin on me, it would have already happened."

Not accustomed to being challenged, Mean Man looks stumped. "Let's get out of here. This stale air is putting me to sleep." Watson stretches thick arms above his head and gives an exaggerated yawn. Then he quickly snatches the beanie off Bunny's head. "Nice lid," he gets out before his jaw goes slack and the blood drains from his face. A collective gasp travels through the onlookers, and Watson drops the cap to the floor like he's afraid he'll catch something. The pack of shocked teammates silently disappear as quickly as they'd arrived.

Bunny scoops up his beanie and, in one motion, snugs it back in place. Raquel's face now a ghostly shade of white, her eyes full of questions, she stares at him. "Don't worry," Bunny smiles. "I'm okay." Fresh energy surging through him, he feels stronger now than he can ever remember. He reaches down, taking Raquel by the hand, and pulls her to her feet. "There's something I've been wanting to give you."

Bunny leans in and awkwardly tries to press his lips to Raquel's. Instead, his only success is bumping into her nose. She jumps, surprised, and as a beautiful smile blooms across her face, she guides him in for a proper kiss. The sound of applause interrupts their moment, and they pull away, red-faced and shocked. Everyone is one on their feet clapping as shrill whistles ring out. Unable to stop smiling, Bunny clasps Raquel's hand, raising it high in the air as he bends low to make an exaggerated bow. "Come on," he laughs, pulling Raquel toward the door. "I've got more where that came from."

thirty-one

"I TOLD you we'd have a talk," TC grins. "And the best way to discuss anything is over a steak and a beer." TC and Bunny stroll under a suspended wood sign that creaks as it sways in the breeze. *Steak Well Done* is a place TC describes as the best restaurant on the planet. It's obvious he's a regular here, and everyone from the hostess to the bartender shouts a greeting as TC and Bunny move toward a seat.

"Wow, everybody knows you," says Bunny. "You bring Ms. Bridget here?"

"Naw," TC says, stretching his neck to see who's here. "These are my people."

The massive horseshoe-shaped wood bar holds the prominent position in the middle of the room. Glass shelves in the center rise above it, loaded with familiar names of whiskey, bourbon, and tequila. Worn, red-leather booths line the walls, and tables fill the space between. The cool dark air of the room is cloudy with the enticing smell of seared meat.

They find a booth that TC's happy with, and Bunny slides in. "Be right back," TC says, walking away. A paper carton brimming with peanuts occupies the middle of the table, and Bunny eyes the discarded shells scattered across the floor. A smiley lady with a mouthful of gum appears beside him. "How you doing, cowboy?" she says, tossing a menu on the table. "Something to drink, honey?"

"Beer... I guess?" Bunny says slowly.

She shakes her head, wagging a finger close to his face. "I don't have any 'I guess' beer, baby, but I'll fix you up." She snaps her gum. "Know what you want to eat?"

Bunny picks up the menu. His stomach growling, he squints in the dim light. "Looks to me like if you don't like steak, you're gonna go hungry." He chuckles and glances up. "I better wait for TC."

"Oh, baby, I know what he wants. Same thing every time. Ribeye, biscuits, and honey. I usually put a spud on the plate, but sometimes he don't bother with it."

"Guess I'll have the same."

"You want your meat cooked?" she blinks.

"Well, uh, don't you do that?"

"Lord, yes, but you wouldn't know it if you're looking at TC's plate," she laughs. "You want brown or red?"

"Brown or red?"

"Meat."

"Oh, brown. Definitely brown."

When she walks away, Bunny rises to see if he can spot TC, but since the light-colored Stetson disappeared down the dark hallway, there's been no sign of him. The server reappears with root beer in a brew-shaped bottle. "Whaddaya think?" she asks, hands on hips. Bunny smiles, giving a thumbs-up and reaches for the peanuts.

He's gone through about half the nuts when TC reappears and sweeps the pyramid of shells to the floor. "Found my friend, Scotty," TC says, crushing a goober between his fingers. "He works in the kitchen."

"Yeah? How do you know him?"

"Worked for me, once. Years ago, right out of high school. He was the best jockey in the business."

"Jockey... like horse racing?"

"Livestock. Selling and buying any kind of meat animal. That guy could squeeze a profit out of a crap deal."

"So, good friend?"

"Naw, not for a long time now. He had a habit—almost died before making up his mind to live. But it took years. That's why we're here." TC gets quiet, folds his hands on the table, and stares at Bunny. "Because my old friend in the kitchen—" He takes a breath. "Is your father."

"Well, hey, just in time 'cause you two look dry, hungry, and way too serious," Smiley says, balancing a tray with steaks and beer. She plops a plate of mostly raw meat and a draft beer in front of TC and hands Bunny another root beer and a plate of brown, as promised. A basket of steaming biscuits, a tub of butter, and a pot of honey replace the peanuts.

Soon as she walks away, Bunny cocks his head, "Father? I don't understand."

TC raises the foamy beverage to his lips and pulls in half the mug before coming up for air. "Nan and Scotty were close. Lovers. Her family went ape shit over that. Scotty was already deep into his dependency, and they gave their daughter an ultimatum. 'Leave him or we'll disown you.'"

Afraid to speak and his stomach in knots, Bunny nervously wipes at the drops collecting on the outside of the glass bottle as TC continues. "Nan's mom and dad didn't know you were already growing inside her when this went down." TC drains the rest of his beer and waves for another. "When she told Scotty about you, he went off the rails, overdosed. Guess he wanted to die."

Bunny picks up his steak knife and savagely stabs the meat. "So, it's like Nan always said. I scared my father away."

"I wouldn't say that. Scotty was a sick man, blamed himself for ruining your mom's life. He did the only thing he thought might help. But Nan's folks took a hard line. They turned their back on her."

Bunny takes a sip and pushes his plate away. His mother's death was so fresh. He's stunned, helpless. "What about the photo? What about you?" The story doesn't make sense of what he's seen.

"That picture was taken at a rodeo. One of those street photographers. You know. I took her out a few times, tried to raise her spirits. Gave her a home. Nan was in a bad way. I think that's when her mind started to fade."

"So, you and Nan?" Bunny's eyes fixed. He holds two fingers together.

"Naw, but she tried that angle. She was desperate." TC cuts into his steak, and the plate pools blood. Bunny sits frozen, watching the ravenous wolf enjoy the kill. "Aren't you going to eat?" TC points with a knife.

"Can I meet him?"

"Who? Scotty? He won't know you. Lack of oxygen when he OD'd—fried his brain. Hell, he doesn't remember last week. That's why he works here. Okay, at flipping meat on the grill, but past that, he's pretty jacked."

"Then why did you bring me here?" Bunny's emotions getting the best of him, his voice breaks. "Just to rub it in my face that me, Bunny Boy Potts, is the reason for three ruined lives?"

TC leans forward, his voice strong. "Look, I know you're disappointed, Red, but that's the stink of it."

Smiley reappears. Raising eyebrows, she points to TC's half-gone beer. He shakes his head and mumbles, "He needs a box," as she picks up Bunny's untouched meal and disappears.

Bunny's stomach is no longer the problem. It's the roar between his ears. The pressure so intense his eyes squeeze shut. He cradles his head. Delirious with pain, his head lolls back on his shoulders, eyes rolling white. "Red, Red!" TC jumps up, shaking him.

And then... it stops.

A deathly silence replaces the noise and pain in Bunny's head. He knows what he must do.

"Water—let me get some water," TC shouts, dashing away.

Bunny bolts from the booth and sprints down the dark hallway toward the kitchen. On the left, light spills from a room separated by a pair of saloon doors. Bunny bursts through with such intensity he knocks his server to the floor. The gasping lady lies on her back, his boxed food now scattered across the linoleum. At the end of the room is a tall man in a yellowed T-shirt and apron, his back to Bunny. He's working the grill, eyes on his task as thick smoke billows overhead. "Scotty?" Bunny shouts. "Scotty?"

"You can't be in here," the lady sputters from the floor.

"This guy Scotty?" Bunny points to the grill man.

"Yes, but he won't answer."

Bunny strides to the grill and roughly grabs the man by the shoulder. "I'm Bunny." He struggles to talk, his voice faltering. The tall man turns, revealing a slack jaw, eyes at half mast, and three-day, dark stubble. He looks back with an empty gaze, clicking the metal edges of the tongs in a nervous rhythm. Slowly, his lips pull back in a monster smile.

"He doesn't talk." Smiley taps her head with a finger.

"I'm Bunny, I'm... your son." He spits the words, tears streaming. Bunny shakes the voiceless man like a rag doll, whose vacant eyes roll like marbles in his head, then wraps his arms around Scotty and holds tight, clinging to the loss he's only just found. He missed it. Whatever the man had to give, gone. His mind a whiteboard wiped clean, nothing left. "But I need you, Dad," Bunny sobs. "I've always... needed you."

thirty-two

When TC asked Bunny if he'd like to work on the ranch, Bunny had been over the moon. Always feeling like an outsider, he longed to belong. Being part of the family, even if it was only for work was a bright spot. The way the Conways seem to care has been a real comfort in Bunny's world.

TC said the two things Bunny needed for ranch work were a truck and a horse. Today, TC is picking him up to find some wheels. The trip into town goes off without a word about Scotty, the brain-altered misfit Bunny learned was his father. After that emotional meeting, Bunny realized the aproned man he'd confronted at the steakhouse had never been a father and wouldn't know how, even if his mind allowed it. During the night, Bunny woke with a clear realization and decided to forget about his past and concentrate on his future.

"Red, the guy who owns the dealership." TC's face breaks into a sly fox smile. "He owes me, so I'm thinking we can get a deal."

"How's that?"

"He has a rather promiscuous daughter that I rescued one night. Poor kid, her face was a mess. An old boyfriend used her for a punching bag."

"What happened?"

"I was with a friend of hers when the girl called, crying. I got there just ahead of the sheriff, so he looked the other way as I took care of a little street justice on the shit boyfriend. The punk tried to leave town after that, bleeding all over himself. Doubt he got very far."

"You must have really liked that girl. You and she ever…"

TC snorts. "Please. Said she was easy. Never said she was pretty."

They arrive at Bellow Motors, the largest dealership in town. Bunny can remember driving past this place many times, but never with the thought of setting foot on the property. The idea of buying a vehicle seemed like something other people did. And now, he can hardly believe it's happening to him. When TC comes to a stop, Bunny is so pumped he almost leaps out the door. TC tugs at his hat brim, surveying the vast lot with row after row of cars. The vehicles in line nearest the street all have a red, white, or blue balloon tied to the front bumper, bouncing for attention on the wind. "Over here." TC points to the far side where lines of trucks wait, wishing for a new home.

Together, they stroll across the lot. "Now, the new models will be up front, but I don't think that's a smart buy for you. A used one in great condition—that's more what you can afford."

"How can I afford anything?" Bunny asks.

"Let me worry about that," says TC.

They start down the first row labeled pre-owned trucks and pass a black one lifted high in the air and a small truck with visible rust creeping from the undercarriage. Next, a blue truck, then a silver model with a big pipe bumper. "I thought that was you, TC," a voice from behind surprises them.

"Mike, how are you, man?" TC greets him with a handshake. "Looking for a good truck for my friend, Red, here." TC claps Bunny on the shoulder so hard he has to take a step forward. "He's going to be working with me on the ranch. He needs something that'll hold up."

"Half ton or bigger?" Mike says. "You don't want new?"

"No, need to keep it real, so he can still afford gas."

"I've got something over here," says Mike. "It's only a couple of years past new and in excellent condition."

TC shakes his head. "That's going to be too rich for our blood, I'm afraid."

"Well now, just take a look and let's talk about it," Mike says, with enthusiasm. "This one here, TC. Let me open her up. Clean as a whistle, almost new." And Mike is right. It's a full-size truck, not a scratch on the body, toolbox already in the bed, and nicely equipped with extras. "Mike, what do you call this color—dehydrated piss?" TC hoots.

"You either like it or hate it, I'm afraid. Manufacturer calls it Banana Run."

"The Runs? 'Bout right." TC snickers as Bunny climbs under the wheel.

"This was a special order for a little lady. She only had it about a year. I'll make you a great deal."

Everything is so clean and shiny. Bunny can't imagine owning something so beautiful. He turns the knobs, adjusts the seat for his long legs, and runs his fingertips over the seats. "Leather," he whispers. "TC, did you see this?"

"What happened to the owner?"

"Got married, moved away, didn't need her truck. Looks like your boy's already fallen in love." Mike smiles and jerks a thumb toward Bunny.

"Ugliest color for a truck I've ever seen," TC answers.

"I'll make you a great deal."

"Damn well better if we have to look at that."

Mike fumbles in his shirt pocket, bringing out a pen and pad. "What you think about this?" he says as he scribbles something and confidently hands it to TC.

TC studies the figure, tugs at his hat brim, and turns to Mike. "How is your daughter doing—now?"

Mike kicks at the ground, probably feeling like he's being pushed over a barrel. "Fine, fine... she's had a couple of surgeries, you know, nose and jaw. Good news is, she looks better now than before." His face opens to a smile, and he scribbles again, passing it to TC. "Best I can do, and that deal is only for you, partner."

"Headed in the right direction at least," TC says, frowning at the number. "Come on, Red." He slaps the hood. "Let's head down to Chevy City. I saw some slick-looking trucks down there."

"Now wait—wait a minute, TC," Mike says, rushing around the hood. "Let me show you the price tag on same year models. You'll see, that's a great deal." Mike points to the paper in TC's hand.

"Come on, Red." TC waves at Bunny, who doesn't move and stares back with a blank expression. Bunny isn't ready to give up on this one just yet, and he doesn't understand this strange, one-sided game. The more Mike tries, the harder TC pushes.

"TC, let me show you something," says Mike, and while they put their heads together, Bunny looks across the lot to the office as two men get out of a car. "Unbelievable," he says, watching as Mean Man Watson and some guy, probably his dad, walk inside the dealership. "I don't need this today," Bunny whispers to himself.

"So, Red." TC's face appears in the open door, interrupting Bunny's negative view. "Let's go up to the office and talk about financing."

"Financing?"

"Yeah, you got that silly, dreamy look plastered on your face. So I'm guessing, this is the one. Right?" Bunny's sudden excitement makes his heart almost leap out of his chest, and he nods ecstatically. "You sure the color doesn't bother you?" TC says, narrowing his eyes.

"I like it," Bunny says. "It's different, like me."

When Bunny and TC reach the office, Mean Man and the older guy with a mostly grey mustache sit across from a salesperson who two-finger-punches away on a typewriter. When Watson recognizes Bunny, a cocky grin spreads across his face, and he discreetly flips him the bird. Watson's head mechanically rotating, he eyes TC and Bunny as they cross the lobby where Mike waits for them at another desk.

Mike pushes some papers across, and TC snags the documents, occasionally asking Bunny for information. He does his best to act as though he doesn't notice Watson's eyes boring into him from across the room, but it's uncomfortable. When TC finishes filling out the form, Mike snatches it away and disappears to the back. "Almost a third of your wages will go to make the payments." TC says. "You sure you're good with that? 'Cause we can do more looking."

"I don't need much." Bunny nods. "Should be okay."

TC nods, stands, and says something about too much coffee, and walks away, leaving Bunny alone. Mean Man sees his opportunity and crosses the room. "Hey, loser, getting your truck?"

"Yup. You picking up your new car?"

"That guy, the big cowboy?" Watson jerks his thumb. "TC Conway, right?" Bunny nods as Watson leans against his chair like they're old friends. "He has that big ranch and three daughters. Jodie, right? In your class. Boy, does that girl have a mouth on her!" Watson rubs his chin. With his goofy smile, he's almost salivating—ready for the kill. "So, does this TC guy know?"

Bunny closes his eyes, praying Watson will disappear. But when he reopens them, the intimidating figure still looms over him. He stands so close Bunny has to crane his neck straight up to see his face. With no choice from this angle, Bunny can't help but see the tremble of the big man's bloated and misshapen lips. Probably the same excitement the Sasquatch feels when his shoe crunches down on a beetle. Watson smiles. "Does he know you call him, 'Dad'?" Bunny's heart pounding, sweat pops across his brow. He considers running for the door.

"Does he know what?" TC says, walking up behind Watson.

Bunny's too-close tormentor flinches and spins with finely tuned reflexes. "Ah... we were just talking cars."

"Were you now? Oh, hey, Watson," TC says. "Speaking of cars, here's something interesting. You probably heard about Red's car engine conking out, right?" Watson's face goes pale, and the smirk disappears. "When I towed that thing home, I noticed some oily smudges on the gas cap and bumper. I had the sheriff come by, and would you believe? He got some pretty good fingerprints." Watson's shoulders slump, and he attempts another step backward, misjudges the placement of his feet, stumbles, and lands on his butt in the middle of the floor. "Careful there, son." TC smiles. "Broken tail bone or criminal record could really mess up an athlete's future." Watson scrambles to his feet and hurries away like an embarrassed child.

TC's still smiling when he reclaims his seat. Bunny stares at him but says nothing. It seems TC has his way with everything. Certainly with women, and today, the way he treated Mike, and now, he even got the best of Mean Man Watson. Stunned and a bit in awe, Bunny watches as TC shakes his head and chuckles. "The look on Watson's face—I tell you, that boy's gonna have trouble sleeping."

thirty-three

Jodie must have been watching out the window because, when Bunny stops behind the Conway house, she appears at the back door on crutches. She grins. "Nice, but interesting..." She gives his truck the once over. "What's this color?" Jodie smooths a hand over the paint. "Popcorn?"

"Yeah, maybe."

"I go back to school on Monday. Thanks to you, Red, I'm behind in my classes."

"Sorry... the last few days with mom and the car... guess I forgot about your assignments."

Jodie shrugs. "Didn't want to do homework, anyway."

"Your dad asked for you to show me around the ranch. Think he wants to put me to work."

"So... guess I'm showing you chores?" Jodie balances on one foot as Bunny holds the door. She pulls herself inside the truck, and he lays the crutches in the back, slides under the wheel, and waits for her instructions. "I'll give you my Dad-speech," says Jodie. "You ready to hear it?" Bunny nods as she clears her throat, attempting to lower her voice a couple of octaves.

"Main thing on the ranch—the animals." She smirks, sarcasm

creeping into her rant. "Keeping them fed and healthy is the gig. There's nine pastures with animals. Cow-calf pairs in most, but we have two tracts with horses. Conways count the livestock." She wags a finger. "That means somebody, Red Potts—" Her face opens with a smile. "Somebody lays eyes on the animals each day. That's the difference between a successful operation and a tax write-off. Conways don't play at ranching while trying to make a living in town." Jodie stops to take a breath. "How did I do?"

"Uh... good," Bunny stammers. "Thought TC was sitting there for a minute. He tell you all that?"

"Yeah, I probably sound like a parrot." She shakes her head and rips off her sunglasses. "I ride with Dad sometimes after school—at least I did before my stupid accident."

"Nice to have a teacher."

"Easy for you to say. You don't have somebody living up your ass." Jodie slings her shades on the dash hard enough to make Bunny jump. "Nothing I do is ever good enough."

"You sure that's what he thinks?"

"Of course." She bites her lip and picks at a soft spot on her cast before rolling her eyes up to look at Bunny full on. "It's because I'm a girl."

"What?" he whispers.

"Yeah." She chuckles and shakes her head. "He blames mom for us all being girls, but everybody knows it's the man's junk that decides the sex of the child." Jodie points the way as Bunny maneuvers through gate after gate. "Always close a gate behind you. Used to be a law in Texas, before outsiders changed everything."

The rolling hills for the Conway ranch are thick with toast-colored growth tossing on the wind. The wayward mounds of grass remind Bunny of a horse's mane as it falls over the neck, first one side, then the other. Babying his new ride, he eases his truck over the rough terrain.

"Red, how old are you?" says Jodie.

"Sixteen, almost seventeen."

"Could have fooled me. You drive like an old fart. Look like it, too, with that shiny bald head," she snickers. "If we don't move faster, it's going to be dark." Bunny bares his teeth, pulls on his cap, and pushes down his foot.

In tract number three, horses of varying colors crane long necks over the bed of the truck to investigate. Bunny climbs up to the edge of the truck's roof, using the prominent position to count the animals. "See that chestnut mare over there?" Jody points out the back glass. "She's not putting weight on that back hoof. I'll mark her to be checked."

They systematically drive on for the next three hours. Jodie makes note of the lame mare in number three, a pair of newborn calves in field six, and a dangerously low stock tank in pasture eight. "Pen nine, coming up, is the last." She sighs and slaps her book closed. "It's the one off the road, close to your house." Bunny turns the wheel, heading for the last stop as Jodie giggles softly. "I saved this one because it's my favorite. My secret place. I'll show you."

When they reach the gate, she taps his arm and stops him halfway out the door. "Since it's on the road, this one has a combination lock on the chain. It's 3-4-0." Bunny nods, steps out, and spins the dial. "Easy to remember," she says. "Dad says the three is because he has three children."

"What's about the four?" Bunny asks.

"Who knows? Maybe a brother from another mother." Her explosive laughter makes him jump. Jodie's voice winding to a giggle, she passes him a peppermint from her pocket.

The vacant hay rack near the gate provides a home for both a red mineral and a white salt block, the well-licked squares now distorted like puzzle pieces. Bunny guides his truck around the tall steel structure and the cattle magically appear. They run from the far side and clamber out of the creek, charging toward the new arrivals. "Do they always come?" asks Bunny.

"Yep. We have nothing for them today, but they always run to see for themselves. Being a cow must be pretty boring." She smiles.

"Grass is almost gone in this pasture," Jodie says, her eyes scanning the area. "Time to put out hay for this group." She reopens her book, making a note.

After a head count and general look-over, Jodie directs Bunny to drive toward the creek that separates his house from the Conway hilltop. "See that big pecan?" She points to towering limbs in the distance. The tree skeleton reaches skyward, the dark arms highlighted against the fade of daylight. "Head for that."

When they reach the tree, Jodie motions to the creek. "We'll walk down there."

"Can you... on crutches?" Bunny asks.

"Oooof, Red, your lack of confidence hurts." She glares. "Hand me my limp sticks." Bunny fetches the crutches, and Jodie shoves them under her arms and hobbles forward, sinking the tips into the soft soil. Helpless, Bunny can only watch, knowing she'd crawl before she'd ask for help.

Near the creek, the trees along the bank are so thick they have to force their way, pushing through the trunks like prison bars. Their efforts are rewarded just on the other side by a small clearing, a narrow space of perhaps eight feet between the confinement of the brush and the steep drop to the creek.

Jodie crutches to the edge, folds her leg, and sits on the hard sand. Her cast and other leg swing in rhythm, dangling over the vertical wall. Bunny does the same, and together, they gaze into the wild and crooked path below. Light bits of sky flicker bright on the slow-moving darkness of twists and turns in the depths. The water fills the depression, molding to the sandy edges before traveling past to disappear downstream.

"My favorite place," Jodie declares, giving a little shiver in the fast-coming night air. Bunny shucks off his jacket and drapes it around her thin shoulders. He feels a rush of pride having remembered that scene from an old movie he'd watched on television.

"I see why you like it," he says. "It's hidden, like being under the covers at night."

Jodie laughs in her easy, accepting way. "I'm the only one who knows this spot except now you." She stares, waiting for his reaction. "We could make this our place. Our secret place, and open meetings with a unique signal." Her voice pitched upward with a giggle.

"Like flashing the peace sign or hook 'em horns?" Bunny curls his fingers, extending the index and pinkie.

"Exactly, except this is a small area." Jodie eyes the dimensions of the space, similar to that of a tiny bedroom. "We need to limit membership."

"Special invitation only."

"Yes, but they have to be acceptable, not just likable. How about the ability to curl your tongue? We both can do it, remember?" Bunny lets Jodie ramble on, smiling at her contagious enthusiasm. "So charter members, agreed?" she asks, her blue eyes pale even in the stingy light. "It's settled then. No one can be added to the Secret Society unless they possess the inherited trait of tongue curling." She laughs as they lock eyes and together display horseshoe shaped tongues.

"Madam President." Bunny raises a hand. "What is the first order of business in the Secret Society?"

"Tell secrets. Things that bother us... you know, *share*." Then her smile fades. Her eyes stare off, looking into space. She picks up a crutch and stabs the sandy ground again and again, the rubber tip digging a scar in the earth. "I'll go first," she says with determination. But immediately her confidence teeters, and she looks to Bunny for encouragement.

Bunny pulls the crutch from her hands. "Sure, you go."

Jodie focuses her attention on a rock within reach and side-arms it down to the water. The *thunk* as it sinks into the darkness ignites her private thoughts. "My mom cries at night." Shocked by her admission, Bunny waits, but Jodie, having surrendered the words, stops to toss another rock. *Thunk.* "I've heard her a few nights when she believes we're all asleep." *Thunk.* "I creep down and hide in the stairwell."

A chilly breeze threads its way through the thick growth to wash over them. Bunny can hear Jodie sniffling, trying to hold in emotion. Her concern, her love for her sweet mom, moves him, and he puts an arm around her. He remembers the pain in Bridget's face when she'd told him about her cheating husband. Jodie must not know. This is supposed to be the place we share things, but telling Jodie about her dad? Can't be right. After a moment, she reins in her feelings and turns to Bunny. "Okay, Red, your turn."

Sudden fear heats Bunny's face. His brain seizes from the shift of the spotlight. He's never shared personal things. Doesn't know how. Why would Jodie or anybody need to hear what's poking at him like a deep splinter? "I don't have anything... sorry."

"Yes, you do," she snaps. "That's not fair. I tell you, but you don't tell me. Not how it works." She narrows her eyes and sets her jaw, silently communicating *go to hell*. Jodie snatches the crutch from his hands. "Guess you don't want to be a part of the Secret Society," she grumbles, stabbing with a vengeance.

But her words, the threat of losing a maybe friend—his first ever—even before the relationship begins is unthinkable. His mind races ahead, searching dark corners. *I've got to say something*, Bunny thinks, *I've got to*. If being a friend means baring his soul, he'll do it. "Okay, okay," he says and puts out a hand, stopping her vicious attack on the ground. "I... uh, met my dad," he blurts. "And he's an idiot."

thirty-four

TC REMEMBERS when the Chateau Apartments were built. He was just a kid when he and a couple of buddies rode their bikes to the construction site at the edge of town. Impressed by the two-story brick building in progress, TC had wondered if he'd ever live in such a fine place. But standing outside the building now, he can only shake his head. The passing years have not been kind, and the once swanky address is now surrounded by trailer parks and a beer barn.

He knocks on apartment door number 215 and shifts from one foot to the other. For a quick second, TC considers hurrying away before the door is answered. He can't shake the worrisome feeling that something is off. He replays the strange phone call in his head. Only the third time he and Shelly had spoken, and her call was loaded with over-the-top flirtations, which naturally got TC's attention. But her voice—strained, almost pleading—didn't jive with the playfulness of her words. If Shelly hadn't reminded him of the hospital where they first met, he'd never have guessed the desperate voice was the same quiet beauty he'd seen twice behind the reception desk.

Several long seconds pass before TC hears the deadbolt slide, followed by the rattle of the chain. When the door swings open,

Shelly forces a smile. TC remembers the perky blond hair, but having only seen her sitting, he is shocked by her tiny five-foot-nothing size. Her face is flushed, with blotchy red patches creeping up her neck. Her tiny chest visually heaves. Wrapped in a fluffy pink bathrobe, she croons her best Marilyn Monroe. "Well, hello there." She attempts a seductive pose, her back against the door, one bare leg cocked to expose thigh-high skin. But the girl just looks uncomfortable.

TC shifts his weight again. This time he props an arm against the jamb. "You exercising? You're out of breath."

"No, just dressing in a hurry." Looks more like *un*dressing, TC thinks and makes a bet there's nothing but skin under that robe. "I just got home," she adds and closes the door behind him and slides the chain back in place. "Would you like a drink?"

"Are you old enough for adult beverages?"

"Jokes," she laughs softly. "You got jokes." Shelly goes to the refrigerator and brings out two bottles. "Beer okay?"

"Beer," he says and hooks a finger around the offered longneck. "Probably help," TC says, certain they both need to relax. He clicks the bottle against hers. "You live here alone?" he asks and takes a sip. Looking around the room, TC pauses, eyeing two coffee cups left in the sink.

She nods, her eyes glazing, thoughts seemingly elsewhere. "Yes... now."

"Now?" TC says sharply. "Something new?"

Shelly looks away. Absentmindedly, she tucks a lock of hair behind one ear. "Broke up with my boyfriend."

The bad vibe rushes back. Beads of sweat pop on TC's forehead. "Don't tell me you asked me over for some kind of revenge setup?" When she hesitates, he sets the beer down and backs two steps toward the door.

Shelly rushes to block his path. "No, no, nothing like that," she gushes and throws her body in front of him. Carefully, she reaches both hands up to encircle his neck, smiling. "I just remembered how cute you were." She lowers her hand and releases the tie of her belt.

The edges gaping, her robe opens just enough to give TC a glimpse of rounded breasts and the dark shadow between her legs. His mind suddenly elsewhere, TC forgets his uneasy feeling and reaches for the prize.

"Wait a minute, would you?" She giggles and leads him down the hall. "How about a hot shower to get in the mood?"

"Unnecessary," TC smiles.

"Come on, silly. I want to wash you," she says, cupping his crotch. While the water warms, Shelly drops her open robe and kneels before him to unhook his belt and let his jeans fall to the floor. TC's enthusiasm now front and center, his eyes trace over her smooth skin. "Impressive," she giggles, then notices his boots still in place and offers, "Allow me." She pats the edge of the tub for him to sit, then facing away, straddles his legs to pull. The bobbing, heart-shaped backside in front of TC is like a red cape before a bull.

When Shelly drops the second boot, the heel smacks the floor with a thud, followed by a distinctive chain rattle at her front door. She sucks a breath, her eyes popping, and grabs TC's arm.

"Shelllleeee," a deep voice screams. "Open this damn door."

TC wastes no time. The forgotten bad feeling now consuming him, he scoops up his clothes. "Back door?" he whispers.

She shakes her head, threading arms into her robe. "Only a balcony—in there." She points to another room, and TC rushes out of the bath, arms loaded. He finds the sliding glass and pushes it open to a small, wood-slatted deck overlooking a green space between this and another apartment building. No stairs, not even a fire escape. Looking over the side, TC estimates it's a fifteen-foot drop to the ground.

Inside, Shelly's voice screams, "Go away, Eric."

"I'm gonna kick it in," bellows a male voice.

"I saw you with that whore," she screeches.

TC tosses the load of clothes, watching them float down and drape the landscaping. A splintering crash inside and TC hops over the rail, clinging on by his fingertips. He grips the edge and, hand over hand, inches to hide underneath, holding onto the wood slats. Heavy boots pound against the deck, and the vibration sends shock waves to TC's fingers.

"Where's that son of a bitch?"

TC squeezes his eyes closed, hoping to make himself invisible, and prays the guy isn't waving a gun. Then the swish of the door sliding closed and the sound of the lock as it snaps into place. Dangling from the balcony, TC looks across to the neighboring building. A dozen windows twenty-five feet away, all vacant except one. Front and center, a blue-haired woman, hand to her mouth, appears frozen behind the glass. TC's half-mast manhood on full display, his equipment waves freely as he struggles to maintain his grip. He's afraid to call out for help, sure that would tip off the raging boyfriend.

His arms numb, TC looks down, considering a drop. Even with his six-foot height and extended arms, he'll have at least an eight-foot fall. Directly below, his jeans, shirt, and drawers lie snagged in the thorny leaves of a holly hedge that extends the full length of the building. Weighing his options, TC thinks he can push off the exterior brick and swing out far enough to clear the dangerous evergreen. The woman in the window, transfixed by the naked TC, seems to have claimed a movie seat. She holds a bowl of popcorn and feeds a handful into her gaping mouth.

TC's arms are like rubber. He's got to get down. More shouting inside, and the door slides open again.

"Show yourself, you cocksucker," a voice slurs. "I'll kill ya, damn it."

TC wills himself to hold on, praying for the door to close, and it does. Between the brick of the building and the holly is a space of perhaps twelve to fifteen inches. TC considers aiming his body for that space, but with nothing to break his fall, he'd probably end up with broken legs. No, better to take his chances with the thorny evergreen and nurse his wounds. Suddenly, TC's grip slips and he drops like a rock into the bush below.

He crashes into the hedge butt first, then rolls to the ground and grabs his pants. Blood beading over his legs, arms, and privates and with no time to worry about injuries, he hurries into his clothes and boots. Afraid to see the damage, he knows he's going to hurt tomorrow. His loyal fan at the window is still plastered to the glass. TC, now in pants, rescues his Stetson from the bush and plants it on his head. Turning directly to the woman, he tips his hat brim, earning him a quick smile and a timid wave.

When TC reaches the corner of the building, he stops to peek into the parking lot. His truck sits unattended, and the half-lit boyfriend is hard at work. A blade flashes as he pounds on the butt of a knife, driving it into the rubber. Air blows out with vengeance. TC breathes a deep sigh and can only watch as the wild man plunges the blade into every tire.

Next on the agenda, how to get home. There doesn't seem to be anything broken, but blood soaks his shirt and the holly's stab wounds are beginning to hurt like hell. TC wonders how he's going to explain this at home. He's not driving away, at least not now. His truck sadly rests on four rims. TC toys with the idea of calling Red. He hates to involve the kid, but he needs a ride. But can he trust him, since it seems Red has really taken a shine to Bridget? Surely the boy can keep his mouth shut. Man to man. He shouldn't have to tell him that.

Finding a pay phone, TC makes the call. "Red, hey man, need you to come get me. Gonna need new tires."

thirty-five

BRIDGET HAS NEVER SEEN her husband so banged up. The man has punctures, bruises, and cuts in places where she'd never dare to look. Even more worrisome, TC has been lying in bed since the night before last. That's something she's never witnessed. He looks so pitiful that, several times a day, she climbs the stairs just to peek in from the hallway and watch him sleep.

Two days ago, when TC limped in the door, Bridget's first thought was he'd been in a knife fight. And from the looks of him, he got the worst of it. He was bent over and hurting, his bloodstained shirt sticking to his skin. Of course, Bridget couldn't help but rush to his side. How he'd managed to get his foot stuck in the stirrup and dragged through a sticker bush was a puzzle. TC has always been sure in the saddle, and he knew that fool stallion, Roman, was only green broke, so what would make him climb aboard when he was all by his lonesome? He must have lost his mind.

Even with TC's sorry physical condition, Bridget has to admit she's enjoyed the last two days. Although he curses a blue streak every time it's necessary to limp from the bed to the bathroom, he's been awfully sweet to her. "Please run me a bath with Epsom salts," he'd ask. "Please bring me a cup of coffee, or some biscuits would be nice." Bridget couldn't say no. Her husband needing her made her feel complete. So putting her hurt aside, for the first time in a week, she curled up next to TC and slept in their bed.

Even from his sick bed, TC tried to run things at the ranch. "Make sure Red turns the pump on for the tank in number six," TC would bark. "Make sure he treats that mare's leg." It was hard for him to let go.

"How about you get better and let Jodie and Bunny handle things for a few days?" Bridget smiles, leaning against the doorway. She hadn't been this giddy and light-headed around her husband in such a long time, she'd forgotten about the wonderful, weightless feeling she now had in her stomach. TC gives her a lop-sided grin before turning his face back into the pillow.

Satisfied, Bridget goes downstairs to the kitchen and hums as she wraps the apron strings around her waist. Creating food for her family is her happy place, and she's going to make TC his favorite thing—her special chocolate cake. She clangs clean plates and bowls, emptying the dishwasher, and doesn't hear her crutch-wielding daughter hobble into the room. "Wooop," Bridget huffs her surprise when she turns to see Jodie at the bar just feet away. "When did you get here?"

"Red just let me off. Asked him to come in, but he said he had a date."

"Really?" Bridget sets down her measuring cups and leans against the counter, suddenly interested. "Who with?"

"The new girl, Raquel. She just started this year."

"Well, that's good news," Bridget says, giving Jodie an enthusiastic wink. But Jodie's hard expression is set, like leftover pizza.

"Maybe..."

"Why maybe?"

"Cause... she's too pretty. She'll break his heart."

Bridget fetches the baking chocolate from the pantry, taking time to think about an answer and hoping to deliver a life lesson to her opinionated daughter. "Sometimes a couple doesn't look like they belong together. Appearances don't tell the complete story. Look at me and your father. TC is a fine-looking man and I'm... I'm... just Bridget. But your father looks inside to really see me. He picked me." Her voice rising with enthusiasm, Bridget is confident she's made her point. She shoves a handful of clean spoons into a drawer before adding. "Looks aren't what it takes to be happy."

"You're not happy, Mom."

Bridget snaps her head around so fast something pops in her neck. "What do you mean?"

"You cry at night when you think everyone is asleep."

Sudden anger rushing up her collar, Bridget glares at Jodie. "You're spying on me?" Her eyes ready to pop, she has to grip her wrist to keep from slapping her daughter. "You don't know what you're talking about."

Jodie shrugs. "Broken hearts are everywhere, like Red's poor mother and father."

"His father? What do you know about that?" Bridget says, sucking in a breath, afraid to hear what's next.

"Red told me he met the man. Some guy named Scotty. Used to work for Dad back in the day."

"Are you making this up?"

"No, the guy has brain damage now, so he's like a functional vegetable."

"That's awful." Bridget clenches her teeth. Even more awful if Bunny believes that garbage, she huffs to herself. Hungry to hear more, Bridget concentrates on setting her anger aside. After all, Jodie is accurate in her observations, but it's embarrassing that she knows. She holds up a pitcher of orange juice. "Want some?" As she fills the glass, Bridget casually continues. "Tell me—how does Bunny know all this?"

"Dad. Is he feeling better?"

Bridget tics her tongue. "Yes, maybe. With your father, it's hard for me to know the truth." Her remark flying over the teenage girl's head, Bridget goes back to her task as Jodie stares into space and sips juice. But the anger pulsing through Bridget's fingers is hard to control, and she drops a plate.

The sharp crash snaps Jodie from her daydream, and she points out stray broken bits as Bridget rounds them up with a dustpan.

"Did, uh, you and Bunny put Roman back in with the mares?" asks Bridget, looking over her shoulder.

Her eyes crinkling, Jodie looks confused. "Roman? He's still over at Blake's place."

"He is?" Bridget presses her lips together.

"Yeah, we took him over last week. Dad laughed about it. Said it was too late in the year, but old man Blake wanted to see if he could get a few offspring and paid good money. Roman will be with Blake's mares till early spring."

"Don't call an adult 'old man,' young lady." Bridget glares.

Jodie shrugs. "That's what Dad calls him."

That attitude—one of the very things that drew Bridget to TC. The idea that he's better than other people and, because of that, can hardly be expected to adhere to the same rules. "That's so TC," Bridget mumbles. No wonder he'd cautioned her not to tell the girls about his so-called horse accident. He said he didn't want them to know their dad had been thrown from a horse. Got the hell beat out of him is more like it.

"I need air." Bridget stumbles to the back door, dizzy with rage. The sharp burst of chill outside clears her head, and she stops to inspect the hilltop now painted in tints of grey. Above her, a dark cloud sits in the sky like a flat brimmed hat floating on a pond. The heavy air is damp, smelling like a small child fresh from the tub. "Going to rain," she mumbles and makes her way down the hill toward the horse barn.

Her face stinging red from the fresh norther, she slides her slender frame through the horizontal bars of the gate without the bother of opening it. Inside the barn, she pulls open the tack room door. There it is—TC's fine, hand-carved saddle. He had driven all the way to Monterey, Mexico, to pick it up. It rests across a wood frame by the only window. The light from the grey outside spreads across the leather as Bridget steps close. She draws a swirl on the seat with her hand and leans in to examine it. The clean trails of fingertips remain where the dust is swept away. "Just as I thought," she says.

She'd been the fool again. Bridget shakes her head and leans against the wall, breathing deep. Her shoe brushes something, and she bends to see in the dim light. The leathery body of a sizable rat is melted onto a wooden slab, the metal bar of the trap embedded into the fur. Stark white of bone peeks through where the hide has split and there, between the sharp exposed teeth, rests a knuckle of yellow cheese. The poor animal must have wondered at his good luck in finding such a treasure. It was a fleeting celebration, the rodent's life draining away, paralyzed by a broken neck. And while he'd lain there, pinned down and waiting on death, did he wonder why he stuck his neck out in pursuit of that delicious cheese? And more puzzling, why didn't he let go? Even facing the end, the rat held onto the prize with such conviction that death could not dislodge it.

"Trapped," Bridget whispers. "No better than this silly rat reaching for a prize. But, Mr. Long-Tail—" Bridget kicks the decomposing mass and sends up a cloud of dust and hair. "I'll be damned if I'm going to lie still, waiting to die."

Bridget's mind calming with resolve, her angst dissolves with the decision. Even her fingers tingle with the new clarity. She can see the other side as bright and clear as if she'd stepped from a thick fog. She's played the wrong part in this production, Bridget tells herself. And everyone knows, being the victim, well, that sucks. It's time to turn things around. But it would be easier with another, an ally, someone else with skin in the game. "Bunny." Bridget's eyes brighten. "I've got to talk with Bunny."

thirty-six

BUNNY KNOCKS on Raquel's door, sweating like he'd just run five miles. The house, a square wooden structure, seems out of place. It's as though the building was plunked down atop the prairie hill with nothing around it but a few trees and toast-colored grasses waving on the wind as far as you can see. Before he left his own home today, he'd changed his shirt three times and brushed his teeth twice, and the way his stomach is clenching now, he just prays he doesn't throw up.

Ever since Raquel said yes to their first official date, he'd been unable to sleep. Worried about making everything perfect, Bunny has spent the last several nights staring at the water spot on the ceiling. He'd decided the irregular brown edges of the stain above his bed made him think of Florida. Not that he's ever been there. Maybe someday. Bunny had imagined the moment he'd arrive to pick her up, playing the details over and over like a phonograph needle skipping on vinyl. But now, standing outside her front door, he looks down at the single rose in his hand and just feels ridiculous.

When her brother, Raff, pulls the door open, he snatches the flower, puts the stem between his teeth, and draws his palms together under his chin. Rolling eyes skyward, Raff gushes in a falsetto voice. "Oh, honey, you shouldn't have."

The friendly humor was the medicine Bunny needed, and now he smiles and takes a breath. "Raquel ready?"

"Yeah, I think so." Raff calls over his shoulder, "Hey, sis, lover boy is here." A Texas-sized grin spreads across Raff's face as he looks past Bunny into the driveway. "New truck? Show me, man."

While Bunny gives a tour of his new ride, Raquel tries her best to creep up behind them, but Bunny can smell her sweet vanilla fragrance even before she taps him on the shoulder. "Hey there, you ready to go?" he says, his eyes dancing at her beauty. Raquel is wearing a white sweater that highlights her long dark hair. And curls. Today her shoulders are draped in soft spirals. "Your... hair." Bunny stutters. His hand flies up to touch the enticing locks, but remembering Raff at his elbow, he shoves his hands in his pockets. "It's different... pretty."

"You like it?" Raquel gives him a shy smile.

"He better. She tied up the bathroom for an hour," Raff says. "You were in there so long I had to take a whiz outside." Raquel swats her brother on the shoulder and makes a face. "What?" he says, throwing up his hands. "Well, you were."

Eager for them to be alone, Bunny helps Raquel in the truck. Noticing the leather, she caresses the seat. "So soft. Love your new truck, Bunny." And together, they drive away, headed toward town.

"I got you something," Bunny smiles.

"I know, the rose. Very sweet. I think a thorn stuck Raff in the lip." She giggles, covering her mouth. "Teach him to grab things."

"No, something else. Open the glove box."

Raquel retrieves a tiny white package tied with a red ribbon. "Bunny, you didn't need to."

"Open it." He laughs. From the box, she lifts a gold chain with two charms. A tiny heart, and the second trinket is the shape of a round rabbit's head with two pointed ears. "I picked the heart because, well, you've stolen mine, and the bunny because... you know." Bunny shrugs.

"I love it! I looooovvvve it," she squeals. Her smile's so big Bunny can hardly keep his eyes on the road. Raquel flips down the visor and opens the mirror to fasten the clasp around her neck. "So special," she says, admiring the necklace, and leans over to kiss his cheek.

Pleased, Bunny is glad he asked Jodie for help in picking something. She'd suggested the necklace and charms and even told him where he could buy them. Bunny also asked Jodie's advice about where to take a date. She said Saturday night is when country kids from the surrounding schools drive into town. Jodie suggested they could get burgers and, naturally, make a couple of trips down the drag. She explained the basics of making the drag, which consisted of circling the east end Dairy Queen on Main Street and then driving back through town all the way to the west end Dairy Queen before making another loop. The point, Jodie explained, was to show off your ride and see who's in town and who they're with.

"Were your folks at home?" Bunny asks.

"Mom was. Dad's still out. He had a semi of alfalfa arrive from New Mexico. They're staying late to get it unloaded."

"I'd like to meet them."

"Mom's shy. She'll hide out until Dad's around. Sort of a cultural thing. Anyway, she gets embarrassed when she speaks English."

"I bet she's pretty... like you."

"That's an odd thing for my boyfriend to say." Raquel cuts her eyes at him. "But yes, Mom is pretty."

"Boyfriend?" Bunny smiles happily. Raquel touches the necklace, then shapes her hands into a heart.

When they arrive at the east end Dairy Queen, there's a long line waiting in the drive-through and a second lane of cars just cruising around the place. The dimly lit parking lot is packed, and groups of kids congregate in twos and threes, lean, sit, and meander around the parked vehicles. The edge of the lot is bordered by the river bottom and thick tree cover that takes over where the pavement ends, providing private cover for socialization. Bunny watches the lighted end of a smoke pass in the darkness of the trees while the identifiable gleam of a tall boy can rises in the streetlamp's light. Occasionally, the hard sound of an engine revving or a sharp horn blast interrupts the loud talk and laughter. But inside the restaurant, the dining room is empty.

Bunny and Raquel order burgers at the counter and slide into a booth. As they wait for their food, they sit framed in the lighted, oversized window, which offers all the modesty of a sponge bath. "I guess all the activity is outside." Bunny grins at Raquel, wishing now he'd ordered the food to go.

When the burgers arrive, Raquel's has onions which she can't stand, so she pushes it away and concentrates on the fries. At her encouragement, Bunny has no problem eating both burgers. "I'm not very hungry," she insists. After polishing off the food, his stomach is so full Bunny has to excuse himself. Moments later, when he returns from the bathroom, Mean Man Watson, Fast Eddie, and a smaller guy Bunny doesn't recognize surround Raquel at their booth. She leans away, uncomfortable, as the three goons hover over her. When Bunny approaches, she flashes him a nervous smile.

"Well, there he is, the loser from Loserville," Watson chuckles. "We're just asking this beautiful girl why she's sitting here all alone?" Watson smirks as his buddies chuckle encouragement. Then he snaps his fingers and points at Bunny. "Figured it out. She feels sorry for you. Am I right?" The king-sized clown bumps knuckles with Fast Eddie and the other grinning stooge. "Rumor is, we won't have to look at your ugly face much longer." He scratches his chin. "Can you give me a time frame on your demise there, Potts?" Watson says, flashing a shark smile. "I mean, you can rest in peace knowing I'm ready to step in and take care of this little hot tamale." With his two buddies blocking Bunny from the table, Mean Man reaches to lift Raquel's chin, but she quickly slaps his hand away. "Fire—I like that in my women," Watson croons.

"You ready?" Bunny says, pushing past the intruders.

Wide-eyed, Raquel gives a nod and quickly tidies up the remains of their dinner. Before they reach the door, Watson shouts. "Hey, girl, call me when... you know." One arm above his head, he grips an imaginary noose. Head cocked at an angle, eyes closed, Mean Man lolls out his tongue. As they rush out the door, he yells at their backs. "I'll be the good-looking guy in the winner's circle." The words echo through the empty room.

Raquel snuggles close as they make their way across the parking lot, loud with activity. "Bunny?" She stops. "What Watson said..." Her eyebrows arch, and she looks frightened.

"Don't worry." Bunny one-arm-hugs her and with the other lifts his cap a couple of inches above his head. "See, hair growing back nicely," he says, chuckling.

They detour around a noisy circle of name callers. The loudest among them starts a shoving match. A black-and-white does a slow roll past them, flashing lights, so the potential fight evaporates. As they near where Bunny parked, he notices the gleam of beer cans lined up on the edge of the truck bed. An off-putting odor steams from the cargo area. The back end of Bunny's pickup is now littered with empties, the aluminum cans shiny with drops stinking of secondhand alcohol. "Assholes pissed in my truck bed," Bunny says through clenched teeth and slaps the line of empties, making beer fly. A chorus of muffled laughter rises from the darkness as Bunny drops the tailgate to free the waste.

"Let's find a carwash," says Raquel. "I've got quarters." She smiles, holding up her purse. That's when Bunny notices the furry keychain dangling from the handle.

"Where did you get that?"

"What?" Raquel strokes the grey-and-white paw, playing coy. "My rabbit's foot? Raff," she laughs. "He said it just made sense."

"Go figure." It's good to know brother Raff seems to be on his side.

Raquel pulls a handful of quarters from her bag. "Dad has this big glass jar at home where he throws his change. When he's not around, Raff and I help ourselves."

At the carwash, they make a good team. Raquel feeds the machine and points out missed spots while Bunny mans the pressurized wand. He directs it skyward, causing a fine mist to rain down over Raquel. "Bunnnnneeeee," she squeals, diving inside the cab.

"Truck looks better," Bunny says.

"And now it doesn't smell like the men's room."

"You want to drive a bit? See who else is in town?" Raquel nods, and off they go. After the second trip up and down the drag, Bunny pulls into a parking lot. He stretches his brain, hoping for an idea of somewhere fun to take Raquel. "You want to go bowling?"

She shakes her head. "I don't know how."

"Me either," Bunny says, disappointed. "Movie?" he suggests, his voice hopeful.

"I've already seen the one showing at the movie house. Dad took the whole family last Saturday." Stumped for ideas, Bunny goes quiet. "We could go again," Raquel says. "I don't mind."

Bunny thinks of TC, his mind focusing on the big red barn where he'd watched TC and Anna-Marie in the tack room. They were enjoying themselves, but then, TC always seemed to know what women want.

The old song "My Girl" starts on the radio, and recognizing the familiar beat, Bunny turns it up. "This is a classic. You know this one?" Lost in the words, Bunny leans close, singing the chorus softly into Raquel's ear. Being so near her, his eyes pore over the curve of her breast and the way her waist cinches in just before the spread of her hips. He's becoming aroused, and the words seem to float from his mouth under their own power. "We could... maybe go somewhere... and make out." But when he hears the request, Bunny's face goes hot with embarrassment, and he hopes he hasn't overstepped with Raquel.

"Yes," she says, lacing her fingers through his, and smiles. "You know a safe place? Somewhere quiet and away from—*this*." Raquel twirls a finger.

Bunny stares at her in the glow from the yellow cafe sign overhead. Again, his eyes focus on her breasts, where he's sure he can see the pulsing of her heart. She is so beautiful. The sudden rush of joy moves him to tears.

"Bunny... Bunny, are you crying?"

"No," he sniffs. "I'm... just... happy. I've dreamed of this for so long."

Raquel takes his hand, placing it on her breasts. "Feel my heart, Bunny. I'm happy, too."

As the song on the radio ends, Bunny starts the truck. "I know a great place we can go. You like horses, right?"

thirty-seven

BRIDGET TAKES out a pen and paper, planning. First, talk to Bunny. Second, collect evidence about TC's obvious unfaithfulness. Third, decide how to move forward. She raises her eyes from the page, looking at herself in her grandmother's antique oval mirror. Bridget's face is plain and uninspiring. Just a square jaw and bland, grey eyes topped by limp hair. All the fine qualities of a beige wall. "I'm forgettable," Bridget moans. "Why did he marry me?"

Since Bunny is gone on a date, Bridget works on evidence. She carefully creeps upstairs past the girls' rooms to look in her own bedroom and check on TC. He's lying in bed, curled away from her, but Bridget can hear his soft snores. On the far side of the room, his jeans are tossed over the reading chair by the window. His wallet must be inside the pocket. She'll have to circle the bed to retrieve the pants. Then she gets an idea. Bridget takes the laundry basket from the bathroom, tucks it under her arm, and crosses to collect all the clothes on the chair. She bends over beside the bed, gathering the pants along with his shirt and socks that have been cast to the side. "How long you going to be like that?" The sudden sound of TC's voice behind her makes her jump.

Bridget whirls to face him. Eyes wide open, he's looking straight at her. "Oh, you scared me." Her hand flies to her breast, and she forces a smile. "Laundry, trying to catch up. See if I can get the blood out of these clothes." She laughs nervously, then notices his underwear on the floor beside the bed.

"Close the door, laundry can wait." TC holds up the bedcover, exposing himself. "Locked and loaded, girl." Bridget grips the plastic basket and holds it like a wall between herself and TC. He must still be sick, otherwise he'd be heading out the door to give someone else a ride on that pogo stick.

"TC—the girls are in their rooms," she says, moving toward the door.

"That's why I said close the door." He turns on his back, making a teepee out of the sheet. "Come on, Momma." He smiles. Normally, this cocky charm would melt Bridget into submission. Hours before, she was fussing over him, feeling sorry he had been dragged by a horse, and would have happily dropped everything and jumped into bed. But now, still stinging from the most recent bullshit discovery, Bridget bolts from the room, feeling nothing but revulsion.

Downstairs, she pulls the phone cord from the hall and locks herself in the powder room with TC's wallet. His billfold is thick with cash and plastic. When she picks it up, several handwritten notes and business cards fall out. Bridget carefully unfolds each paper and lays out the business cards. On the first of the two ragged notes, the name Troy Roberts is scribbled with a series of digits. On the second, just the word Al, followed by another phone number. Bridget first calls Troy, to learn he's a used farm equipment parts dealer. On the second call, a woman answers. When Bridget asks for Al, she says, "He's pumping. Can I help?"

"Pumping?" says Bridget.

"You got one needs doing?"

"One... sorry, is this a business?"

"Honey Pot Septic Service. We can probably get to you in the morning."

Bridget hangs up without a reply. She fans out the business cards from TC's wallet. The first one is from the sales barn, another is the new bank that just opened in town, and the last card is from the hospital and reads "Shelly White, friendly face at the front desk." Stupid, thinks Bridget, shouldn't it just say receptionist? Looking at the card from the hospital, she remembers the poor boy who got his hand caught in the auger at the mill. But when she turns it over, in blue ink and written in TC's hand, it says "Tuesdays."

She takes a seat and hangs her head between her shoulders. Her face pointed at the floor, Bridget mutters, "No, no, no." She hates what's happening, and now she's become a snoop? Oh, plenty of women brag about trolling their husbands' pockets, suspicious, always on high alert. But that's not Bridget. That type of marriage would be strained and disgusting. Imagine living twenty years like that! But it's impossible to go on as though none of this has happened. How can she ever feel the same? Even so, Bridget knows she's no sleuth, and in fact, she's appalled by even playing the part. "A professional," she says out loud, and brightens with the thought.

Bridget searches for an expert. She finds little in the way of private investigators in their local area, but one name shows up. Jay Henry's image smiles at her from his yellow page advertisement, looking young enough and fit enough to be up for the job. Even though it's after hours, she dials the number.

∼

Bridget is doing her best to get a read on Jay Henry. He sits across from her in his blue polo and ball cap, but the man is almost miniature. When she'd arrived and he'd stood up to greet her, she had towered over the fire-hydrant bit of a man. Perhaps the size benefits him, allowing him to do his job unnoticed. But something about him makes her wonder just how long he's been doing this. His tiny office, if you can call it that, is located at the back side of an industrial park. The single room seems to be an afterthought tacked onto the rear of a garage, where a loud Chicano tune blares through the adjoining corrugated metal wall.

"I hope you don't wear that cap while you're working a job." Bridget yells, pointing to her own head.

Henry snags the lid off and studies it for a beat. "Gift from my dad," he shouts, just as the annoying melody grinds to a stop. "Taco time," he chuckles, then continues in a normal voice. "Some folks have name plaques on their desk. You know, in case they forget who they are." He smirks, animal-like teeth flashing inside a crooked smile. "But me, I put my cap on in here so the client doesn't forget my name." He tugs at the bill, reseating the grey felt branded with one huge, menacing eye and the words Henry Investigations. His face morphing to serious, Jay Henry leans forward on his elbows. "So, Bridget, what brings you to see me?"

"My husband."

"Mmmmm... An asshole, huh?"

"How did you know?"

"Only the wives of assholes sit across from me."

"Really?"

"Yep, all of 'em. Except for this one lady who didn't know her husband was an asshole. She just thought he was gay, but he was doing a college coed, so, he was one, too."

"Well, my husband..." She smirks. "Likes women alright. Too much."

"That's pretty universal."

Bridget narrows her eyes. Even if he is the only investigator in Willow Creek, she's not convinced yet.

"I'll need a bit more information." He opens his notepad and takes the pen from the holder. "Full names, you and your husband."

"My husband is TC Conway, and as you know, I'm Bridget... Bridget Conway."

Henry stops looking up, he leans back and takes a deep breath. His eyes glaze over as he focuses on the space behind Bridget. "TC Conway?" he whispers.

From the reverent sound in his voice, you'd think Bridget was married to JFK. Wide-eyed, she nods. "Problem?"

"Hardly seems fair. Taking your money, that is."

"Wha... what does that mean?" she sputters.

Henry's face reddens like she's caught him in a private moment, and he leans forward. "I mean, the man has a reputation."

"What do you know?" Bridget snaps. Her fingertips turning white, she squeezes the arms of the chair. "Does everyone know? Everyone but *me*?" Her voice breaks with emotion and she swallows hard, gulping air.

"Calm down, didn't say that," Henry says, putting up a hand. He sighs loudly, drumming his fingers against the desk, then mutters almost to himself. "I need the job."

"There are other women, but I need concrete evidence." Bridget's voice escalates. "We have children, property... I'm not the bad guy here!" she shouts, fending off tears.

"Photos, written communications, involved parties, et cetera," Henry says, twirling a finger, his voice a singsong. He pulls a box of tissues from a drawer and pushes it across the desk.

"Guess you've seen this kind of thing hundreds of times." Bridget sniffs and blows her nose.

"Plenty." Henry squints at his screen. "So, do you work, Bridget? Outside the home, that is."

"You mean where I make money? No, but they should pay me. I do everything for everybody. 'Bridget, go pick up this part in town. Bridget, make me some biscuits.' I'm sick of doing my part for a cheat."

Henry stops writing and scratches his chin. Her last news seems to have derailed his thoughts, and his eyes lock into the space behind her once again. He stares without blinking and with such intensity that Bridget turns to see what he's looking at. Nothing behind her but a dark corner furnished with dust and cobwebs. "Maybe we should explore, how am I going to get paid?" He rushes the last words, sucks in another breath, and avoids her eyes with something in his desk drawer.

"That won't be a problem." Bridget's words are icy.

"Okay, great." His voice flat, he studies her across the desk. Face distorted, he gnaws the inside of his cheek, then suddenly sits up to rub the back of his neck. "I'm going to need a sizable retainer up front. Two thousand now plus expenses when we settle up. If I don't have to tail him out of town, more than likely, that'll be the lion's share the first couple of weeks. Might have enough evidence by then. You'll make the call."

Bridget looks across the desk at Mr. Henry with something between hope and distrust. She's struggling to decide if she should go through with this. Is this guy for real or just another man ready to take advantage of her? His flippant attitude doesn't give her a warm and fuzzy vibe, and this place is nothing but a dump. Still, this is a guy who makes his money by peeking into windows and taking dirty pictures. Guess that's a type of business that doesn't demand a plush office. Bridget fights with the decision and realizes, if she goes forward now, she's reached a point of no return with both her marriage and her family. If only TC would show some remorse, stop the lies rolling in faster than a thunderstorm, and just be her husband. *If only...*

Eyes focused on her lap, she picks at a ragged cuticle and whispers to herself, "I can't keep going. Not like this." Mechanically, she reaches across to the desk phone and makes a call. "It's me. Will you talk to this private investigator, please? Yes, I'm finally doing it. He needs a retainer." Bridget pushes the receiver toward Henry. "Talk to my dad. He's the one with all the money."

thirty-eight

"You ever feel like something is off?" TC says, calling from his office in the barn.

"You mean like when the humidity is high and my hair won't do right?" Darleen giggles.

"Yeah, that's a quote from Nietzsche, right?" TC snorts.

"Who?"

"Never mind." TC shakes his head and tries to focus on Darleen's generous curves and not the empty space between her ears. "I'll be at your back door in an hour or so. I've got to do a couple of things first, so keep your panties on for now." He chuckles.

"Well, hurry. It's wrong to keep a girl waiting," Darleen coos. "And TC, whatever is bothering you, I'm going to make you forget all about it."

The last two days, TC has ventured out of his sickbed, able to run a few errands. But each time he drives away from the ranch, the nagging, uneasy feeling returns. It almost seems like he's being watched. Both days he remembers seeing a small white car in the rearview. He probably wouldn't have taken notice of the nondescript vehicle—after all, there're plenty of white cars on the road—except for one thing. There is an unusual horseshoe indention in the middle of the front grill. The sunken place, combined with the bent chrome, made the car look like it's smiling. Probably nothing, TC reasons and takes a deep breath of cold air as he leads the filly back to the barn. His body is still stiff and sore, but it's good to be out of the house and away from his wife's snarky looks. Bridget just can't let go of the business with Anna-Marie. But that girl is long gone, and after TC almost broke his neck at Shelly's apartment, he's gone back to his steady Darleen. They still manage to meet up on her days off from the feed mill.

TC locks the stall gate behind the filly. She's the little beauty he's getting ready for Red. He props his elbows against the wood, watching the hungry girl dig into the pail he'd filled with oats. "You're going to make a fine saddle horse." He reaches through the slats to stroke her lean, shiny neck, his heart swelling with pride as he reflects on the trade he'd made for the unique animal. "Those cowboys said you were too small, but we'll show them. Coming along, aren't you, girl?" TC gives her a final pat and turns toward the truck for his drive into town.

When he reaches the intersection of the highway to turn south toward Willow Creek, he gives a quick look in the opposite direction. About a quarter of a mile down the highway, he catches a glimpse of white just barely visible behind bushy growth in the bar ditch. TC whips his truck through the turn, headed toward town. Watching in his mirror, he sees a white car rush out from behind the greenery, climb onto the highway, and trail behind him.

"You're shitting me," TC says, his eyes glued to the mirror. He slows to fifty, and the car slows. He turns onto a county road, taking a shortcut, and the car turns as well. Never getting closer than a quarter of a mile, the smiling white car pursues, stuck to TC like a whiny kid brother.

He stops at the bank. The other driver pulls to the curb half a block away. When TC leaves, going to fill up with gas, he loses sight of the pesky shadow. "Good. Maybe they've had their fun." But as he exits the station and turns toward Darleen's on the edge of town, the white car magically reappears. "What's with this Chevy?" TC growls and spotting a pay phone, he whips his truck over, calling Darleen. "I'm being followed."

"What... you sure?"

"Yeah. Here's what I want you to do. Go to the feed mill and write me a ticket for twenty bags of that calf starter. Tell Laguin to have the boys load it on a pallet and be ready. I'll drive around back to the covered loading dock. Soon as I stop, I'll have the driver's door open next to the building, and you shoot out the door into my truck and scrunch down in the floor."

"Are you joking?"

"Dead serious. The boys will load the truck, you stay down, and we'll vamoose to the ranch. That shit-can Chevy can't follow me on my own land."

"TC, that sounds crazy. But you know I love adventure."

According to the plan, TC takes his time winding through town and drives through the Beer Barn, where he has them ice down half a case while he waits for barbecue sandwiches from their grill guy. Then he drives to the feed mill, taking note that the relentless white car is still back there. When TC drives onto the lot, he whips around back of the building and pulls under the covered dock area. Darleen rushes out, almost knocking him over, and sails inside where she hunkers down in the passenger floor. The truck makes a gentle squat as the forklift deposits the load inside the bed. TC slams the tailgate and they're on the way. "Stay down," he says, smiling at Darleen, folded in the floor. "There's lunch, if you don't mind eating down there." TC nods toward the bag on the seat.

The white car follows them out of town and stays on them until TC turns off the highway on the county road to Conway Ranch. "Good. The asshole has stopped." TC smiles at Darleen and pats the seat beside him. "Join me."

Darleen climbs up, beaming at their success in dodging the pesky party crasher. "You did it." She claps softly and leans close to give TC a hug. She gathers the discarded, sauce-soaked lunch wrappings, bags the trash, and looks up, suddenly interested in the countryside. "Where're we going?"

"Oh, I've got this place in mind." He grins. "Beautiful pond, so clear you can see tadpoles wiggling. We'll get on the back side, out of the wind, make a little campfire, see what happens."

When TC and Darleen cross through the last gate off the road, the pond water gleams bright with reflection of the day. The elevated high bank of the pool spans the valley and fills the distance between two gentle hills. Mirror images of willows trees rooted by the water's edge languish on the liquid surface. "TC," Darleen squeals. "It's so beautiful! We gonna skinny dip?"

"Little chilly to dip a skinny," he chuckles. "But," TC says, getting serious, "I am ready to see you without those clothes." He turns the wheel, circling behind the dam to hide his truck from the road. They collect branches, stacking them in an upright triangle to build a campfire. Once the dry wood is popping, TC fetches a quilt from behind the seat and spreads it on the ground. Out of the wind, bedded down next to the flames, the cool of the fall day is no longer an issue. They quickly shed their clothes, and the sun does its part by sending a welcome warmth across bare skin. TC finds her secret spot and teases with kisses before his tongue ignites a series of pleasure spasms. Moving to her breasts, he kneads the fullness, hypnotized by their buoyancy, then mouths the generous orbs, her erect nipples saluting in the breeze. He carefully lifts her legs over his shoulders and dives deep, hungry to provide a second round of lady pleasures. When her moans subside, he pulls her up, filling her body with his own explosion of euphoria. Panting with exhaustion, TC rolls the quilt over them to share the warmth and comfort.

All afternoon they make love, finish the beer, and laugh by the fire. Giddy, they doze, satisfied by the release of the day's drama and desire. Light fading, the sun calls it a day. "Getting late," TC says, gently shaking her awake. "Your old man gonna be pissed?"

Darleen frees her arms, stretching outside their cocoon and

laughs softly. "Nah, we got a late start, so I told him I might be out—dinner with a girlfriend."

"Smart girl. I'm impressed. But guess we need to head that way." TC stirs out the remains of the dying fire as Darleen sacks the empty bottles and they load into the truck. "Since you're supposed to be at dinner, guess I should spring for some food," TC says. "It seems my wife has quit cooking for me, anyway."

"Trouble in paradise?" asks Darleen.

"You could say that."

"Probably cause you're such a slut." She grins.

"Hey—" TC cuts his eyes at her. "You weren't complaining earlier."

They drive away from the postcard scene, locking the gate behind them. Their spirits high but appetites now ravenous, TC and Darleen playfully try to shout each other down with their dinner preferences. But the silly game stops abruptly as the headlights shine on someone walking beside the road. The outline is diminutive, perhaps a hefty child, but why would they be alone in the dark? TC slows as the walker puts out a hand, thumbing for a ride. "Hey there," TC says, rolling to a stop. "Need a ride?"

Whoever it is, covered in a dark sweatshirt, the hood drawn tight around the face. "Yes, my car is up ahead, if you could just take me there." A polite male voice floats out.

Feeling no pain, TC is glad to help. "Sure, hop in." He pulls Darleen close to make room as the hitchhiker jogs around the back and slides in the passenger side, cradling a loaded backpack.

"Hope this isn't out of your way," says the hooded man.

"No problem. Going that way, partner."

"Y'all live around here?"

"My spread is back down the road." TC jerks his thumb over his shoulder. "Just taking Darleen home."

"Oh, sorry, ma'am... to interrupt your trip, that is."

"Please don't *ma'am* me. I'm not that old... yet." Darleen giggles.

"I guess I assumed... you two... aren't married?"

"Oh brother, I pity the woman who'd throw in with this one," Darleen says and playfully slaps TC's leg. In her enthusiasm, she topples the sack of empties underfoot. Glass bottles roll and clang, the last sips spilling out, soaking the barbecue trash. A sour beer smell rises from the floor.

"Y'all been to a party? Beer and barbecue—am I right?" the guy says.

"How did you know?" Darleen cranks up her giggle but stops with a gasp as TC delivers a quick elbow to her ribs.

"What happened to your car?" TC's voice has an edge now, irritated by Darleen's loose comments.

"Oh, nothing. I just had to check something. That's the spot on the right... there."

TC slows, swerving to a stop at the turn-in, and the small man climbs out. "Thanks a bunch. Saved me some legwork," he says, revealing the tiniest flash of a smile.

Troubled by the hitchhiker and his strange reply, TC waits for the guy to clear the truck then spins the wheel, backing to shine headlights into the dark pull-off area. "Son of a bitch," he groans.

"How cute! Look, that car's smiling." Darleen points out the windshield.

"Just my luck," TC forces through gritted teeth. "It's that shit-can Chevy."

thirty-nine

THE HOUSE SQUEEZES him like powerful arms, shaking him awake. Bunny jumps from his sleep, sheets soaked, face slick with sweat. His bare feet slap from room to room, but he finds no one.

It's her. He's sure of it. Nan. The house has consumed her, digested her very soul. The familiar walls, the sag of the roof—once a comfortable old friend, now suddenly alien. More than that, it knows. The house knows his anxiety, his loss of a mother. Painful. She'd been his only human link and the very mold that'd shaped his world. She talks to Bunny, not in the usual way, but comes to him as an unexplained blast of cold, a sudden off-smell, or sometimes the house just breathes out a tired groan. The tiny offerings of comfort are not lost on him. A touch, a remembrance—*I'm here*. Oh, how he'd longed for the attention! It certainly didn't exist when Nan was alive. Perhaps now, it's her spirit working to compensate for neglect and earn passage to a better place.

Sleep for Bunny since Nan passed has become both terrifying and wonderful. He is literally afraid to close his eyes. It was very much the same when she was alive—his sleep was always on edge, never knowing when Nan might wake in a fit of rage. But now, the comfort of the little home has become the erratic personality of his mother.

Many nights, Bunny completes the same ritual he has for years. He escapes outside.

It feels like he's just closed his eyes when Bridget touches his shoulder. "Bunny, Bunny, why are you out here?" He pulls the blanket off his face to squint up at her.

"What time is it?"

"Early. Thought I'd check on you before you left for school." She bends over him, spine curved like a gooseneck lamp, back to the rising sun, her face shadowed in the dark. Feeling a pain in his hip, Bunny fumbles under his body and tosses a rock away. The frantic mob sound of cattle calls prods him to sit up.

Across the fence, TC pulls into pasture number nine on his regular morning routine. Bunny watches as, truck loaded with still-green bales of hay, TC snip the wires before heaving the heavy bales into the feeder. The hungry cattle swarm like angry bees, fighting for position. Boss cows claim a place at the troughs and are soon rooted to the earth like concrete pillars while the smaller, younger animals employ the rush-and-grab method, hoping to secure a mouthful before receiving an aggressive head-butt to move along.

"Who's your friend?" Bridget points.

"Oh," Bunny says. "Didn't know he was there." He stares dumbly at a half-grown white kitten curled and content on the end of his blanket.

Bridget squats beside the still-sleeping fur ball and gives Bunny a hard look. "You're not going to hurt it are you?"

Bunny sheepishly reaches for the kitten. "No," he says. "Nan sent him," he says with confidence and presses a tiny pale paw between his thumb and forefinger, smiling at his creation of tiny Wolverine.

"Your mom?"

"Yeah, she's hanging around the house, keeps waking me at night."

"Bunny... you okay?" Bridget cocks her head, staring like she can see into his brain.

"Just tired." He brings the kitten close to his face. "When did you get here, big guy?" The kitten mews, then yawns and rolls out a pink sandpaper tongue between needle teeth. "I think I'll call him... Casper." He coos into the tiny face, laughing at the whisker tickle against his nose.

"Casper, like Wyoming?"

"More like the friendly ghost."

Bunny stumbles to his feet. One hand around the kitten, he drapes the blanket over his head to block the sunrise and morning chill. Bridget reaches in, planting her wrist against Bunny's forehead. "No fever." She knits her brow. "Do you need to talk to someone?"

"About what?" He shrugs, thinking that, in the light, she looks like the one who's sick.

"Gee, I don't know." She bugs her eyes. "Ghosts... or maybe you sleeping on top of the dirt mound of your mother's grave?"

"Makes me feel close to her. Sometimes, the house is just too pushy."

Bridget gives Bunny a side-eye glance. She looks concerned and seems to be trying to decide if he's telling the truth.

"What?" Bunny grins, but seeing that she's all business, loses the smirk. He decides to stay quiet, knowing Bridget has more to say.

"The child welfare people are snooping around. They know you're a minor and on your own. I'm hoping to find a blood relative to help you get the emancipated minor status." Bridget explains.

"They call you? The welfare people?"

"Uh, no but they've been asking around—I bet. Everybody knows it's just a matter of time, really, until they come."

"You could ask my dad."

"Really?"

"He works the grill at the Steaks Well Done place in Willow Creek."

"Yeah, about that... not so sure that guy is your dad."

Wide-eyed, Bunny nods. "You know him. Scotty. He used to work for TC."

"Yeah, thing is... I don't. Nobody like that ever worked for TC," she snaps. Bridget takes a breath. She tries a smile, but only one side of her mouth seems on board and a sneer crawls across her lips.

"But... TC said..." Bunny manages before Bridget cuts him off.

"I don't give a damn what TC says. Lies, all lies," she shrieks. Backhanding the blanket off Bunny's head, she steps close. Conditioned by Nan's erratic behavior, he throws up an arm in defense. Bridget's jaw drops. She looks him straight in the eye. "Dammit, I'm trying to you help you, Bunny. I don't want you to go live in a crappy orphanage."

Shocked by this new, violent, foul-mouthed version of Bridget, Bunny's response is little more than a whisper. "Could that happen?"

"Sure it could." Bridget reaches for Bunny's arm and tugs him behind her like a confused toddler. She strides across the yard to the fence line that separates pasture nine from the Potts' place. "Let's just ask him," she says, windmilling an arm overhead to signal TC.

TC, already back in the truck but seeing her wave, circles around. He drives close, then walks over. "What's up, Momma? Kid wet the bed?" TC chuckles at his own humor.

Bridget clutches the top wire, careful to grab between the glistening barbs still wet with dew. The vibration causes the tiny, sun-filled diamonds to drip their riches below. "TC, Bunny just had his first date with a girl." Bridget smiles sweetly. "He could use some fatherly advice."

Caught off guard, TC's eyes grow large before his face crinkles with concern. "Don't know about the fatherly part," he says slowly. "But I'll help—if I can." A silent observer, Bunny calmly strokes the kitten's white fur, wondering what his love life has to do with an orphanage.

"Great," she says dryly. "Bunny likes this girl, you see—a lot. But he needs advice on how to get in her pants. You're the master at that sort of thing, so thought we'd start at the top."

"Bridget," TC shouts, his eyes suddenly smoking with rage. "You're embarrassing yourself."

"I'm already the joke of the county, you asshole," she scoffs.

When TC turns away, Bridget realizes she's losing her audience. She bends down, grabbing a handful of dirt clods that she heaves across the fence. Ducking the debris, TC straightens, his face paper white.

"TC, who's the new girl you've got your eye on?" Bridget's voice teases, amused by her attack. "I hear she's a real dark-haired beauty. Oh, what's that name?" She snaps her fingers with a fresh memory. "Raquel, wasn't it? Yes, Raquel."

Bunny gasps. He can't believe his ears. Bridget tilts her head, smiling at TC. "I'm sure of it." Now Bunny's rush of anger strains his insides like an overblown balloon. He's ready to explode. His hands shake so violently he has to fist them as he holds his breath. *Is TC really after Raquel? My Raquel?*

TC stares across the fence with an expression Bunny has never seen. His eyes lock on Bridget, narrowed to slits. TC's jaw pulses, lips so tight they're colorless. His face a mass of hate, he spits through clenched teeth, "Bridget, have you lost your damn mind?" He shakes his head and stalks to his truck.

As soon as TC drives away, Bridget turns to Bunny, who is so weak he has to bend at the waist and gasp for air. As he juggles the kitten, the frightened animal lightning-strikes with tiny claws. Bunny jerks away, and Casper scampers under the house. Still catching his breath, Bunny looks at the rail-thin woman who hovers over him. She's drawn, with lines under her eyes he hadn't noticed before, her face a pallid shade of yellow. "Aren't you afraid to go home?" he says.

She nods but refuses to look up as she bites at a nail. "The girls and I are staying over at my dad's house." Bridget releases a weak laugh. "My daughters think I'm the problem. I'm the one interrupting their perfect lives. Guess I'm getting good at being hated."

"I don't hate you," Bunny says softly.

"Good, that makes one." She puts a hand on his shoulder. "Glad you've got my back. I'll let you get to school."

"But what's the point?" Bunny says, his voice slow and distant, like it's forced through a paper tube. What could any of this matter? Raquel is his future and without her, he'd just as soon live with strangers, or not live at all. Maybe that's what Nan wants—for him to be with her. Bunny stares into Bridget's once soft and kind grey eyes. There's a hollowness in her now, a gaping wound he's seen before. It's the same dark void that lived in the eyes of his own mother. His body throbs, his energy crashing, he's tired. "If Scotty's not my dad, then..." He shrugs. "Then there's no one."

"But, Bunny, there is someone," Bridget says. "And you deserve to know who."

forty

THE IDEA of TC putting his hands on Raquel blinds Bunny with anger. He drives like a madman toward the school, desperate to find her. "I've got to see her." He pounds the steering wheel, his foot jammed all the way down, trying to make up time lost from Bridget's disturbing visit. He slides to a stop and races inside the building. But Bunny is late. Everyone is already in class.

Focused on stopping TC, Bunny walks through the vacant hall straight to Raquel's classroom. He pulls the door open, oblivious to the biology class in session. "Excuse me, Potts," Mr. Jenks says, holding an open textbook in midair. "Why are you here?"

Ignoring the question, Bunny strides quickly to Raquel, who gapes at him from her center row desk. He latches onto her arm, attempting to pull her from her seat.

"Bunny, what are you doing?" she huffs, snatching her arm away. Her cheeks flushed, Raquel's eyes dart rapidly, her classmates filling the room with whispers.

"Come on." He insists and tugs again, this time so hard you can hear the bones of her wrist pop.

"Potts," Mr. Jenks magically appears beside him. "You want to explain yourself?"

"I've got to... to... talk to Raquel." Bunny stammers and looks at his shoes, stoking giggles from the room.

"Fine, but after my class, on your time," Mr. Jenks says. He unwinds Bunny's fingers from Raquel's arm. "Potts, if you disappear by the time I count to three, I'll not bother the principal with this impromptu interruption. One... two..."

When Bunny reaches the door, he sits in the hall waiting for class to be over. He can't risk missing Raquel, but he keeps a watchful eye, ready to disappear if necessary. If Principal Pemberton makes an appearance, Bunny plans to duck into the boys' room next door. About halfway into the torturous wait, Mrs. Matthews, the ancient history teacher, begins her familiar limp-step down the length of the hall. Her feet and legs don't match, one normal, one shriveled. Polio, they say. Her curled fingers around a student's bicep, he towers over her. The boy in trouble wears a goofy smile. From the determination in her face, Bunny knows Mrs. Matthews is taking him straight to the principal's office. Bunny can almost hear her say those exact words. As they approach, he gets a scornful look from the teacher, who probably thinks Bunny is being punished and banished to the hall. As they pass, Bunny notices the back of Mrs. Matthew's skirt is caught up in the waist of her baggy undergarments making him duck his head to hide his smile.

As soon as the bell rings, ending the period, Bunny leaps to his feet, eyes glued to the door. The students file into the hall. Raquel is one of the last out of the classroom, and when he steps in her path, she gives Bunny a wild look. "What's the matter with you?" Raquel says, her eyes shrinking to slits.

"We need to talk. I've got to warn you."

"So you break into my class?"

"It's TC."

Her face is a question mark. "Jodie's dad? The nice man who gave me a ride home, twice," she says, holding up two fingers.

"Yes, him," Bunny shouts, drawing unwanted attention from Mr. Jenks, who's stepped into the hall. He pulls Raquel closer to talk, breathing her sweet smell, like warm vanilla wafers. The shine of the necklace he'd given her is visible under the lace of her blouse. Bunny's pride swells at seeing his gift staking his claim, and he double-downs with awkward insistence. He stares into her eyes, hoping to show his concern, but Raquel's look back is trouble. She's upset. "You have to listen to me. TC uses women."

She glances to Mr. Jenks, who watches from the door. Her sad eyes seem to beg for help, and Raquel takes a step back, keeping her distance. If he could just make her understand. Bunny tries again, reaching for her arm. That's when the teacher walks over.

"Potts, if you don't walk away, this is not going to go well. Stop harassing Miss Martinez. Now!" Forced to retreat, Bunny can feel them watching as he weaves this way and that to disappear among the crowd of noisy students.

It's lunchtime when Bunny tries again. When he pulls Raquel from her seat at the table of friends, she tugs her arm away. "Why are you acting like this?" She glares, her eyes angry and hurtful. "Everyone is laughing at me."

"I'm sorry... but I think... I mean, I heard... TC is interested in you," Bunny blurts.

"Ridiculous. Wouldn't I know if he was?"

"I'm... *worried*. Raquel, you don't know what he's like." Bunny sees a couple of buttons are undone on her blouse, and he reaches to close them. "Your necklace?" he gasps, staring at her bare neck.

"Oh," her hand flies up. "I, uh, didn't wear it today."

"But... I..."

"Leave my buttons alone." She swats at him. "I'm a big girl. I dress myself."

Bunny pockets his hands and looks at the floor. He hadn't expected this and now is stumped. But she's so innocent, he has to protect her. TC has a wife and plenty of women. He can't have Raquel. Bunny won't let that happen.

"Bunny, I care for you, but sometimes..." Raquel takes a deep breath to gather her thoughts as her hands nervously flit at her collar. "Sometimes it's like, like you're choking me. You take me home from school, I see you at lunch, you call me when we're not together. Bunny, I'm still the new girl here at school. I need the chance to make friends." Her face sad, she looks back at the table of her schoolmates. Raquel sighs, straightens her shoulders, and focuses her apple-green eyes on his. "We should take some time off. I need space to breathe."

Her words rush at him, ringing his ears like a slap. Thinking he couldn't have heard that right, he stares back dumbly. "What? Raquel... what are you saying?" he stammers. "You can't mean..."

She flips her dark hair over her shoulder and spins on her heel before looking back. "Bunny, please stop bothering me. I can't do this."

∼

JODIE'S PHONE call wakes TC from a dead sleep, and the familiar quivering sound in his daughter's voice kicks him into high gear. "Dad, please come get me." No doubt about it, she's been crying.

TC runs out the door and races toward the Watson place. Checking the time, he sees it's after midnight. Jodie said she and a friend got a ride to the after-game party. That's just like Jodie, trying to fit in. She'd missed so much school with the accident, she probably wants to make up for all the time she'd spent stuck at home.

The Watson place sits aglow like search lights are scanning the walls for escaped prisoners fleeing into the surrounding darkness. TC parks and is apparently too late for the handy valet service. He walks past several departing guests searching for their own rides. The party seems to be pretty much over as TC strolls through the house without seeing a single soul. When he looks out the back door, Jodie is slumped over a bench, hugging one knee, her cast propped on the seat beside her.

"Oh, Dad." Her words tumble out. Relief in her watery eyes makes TC glad she'd called.

"Where're your crutches?" he says, glancing under the bench.

"Drowned," she says. "In the pool." Her sarcasm a weak disguise, she's still fighting tears. "That horrible Perky Peterson and her best friend July made fun of me and stole them. One girl slipped on the diving board and almost fell. Crutches went into the water. I had to hop to the back door just to call you."

"Say what?"

Her mouth forming a perfect upside-down horseshoe, Jodie's luck seems to have run out. "Down there." She points. TC walks to the end and can just make out in the deepest water the ripple image of two crutches forming a perfect X at the bottom of the pool.

TC scans the mostly deserted backyard where a few hardy party-goers still huddle around a dying fire pit. "No takers on helping a crippled girl in forty-degree water, I guess," TC shouts at their backs. A couple briefly look his way but are quick to turn back to the fire. He spies a net on a long pole and, after a few tries, manages to drag the wood crutches out. He shakes off the water and helps Jodie to her feet. "Didn't you say you came with somebody else?"

She nods. "Raquel. The girl Bunny likes."

"Of course..." This night just got weirder. TC remembers just how ripe for the picking that beauty is.

"She and Bunny broke up, I guess." Jodie shrugs. "This group of kids leaving the game asked if we wanted a ride to the party and Raquel said, 'Sure, if Jodie will go.'"

"Does your mother know where you are?" TC's eyes drill Jodie. She nods but, reluctant to discuss, directs her attention to the crumbling plaster on her foot. "I want to come home, Dad," she whines.

"I want that, too." TC squeezes her shoulder.

"I hate it at Granddad's." She wrinkles her nose. "I have to share a room with big slob Meredith. And Dad—" Jodie bugs her eyes. "She farts in her sleep."

TC chuckles, "Your sis better lay off the Mexican food. And your mom, well, she just needs to stop acting crazy." He pushes up his hat brim and glances around the empty pool. "Okay, so where is

Raquel?" he says, hoping the girl will magically appear. The thought of seeing that pretty face again might make this dismal evening worthwhile.

"When we got here, I had to find the bathroom. When I came out, she'd disappeared."

"So you haven't seen her for how long?"

"Hour." Jodie shrugs. "Maybe longer." TC's eyebrows shoot up. "I know, rude, huh? I've been stuck by myself." Jodie shivers, hugging her thin shoulders in the night air.

"Come in out of the wind. Let me find her." TC helps Jodie maneuver to the house and finds her a seat. He begins the search by striding room to room to look in each doorway. In a stuffy space with a gaudy chandelier and dark wood walls, smoke curls toward the ceiling from the other side of a high-back sofa. TC calls, "Raquel." Immediately, two heads pop up over the back of the sofa. A boy and girl wearing the same "oh shit" expression, their big eyes waiting on TC's next move. "No smoking in here, you pot heads," he barks, then turns away to continue his search.

In the kitchen, he almost steps on a hand. The hand is attached to a boy sprawled on the floor behind the breakfast bar. TC traces the putrid smell in the room to the sink splattered with thick, brown vomit that reeks of sour beer. The comatose kid below snores fitfully. His open mouth is partly pressed against the tile, his face in a pool of spit. TC assesses the boy's age at about sixteen. "Don't worry, you'll feel worse in the morning." TC chuckles, nudging the boy's shoulder with his boot.

Now TC climbs the stairs, apprehensive about searching in private areas. It was a closed bedroom door, he remembers, that had gotten him in trouble his freshman year of high school. Dee Dee Wilson's irate father had almost broken the door down before he dragged TC off his daughter and threw him out into the street. He flinches now, thinking of the embarrassment and the cold as he was forced to run home wearing only a pair of argyle socks he'd received for Christmas. But the memory of the girl and the forbidden act still excites him. And twenty plus years later, as TC ascends to the second story, he eagerly expects the possibility of finding a willing Raquel behind one of these doors.

At the top of the steps, a long hall stretches before him with rooms on either side. The overhead lights are blazing, but the doors are shut. "Bedrooms," he huffs under his breath, stopping outside the first closed room to listen. No sound. He tries the knob and the hinges squeak as he pushes the door open. "Raquel," he calls softly into the dark. As his eyes adjust, a woman with curlers in her hair sits up in the bed. Quickly, TC closes the door and moves on.

When he opens the next room, a white, shaggy dog with an enormous head rushes out straight at TC. After a quick pet, the friendly animal lumbers away, his nails clicking against the floor. The room across the hall is locked, and TC is beginning to think Raquel must have already gotten a ride home. Only two more doors remain. TC opens the next and calls again, "Raquel." No answer.

Just as he starts to pull it closed, a weak reply comes from somewhere in the dark. "I'm, I'm here."

"Raquel?" The only light in the room filters around the space at the edges of closed blinds. He feels for a switch and illuminates the room. A rug, a desk, walls of signed game balls and framed jerseys, and crumpled on the floor beside the four-poster bed is Raquel.

forty-one

BRIDGET'S SKIN is already crawling, and she hasn't even walked inside. The giant pink neon cowgirl with three red, flashing stars covering her nipples and hoo-ha is so scandalous she feels dirty just looking at it. For a moment, Bridget considers driving away. Can you imagine insisting on a meeting at this time of night? Here? Nothing good happens after midnight and especially in a place like this. But with Jay Henry's words still fresh in her ears, she reluctantly turns the wheel toward the graveled lot.

A muscle-guy with sleeves rolled above bulging biceps stands beside the entry gate. He bends down, looking, so Bridget lowers her window. "Three dollars, Miss," he says, thrusting a meaty hand.

Bridget blinks at him. "To park?"

"Three dollars to park, yes."

"But I haven't even gone in."

"Yeah. Boss found customers using the parking lot to jerk off, turn tricks, and sell drugs. So, gotta pay to play."

"Sounds like a lovely establishment," she huffs, rummages in her purse, and finally produces three singles. She hands it over, spins her wheels and peppers the guy with loose rocks. Fortunately, there is a parking space right near the building. But when Bridget steps from her car, she notices several people milling around outside in the semi-darkness of the lot like the half-dead. She must be out of her mind to even be here, but she sprints across to the building.

At the door, a scary, tattooed person of sex unknown demands another five dollars. Bridget wonders, at this rate, how does anyone have money to spend inside? Finally through the door, a rancid cigarette odor topped by notes of locker-room ball-sweat greets her. She follows ear-splitting music down a short hallway that empties into a barn-sized room with soaring ceilings. The thick purple hue of the space makes it impossible to define more than body shapes at the tables and a line of butts parked at the bar. *Swish*. A rush of motion grabs Bridget's attention as the flash of a naked girl balanced on a swing sails overhead. *Swish*. She pumps her legs, pointing black stilettos to the dusty rafters.

Across the room, someone frantically waves and Bridget threads her way through crowded tables where a rowdy male audience hoots and whistles. On stage, a girl with jiggling parts and generous curves rips free a tiny pair of ruffled panties, leaving her body bare, save a pair of knee-high western boots. The performer slingshots the tiny bit of cloth into the crowd, where it snags in Bridget's hair. In the melee that follows, Bridget is knocked to the floor and scrambles on all fours, her fingers sticking in god knows what.

Hands pull her to her feet, and when Bridget turns, she's staring straight into the boyish face of Jay Henry. "Glad you came." He smiles.

"Wish I could say I was thrilled to be here." She fans her fingers, unsure what to do with them.

"Yeah, I'm waiting for someone." He points to a table.

"You better not mean one of these, these girls."

"You can say stripper. They're professionals."

They take a seat at a tiny table, the farthest from the stage. Bridget notices that, from this angle, you can see the entire room. The stage show seems to go on break, and thankfully, the obnoxious music recedes to background noise. Straining into the purple haze hurts Bridget's eyes and makes her feel woozy even though she's had nothing to drink. The fight she'd had earlier with Jodie about going to some party is still fresh on her mind. Jodie, she's the one who always has to push, complaining every five minutes about how much she hates staying at her grandparents' house and, "Why can't we just go home?"

"Something wrong?" Jay asks.

"No, just feels like I'm looking through water. What's with the lights?"

"Not really the kind of place where you want to see and be seen," Jay says. "You said you had something to tell me?"

"You remember the boy I told you about, lives at the edge of our ranch. I think my husband might be the boy's father."

"Well, that's possible, I guess."

"My dad, the one with the money, hates TC. He called him out right before he walked me down the aisle. I'll never forget the look on TC's face when Dad told him, 'Conway, I don't trust you half as much as a yeller dog.'"

"Weird, but... pretty awesome." Jay chuckles and pumps a fist in the air. "Go, Dad!"

A pretty girl in a red cowboy hat and toddler-sized Daisy Dukes appears at their table. "Oh, hey, Bridget, this is Tammy—the girl I was waiting for."

"Yeah, it's supposed to be my break time." She snaps a chaw of gum, pumping red lips. "But since I'm out here on the floor, let me get your drink order." Tammy whips a look over her shoulder in the direction of the bar. "Or at least pretend to." She smiles, zeroing in on Jay, her head tilted slightly to the left.

"Tammy, you ever know a guy named TC Conway?"

"TC," she says, rolling the name in her mouth like mystery meat. Suddenly, her eyes widen. "TC. Tall? Big Stetson?"

"Bingo."

"Hadn't heard that name in years. He used to hang around the house when I was a kid. Momma was crazy for that cowboy."

"So what happened?"

"Nothing. He just stopped coming. Momma cried buckets. She thought they were going to tie the knot, but she said TC wouldn't get off the gravy train."

Bridget steadies herself, elbows anchored on the table. The words explode in her brain. It's true her dad bankrolled the ranch for TC, but she can't make the parts line up. This happened when this girl was a child. How is that possible?

"Could you bring us a couple of soft drinks?" To Bridget, he asks, "Cola okay?" Bridget nods approval.

Tammy frowns and taps her pen against an order pad. "Jay, it's still three-fifty apiece, even without alcohol. Don't you want a little rum or Jack in there?"

"Thanks, but I'm on the clock." He smiles, and she scurries away, red hat bobbing toward the bar. Jay must be reading the question plastered on Bridget's face. "Best I can figure, that happened probably eighteen or nineteen years ago."

"We've been married nineteen years in June." Bridget sighs. "The boy... he's sixteen, almost seventeen." She studies her hands now balled into tight fists. "TC hit the ground chasing, I guess, soon as we got married."

"Oh, I'd say he's probably been juggling women since puberty," Jay says. "Don't make this personal."

"*Personal*—did you really say that? How can you be so, so, *calloused*? You a married man, Jay Henry? Children? I don't see a ring on that finger," Bridget snaps, frowning across the table at his shallow statement.

"I just meant—" Jay shakes his head. "TC would be doing this no matter who he married."

Bridget twists her fingers on the table, letting the flash of anger calm. "Have you found anything?"

Jay plops a manila envelope between them. "Didn't take long. He's been a busy man."

"Do I even want to see this?"

"Probably not, but that's why you hired me."

Bridget opens the top and fans out several photos. For the first time, she appreciates the weird purple haze in the room. The images are so painful that, even in the dim light, the shock is overwhelming. She glances, then clutches her stomach, grabs the manila envelope, and, spreading it open, vomits inside. Bridget folds the top, wipes her lips on the back of her hand, and blinks up at a wide-eyed Jay. "I know this woman," she says stiffly and shoves the photos in her purse. "She works at the feed mill."

Tammy reappears with a tray and two drinks she carefully places on the table. "Anything else?" She bubbles a smile.

Bridget pinches the top of the envelope and pushes it toward the girl moon-eying Jay Henry. "Could you be a dear and toss this?" she says. Tammy accepts the drippy package between two fingertips, holds it at arm's length, and hurries away like the thing is on fire.

"Really?" Henry makes a face.

"Was that mean?" Bridget mumbles. "I can't tell anymore."

"So that was the daughter. Would you like to meet the girl's mom? You know, one of the old girlfriends?"

"Is this fun for you?" Bridget stabs at him with a hard look. "Your sick entertainment? Torture the client?"

"It's just... the testimony of a spurned ex is something a judge will listen to. Sorry, I know this is bad, but it'd help your case. Come on, I'll introduce you." Henry stands and takes a big slurp from his glass. Bridget leaves hers untouched. "You don't want your expensive soda?" he asks.

"Afraid not. I'll probably need to pick up some delousing products as it is."

"No worries." He shrugs. "You're paying, anyway." Jay leads the way across to the bar, finds a vacant spot, and leans in. A woman draws beer from a tap, but looking up, notices Jay and gives a nod.

"Jay, why are we at the bar? I'm not consuming anything in this place of filth," Bridget rails. The lady bartender appears, drying hands on a towel. Her face brightens as she smirks at Jay. A game of chicken. Who'll speak first? The woman has some miles on her, but even now, Bridget can see she once was very beautiful. Honey colored hair, nice tan, the old girl looks like she knows her way around a gym.

"Cathy." Jay loses, breaking the silence. "Somebody I'd like you to meet." His head rotates mechanically toward Bridget, who would like nothing more than to disappear. "This is Mrs. TC Conway."

The immediate hateful stare directed across the bar lands squarely on Bridget, who shifts from one foot to the other and fumbles with her purse. The bartender flips the damp towel across her shoulder, leaning forward. Her eyes narrow to slits, her lips curl into a grimace. "Well, now, whaddaya know? Something the bastard didn't lie about. TC told me he'd married a homely girl." She gives a knowing smile, takes down the towel, and begins polishing the bar between them. "Let's see, now..." Her eyes roll up from the busywork, sparkling with new thought. "Your daddy... he has money, right?"

forty-two

RAQUEL CAN'T STOP CRYING. The waterworks started once they reached the truck. But what's weird is, she wasn't crying when TC found her by the bed. Turning it on now seems more like a smokescreen. The girl doesn't want to talk. She dries up long enough to sputter a pitiful request to spend the night with Jodie. "What about your folks?" TC asks.

"I'll call Mom," she mutters. "Dad will be asleep. Tomorrow is Saturday, Dad's day off. If I get home early in the morning, he might still be asleep."

Her clothes are a mess, her blouse is ripped open. Poor girl has to grip the material together just to cover herself. "What happened in there? Do we need to go to the cops?" TC asks, only making her sob louder. Gritting his teeth, TC squeezes the wheel and drives on.

Jodie taps him on the shoulder. "Dad, please go to our house. I'll call Mom when we get there." He understands she means their hilltop home and not his father-in-law's place, where the girls and Bridget have taken refuge.

He drives on, feeling uneasy about what went on at the party. "So, that was Watson's bedroom?" TC says, watching the stark white line of the blacktop roll past like milliseconds on a timer.

Silence for about a mile, before Raquel squeaks out an answer. "Guess so. It was a game." She sniffs. "Two girls gave me a note. Said if I wanted to belong, I could become a familiar."

"Perkie and July, I bet." Jodie groans. "I know that game."

"Jodie, don't tell me you've been involved in this kinda thing."

"Daaaad," she says, then hangs her head, her voice dropping to almost a whisper. "I'm not... pretty enough."

"Blame your mother for that," TC snaps at his daughter, turning to Raquel. "What about this note?"

"It said go upstairs and knock five times on the third door. No talking, or I'd be out. The door opened, the room was dark, lots of people bumping into me." Raquel huffs a breath, wiping at her face, and Jodie pushes a fistful of napkins toward her. "Somebody fell against me, my blouse ripped."

"Sounds like a Roy Orbison orgy," TC says.

"Who?"

"Never mind."

"Someone outside screamed five minutes, I got pushed to the floor, and—" Raquel folds over, hugs her knees, and moans. They ride on in simmering silence until TC passes the turn to the Conway's house. Jodie quickly asks, "Where're we going, Dad?"

"Sheriff's," TC grunts, his eyes glued straight ahead. His decision is met with a chorus of protest.

"You can't," Raquel wails. "My dad will kill me. My family." She cries and bursts into a new set of tears.

Jodie chimes in. "Dad, you'll ruin it for her at school."

"What happened is not okay," TC shouts. "We have to report this. Only a coward would use such a trick. And this, this sounds about as satisfying as jerking your own chain." TC pounds the wheel with his fist. "This isn't about sex, it's about power. Any of those football players holding a grudge?"

"Grudge? Against, *me*? I uh, slapped Watson... once. He tried to pull me away from Bunny."

"Sounds like, if he couldn't have you, then he'd just as soon piss the pot."

"Dad?"

"Was that him, you know, in the room?"

"I couldn't see anything." Raquel mutters, but TC is sure the girl's holding back.

"Dad, please." Jodie tugs at his sleeve.

"Evidence will be gone if we don't go now."

"It's her decision, her life," Jodie insists. TC jams on the brake and spins the wheel. He's fuming at the go-along attitude of the girls. But for now, he'll wait. Justice often comes out of left field, anyway. He may have to deal with that self-entitled football punk himself.

When they reach the house, TC shuts off the engine and pulls his watch from his pocket.

"What time is it, Dad?" Jodie asks.

"Early," TC says, squinting at the open timepiece. "Little after one o'clock." The girls disappear up the stairs, taking refuge in Jodie's room. TC pours himself two fingers from a bottle of a single-barrel scotch he's been saving. He escapes outside, hoping to cool his rage and replay the information. His appearance in the backyard brings life to Rowdy and Sugar, and the two dogs creep from the shadows to beg for attention. Taking a seat on the low bench under the tree, TC removes his hat, leans his head against the trunk, and closes his eyes, thinking.

Raquel has been molested, but the crime was cleverly disguised as a simple game for cool kids. Dark room, unknown participants, that's a slippery slope for placing blame. Besides, she'd accepted the invitation, put herself in the situation. No talking, so she never cried stop. Raquel is hiding behind what this'll do to her family, and like a frat pledge, the other side of hazing is the goal. She must have felt like a nobody and would rather forget what happened with the hope of becoming popular.

TC swirls the mellow liquid, noticing a glow through the glass. Across the meadow, a light burns inside the Potts' house. "Doesn't that kid ever sleep?" he mutters, scratching Rowdy behind the ear.

~

Bunny is tired, so tired, but Nan will not let up. She makes an evil game of the darkness. He tries to sleep with a light on, but even then, her sinister heckling climbs from under the bed and tightens around him.

"You know what to do," a throaty voice breathes in his ear.

Bunny jumps awake but finds he's all alone. When he does manage sleep, violent dreams reach inside his brain, twisting it like taffy at a pull.

"He took your girl," the voice hisses.

Bunny leaps from the bed, certain a coiled snake is waiting under the pillow.

Wrapped in a blanket, he leaves the house to lie beside her grave. "You happy now, Nan?" His words billow a white fog into the night. Outside, Bunny doesn't hear the voices. The hard ground is unforgiving, but at least he can find peace. Casper darts from the tin underside of the house, his pink nose making a wet stamp against Bunny's cheek. "Hello, buddy." He strokes the tiny head that pushes against his hand, then raises the edge of the blanket. The kitten disappears inside, curling next to Bunny. "You won't leave me, will you? Not like everyone... my dad, Nan, and now... even Raquel." Bunny closes his eyes, listening to the kitten's motor of contentment and falls asleep almost instantly.

Hours later, the fireball of sunrise creeps under his eyelids, prying Bunny awake. Muscles stiff and painful, he kicks off the blanket to stretch. The sudden action startles the sleeping kitten, who bolts away. Bunny chases after him but is only able to catch an occasional glimpse of white darting in and out of the thick growth of the ditch. He walks on, nearing the main road, but hasn't seen the kitten in several seconds. "Here, kitty."

There's a truck sound from the road. The engine noise builds as it approaches. "Here, kitty," Bunny says, plodding along. No sign, and he's reached the intersection. He stops, waiting for the truck to pass. Just feet away now, the engine's roar is loud. A flash of white jumps out of tall grass. Bunny runs blindly after it and almost broadsides the truck with his body. Breaks squeal, tires skid on gravel.

TC steps out, watching Bunny, on hands and knees, scoop up the broken kitten. "Sorry, man, he ran right under the wheel." Fur dripping, loose and limp, Bunny's hand now a garish red, he one-finger-strokes the tiny ears. "Thought you had a thing against cats." TC smirks. "Did you like this one?"

"Bunny." Her voice floats from the front of the truck, and he snaps to attention. Raquel is there, her brow knitted, her face fresh with the glow of just awake. She holds her blouse together, staring at Bunny.

"Raquel?" he gasps. "What?" His brain can't make sense of this. He returns a look so icy it could chill a drink. Raquel just got out of TC's truck and is standing in the middle of the road, and it's barely sunup. A dark disgust creeps up from Bunny's stomach and plants a sour taste in his mouth. "Why are you here?" His scornful words edgy and cold, he can almost hear Bridget say *I told you so*.

Raquel points to the lump of fur. "Is he... dead?" And now, she's pretending to care.

Bunny glares. "What's it to you?"

Smart enough to keep her distance, the girl has gone mute. TC butts in. "She spent the night with Jodie. Just running Raquel home early, you know, before Saturday morning cartoons." *Does he think this is funny?*

"Why is your shirt ripped?"

Raquel looks down, adjusting herself. "Long story," she stammers, her cheeks blooming scarlet.

Bunny squeezes the dead kitten, making fresh blood ooze

between his clenched fingers. He steps in front of TC and jabs a finger into the cowboy's chest. "You killed my cat!" he spits. His face twists in disgust, like the surprise of an unflushed toilet. Anger flooding through his fingers, he squeezes again and the tiny head pops free of the body and bounces unnoticed at his feet. "And now, you sick fuck, you've ruined my girl."

forty-three

Bridget doesn't drive back to her dad's when she leaves the strip club and the hurtful company of Jay Henry. Feeling like a gutted catfish, the unknown parts of her life are suddenly splayed out on the table for the entire world to poke through.

Blind with shame, she puts on her shades even though it's still dark outside and races her station wagon back into Willow Creek, parking in front of the feed mill. It's hours before dawn and even longer until the business opens, but Bridget is wired like she's chugged a pot of coffee and has only one thing in mind—confronting Darleen.

She knows there's no use in attempting sleep or even going back to her father's house. That would involve a mandatory, lengthy question session, and she can't bring herself to face that—not now.

When the first light of morning invades her space, it feels like she's just closed her eyes. Bridget has nodded off during her wait for daylight and groans, clutching a stiff neck as she lifts her head from the steering wheel. She does a quick check of the time, knowing the mill opens early to accommodate farmers and ranchers. But that's still more than an hour away. She doesn't have to wait long before a group of boot-wearing gimme caps congregate outside the front door to moan about the lack of rain and dried-up stock tanks.

Half past the hour, a red truck pulls up beside Bridget. When she looks over, she's staring right at the woman whose face is contorted with pleasure in the stack of photos in her lap. Darleen smiles and waves at Bridget, her hand like a flag on a breeze. You'd think they were close friends. Sharing her husband with the girl, well, guess that qualifies for the close part. "Good morning, you dirty whore," Bridget mouths through the glass. "You better not have the clap."

Darleen climbs out of her truck, and Bridget can't help but notice the outline of her man-killing figure in those tight jeans. But with a red bandana tied in her dark hair, she looks the picture of an innocent country girl. Key in hand, Darleen threads her way to the door, skillfully deflecting the playful banter of the waiting male customers. Bridget watches the porch empty as the people file inside. There's no reason to hurry. The "meet at the mill crowd" of farmers and ranchers live solitary lives of animals and machinery and will enjoy the conversation and coffee for a bit.

After a few minutes, allowing time for the coffee to brew, more locals arrive, including Momma J, who hobbles past Bridget's car to the front door. Poor Jean looks like her hip is really bothering her. Guess she's working with Darleen today. Satisfied the counter must now be shoulder to shoulder, Bridget picks up the group of photos Jay Henry presented her last evening and steps from her station wagon.

The friendly bell on the door jingles when Bridget pushes it open. Heads turn and hats tip with nods of recognition. Bridget knows these people, where they live, who's been sick, and the names of their children. She knows their politics, their family members who've passed on, and which rancher has the best bulls for sale. And most important, they know Bridget and TC. Heck, TC is a majority stock owner in the feed mill. This is the perfect stage for exposing his horrible actions.

"Oh, Miss Bridget!" Momma J smiles across the counter. "Thank goodness for another woman. I've been struggling to stay afloat in this rancid sea of men."

"You love us, Jean," someone calls from the back, and Momma J answers by tossing a sugar packet.

Directing her words to Bridget, she raises her eyebrows. "See what I mean?"

Bridget weaves her way to Jean. "I thought Darleen was here."

"She is." Momma J jerks her thumb. "In the back, girls' room, probably." Then she leans across. Concern crinkling her eyes, she takes Bridget's free hand between both her own and looks into her face. "What's the matter, baby? You sick? Them some serious bags under your eyes, girl."

Surprised by the comment, Bridget tugs her hand away. "Just not sleeping," she says, trying to smooth her hair. But her fingers shake, so she double-hand-clutches the stack of photos against her chest.

"Something for Darleen?" Momma J points to the papers. "Want me to give it to her?" But Bridget just shakes her head, lost in the surrounding din of conversations.

"Ya'll see my truck?"

"Yup, done a number on ya bumper."

"Somebody can't back."

"My son. Teenagers, I swear."

"Hey, that bull you sold me. Can't keep that dang fool fenced."

"You figuring out why I sold him?"

"Did I tell ya? Gonna be a grandpa... again."

"Better tell them kids what's causing that."

The voices fight for attention, and Bridget moves from the pack to take refuge against the wall. Minutes tick by, and she tunes out the noise to concentrate. She has to show them. They need to know Bridget Conway is not a whispered joke. She is not the one out of step here. Bridget has been wronged, and it's time for the world to see that.

After what seems like an eternity of waiting, some men finish their coffee and collect sales tickets from Momma J. Darleen quietly returns to the room from the hallway, and Bridget watches as she smooths the front of her blouse and rights her collar. Her bandanna is missing, and her dark hair is messy and draped across her shoulders. She makes her way behind the counter, smiling at friendly faces who shout, "Where you been?" Her quiet entrance brings new life to the room, and the playful banter rises.

"Can't a girl have a bathroom break?" Darleen fires back. She offers to refill empty cups and snags a cap from one admirer before quickly snugging it down on her own head. Her eyes light up when she sees Bridget across the room. "Hey, come join the party." She signals and lifts the glass pot offering morning joe. But Bridget only shakes her head and pushes off the wall.

Bridget's serious-lack-of-sleep face works like magic to part the crowd. The men step back and seem leery her sour expression will rub off. Darleen's face changes, too, and she watches Bridget with guarded anticipation. The smile is gone. Darleen sets the coffeepot down.

"I've got something you might like," Bridget says.

"For me?" Darleen smiles to lighten the moment. Conversations have dried up. The room is so still you can hear Bridget sliding pages from her stack.

"I think he captured your best side," she says and fans the images across the counter, facing the customers who strain to look over her shoulder.

Darleen lifts a picture and brings it closer. An audible gasp travels through the curious onlookers. Whispers of "Who is it?" and "Oh, my." Darleen's face goes pale, her lips draw together. She tosses the photo back to the counter like she'd accidentally picked up a snake. Momma J limps close, leans in, and asks, "What is it, love?"

"Darleen, tell me if I'm wrong, but isn't this my husband's head between your legs?" Bridget picks up another photo. "Yes, I was right. Here, you can see his profile in your bush."

Bridget's twisted pleasure watching Darleen squirm is interrupted when TC appears from down the hallway. "My lord," she whispers. Putting two and two together explains where Darleen has been. TC spies Bridget and hangs back, sizing up the weird hush that's fallen over the room. She gathers her courage and shouts, "Hey, husband, come over! This will interest you, too."

TC takes two steps forward before a tearful Darleen rushes past him, bolting from the room. Coffee-drinking customers, shocked and silent, seem shamed by the spectacle. They want nothing more than to distance themselves from the stink in the room. Muttering, they shoot glances at Bridget, seeming to forget why they came, and make their way to the door.

"What's this?" TC says, coming close. He eyes the images for a beat before his brain catches up. When he raises his face, the pain in his eyes stabs Bridget's heart. She wants to hurt him. She wants him to feel what she feels. But... her love—the thing Bridget thought dead—breaks the barrier she's built. Witnessing TC's pain is worse than bearing her own.

Momma J tics her tongue. "Well, that was something," she says. "Mean as hell, I'd say." Her faded-blue eyes glare across the counter at Bridget as she shuffles past TC, making a somewhat hasty retreat to find Darleen.

Now it's just Bridget and TC left in the room.

"Why?" TC raises his voice, his eyes red with anger, jaw clenched.

His reaction leaves Bridget reeling. She feels cheated. Where is her deserved sympathy? His soulful apology? "Do you... love her?"

"That lady—" TC slams a fist on the counter. "That lady is a damn fine friend."

Bridget grabs a handful of the graphic photos and throws them in TC's face. "A friend?" she smirks. "Words of a first-class asshole."

TC heaves a deep breath and clutches the back of his neck, an uncomfortable tell Bridget knows so well. "What do you want?" he says softly, refusing to look at her.

"Stop screwing around," she screams. "I'm your wife, damn it. You married *me*." She thumps her chest.

"You knew who I was. I haven't changed."

"But I... I want all of you. All of you or nothing."

"All or nothing," TC sneers. "Bridget, old girl, you're not qualified to fill that job."

Her anger explodes with his hate-filled words. Quick as a cat, Bridget climbs on top of the counter, kicks two fat sales binders to the floor along with order pads, a cup of pens, and a stack of logo refrigerator magnets. Dodging flying counter goods, TC makes a grab for Bridget's busy feet. But she jumps from the counter on top of his head. Spinning like a whirling dervish, he tries to dislodge her. But she two-hand-smashes his Stetson past his ears, busting the crown and covering his eyes. Grabbing his head between her legs like a saddle horn, she rides his shoulders, her boots jack-hammering blows to his ribs.

Eyes covered by the hat, TC grabs at her feet as Bridget snags one of the pegboard displays off the wall. The heavy panel crashes down, the hard-edge sails making a direct hit just above TC's ear. Knocked silly, he stumbles, dancing on electronic cattle prods and tubes of worm medicine that skitter across the floor, then crashes into the counter.

Thrown from her ride, Bridget rolls across the surface. TC rips off the ruined Stetson. A river of red runs down the side of his face and drips from his jaw. He grits his teeth and dives at Bridget, muscling her in a bear hug. She kicks like a mule as TC drags her toward the front door.

"Son of a bitch," Bridget screams and braces a boot against the jamb of the open door.

The fight noise carries outside where the stunned parking lot crowd gapes with open mouths. TC throws a shoulder into her back, breaking her foot brace loose, and Bridget flies through the opening, her body landing in a heap on the dock. The door lock clicks at her back.

Shoulders heaving, she struggles to her feet. "TC—" Her defeated words are pathetic. Bridget pounds her fist against the glass door. "I hate you. I wish… I wish you were dead."

forty-four

DREAMS. Something Bunny has never given much thought. He's accepted his life although often thought of ending it. Doesn't spend too much time worried about things he doesn't have, or people he's never known. If you've never tasted chocolate, it's impossible to crave it. But then Bunny saw Raquel. He sat beside her on the bus and drank in her delicious smell. She'd held his hand. They'd laughed, and he'd shared the softness of those red lips. Memories sweeter than chocolate. Raquel became Bunny's dream.

And now, there's only one thing for Bunny to do. Get even. But that can't bring Raquel back to him. And if it could, now that TC has taken her innocence, Bunny could never feel the same way about her. TC has stolen his dream and, like any dirty thief, he must pay the price.

Since seeing TC with Raquel, Bunny can't think of anything else. He's not closed his eyes or even thought about food. The plan he's been hatching for the last two days is simple. He's gone over and over it a thousand times. Just like a memorized speech, every detail is etched into his brain. TC is too smart and too strong for a one-on-one. Instead, Bunny will need to catch him when he doesn't suspect a thing.

It's now first light on Monday morning, and Bunny stares at the clock. In about an hour, TC will pull up to the gate in pasture nine, next to the Pott's place. His pickup will be loaded with hay for the cattle. Every morning, same thing, same time. But today will be different. Bunny will be ready and waiting.

At the water well shed, Bunny wiggles the heavy pipe wrench off the hose bib. There's never been a proper handle, at least as long as he's been showing up for a drink. But in his search for a substantial, weighty tool to grip, the wrench was his best option. In the lean-to barn, he collects the paint bucket filled with gasoline and pushes the lid down. He pats his jeans pocket for the matches. Yes, he's all set.

Bunny leaves his truck parked at the house and carries only what he needs. The grey, pre-dawn light is just enough for walking, and when he gets close to the creek, he disturbs the bedded-down cattle camped there. Cows rise up, back legs first like off-center triangles, the flattened earth under them steaming with their heat. The thick undergrowth here is a windbreak for animals against the cold of the near-winter day, and Bunny knows that he can't be seen in the shadows.

The wait isn't long before TC appears at the gate. Truck loaded with hay bales, the engine purrs, puffing grey clouds of exhaust skyward. Bunny holds his breath as the morning ritual unfolds. TC drives beside the hayrack. He climbs to the top of the stacked hay and seems to strike a pose, looking over the pasture. The cowboy's lean silhouette against the light sky is impressive. "Cock of the walk, huh?" Bunny whispers. TC flexes fingers into work gloves and slides a pair of wire cutters from his back pocket. The cattle are swarming now, they bump the side of the truck and tug stolen mouthfuls from the bound bales.

Deserted by the cows rushing to the hay, Bunny continues his watch alone from the tree cover. He checks the sagging front pocket of his hoodie. It bangs against his legs with the weight of the heavy pipe wrench. He picks up the gas-filled paint bucket and listens to the snip of the wire as TC cuts the bales open, then the grunt when he heaves the heavy hay into the rack. This is a critical time. While TC works, the cattle make noise, giving Bunny his opportunity to cross from the creek to the truck without being noticed. Slowly, he steps from his cover to the open field. The distance is less than a hundred yards, and Bunny is careful to stay at TC's back.

When Bunny reaches the truck, he stoops down to stay hidden in front. He rises up just enough to peek through the windshield and back glass. TC stops for a moment, folding loose wires. He stares across to the Potts' house, his warm breath white in the cold air. Bunny's decision to leave his truck parked at home was spot on. TC doesn't suspect a thing.

Bunny stays low and peeks around the corner from the front of the truck. Once the hay tossing resumes, he stows the gallon paint can under the bumper, then army crawls down the side of the truck opposite TC. When he reaches the passenger door, Rowdy jumps at the glass and barks wildly from inside the cab. Bunny dives, scrambling to hide under the truck and praying he wasn't seen.

"What is it, boy?" TC says. "Rabbit, you see a rabbit?"

For a moment, all is quiet, then the chassis rises as TC steps down and walks around to check on Rowdy. Inches away, his shiny boots stop beside Bunny, who's holding his breath under the truck. Close enough to smell the fresh polish, Bunny is frozen with fear. "What's a matter, boy? You gotta stay inside, buddy. Cows don't need herding." A work glove drops to the grass by TC's feet. The brim of a Stetson dips into view as he retrieves it, TC's hand so close to Bunny's face he can count the hairs on the cowboy's knuckles.

Holding his breath, he waits for TC's return to his work. He could still stop and slink back to the cover of the creek. No one would even know. But he's come so far and Raquel—what about payback for Raquel? The bed dips, the work resumes. Long minutes pass. Bunny stays hidden. His hands shake so hard he traps them under his body against the ground. Rowdy calms. Boot heels scrape against the metal above his head.

"That ought to hold you gals." TC chuckles. Steps thud toward the back.

One deep breath and Bunny crawls into the open. Squatting below the side, he squeezes the wrench and waits for the rise of the truck.

When the first boot crunches dry grass, Bunny rushes around the corner. He draws back, slamming the heavy tool into TC's skull. There's no sound, no grunt, no groan—nothing.

The cowboy drops. From the cab, Rowdy rages. Frantic, the dog digs at the glass.

Bunny races for the gas, soaking unconscious TC head to toe. Sharp fuel smell alarms the cattle, who stop eating. Nostrils flaring, they inch closer. A match is tossed. The sudden flash huffs across the body, a brilliant flame. Cows run, tails lifted high, to the creek.

That's when TC comes around. Engulfed in fire, his screams are insane. Hands covering his face, he rolls on the ground. Fiery clothing sets the pasture grass burning, the wind guiding it away from the truck.

Bunny can't listen, can't stand it. He covers his ears and shouts, "He's a bad man, a bad man!"

Someone might hear the screams. Someone might come to help. And if not, the smoke rising off the pasture will send up an SOS for miles.

He knows it won't be long, but Bunny can't look away. Reflex thrashing goes on even when it isn't possible. The flames eat the flesh, and a man becomes nothing more than a smoldering log.

He squats beside the blackened lump, heat pulsing from its surface, shiny and brittle as coals on a grill. The clothes have burned away, and only a ghostly red sheen of melted long johns remains. Boots still aflame, the leather soles curl and lick open like panting hounds. Inside, the tissue flickers red, the wink of a missing eye. Forearms over the face have melted into the features, swollen and bubbled as campfire marshmallows. A charred half-moon of gold smiles up at Bunny—TC's precious watch chain.

The stomach-turning smell is so powerful, he gags and stumbles away, vomit spewing onto his shoes. The charred odor is as sweet and sharp as swallowed syrup. Wiping his mouth on his hand, he screams at the dead man. "Why... *my* girl... why Raquel?" Suddenly, he turns and kicks the corpse. The jet-black surface shatters, the impact making an oozing wound. "This is for Raquel, you sick bastard." Bunny hawks a wad, the well-aimed spittle answered with a sizzle.

In the distance, an engine roars. He hurries now, grabs the paint can and the wrench. The sound stronger, it's almost on him now. Bunny sprints to the cover of the creek. He'd never be able to make it home before the visitor arrives.

A flash of yellow and a school bus squeals to a stop at the pasture gate. Nothing for several seconds. Then the driver steps down, reaching back to help someone. Bunny gasps when Jodie hobbles out on crutches. Windows full of eyes, the school children are glued to the glass. At the gate, Jodie spins the combination. She and the bus driver walk through the burning grass to find Rowdy in the truck. But the hardest part is the sound of her voice, clear and strong, splitting the still of the cold morning. Jodie, calling and calling for Dad.

When they free Rowdy, he runs nose-down and quickly locates the blackened mass they'd passed right by seconds before.

They stare in disbelief. Rowdy beside what's left of his master.

And Jodie—sweet Jodie—drops to her knees.

forty-five

ABOUT TWO WEEKS after the funeral service, Bridget pulls a handful of mail from the box. She scans the stack of business letters, each one addressed to TC. "He's gone, but I'm still invisible," she huffs. Bridget shoves the envelopes into her pocket and hurries back to the house.

She's feeling edgy about the sheriff's visit. She's known Don Cutco her whole life, voted for him when he ran for office, and even contributed to his campaign. Don had called earlier, saying he'd like to come by, and is due to arrive any minute now. His call this morning was what finally made her get out of bed. Buzzing around her house like the old Bridget, she feels better—*useful*. The sheriff must have news about TC's murder, and Bridget is so anxious she's already straightened, fluffed, and wiped every clean surface.

When she walks into her kitchen, the rich smell of sausage upsets her already nervous stomach. Ignoring the wave of nausea, she peeks into the oven, proud she hasn't forgotten her manners, and sets out mugs and plates, ready for her guest. TC's melted watch chain on the bar draws her back to the awfulness of the last two weeks. Bridget can't remember most of it. If the girls hadn't been there to thread her arms into sleeves and slide a comb over her head, she would have just stayed in the bed, pulled the covers over her head, and prayed to stop breathing. The funeral home had returned the chain and, although the links were fused, it was truly the only thing from the fire she could recognize. It was bad enough being told of her husband's death, but if dental records hadn't proven it was him, Bridget would never have known it was TC she'd put into the ground.

Most nights, she dreams TC is still alive and she's discovered him nose deep between a shapely pair of mystery legs. When she screams out, Bridget wakes, swimming in her own sweat. Picking up the gold piece, she rubs away some of the char before the empty feeling wets her eyes. "Enough," Bridget scolds herself for breaking the promise. "No more tears." She takes a deep breath and slides the stack of mail under the misshapen lump, promising to deal with that later.

A knock at the door and Bridget sprints to open it.

"Good morning." Sheriff Don smiles, his round face shaded by the brim of his hat.

"Come in, come in, Don." Bridget leads him down the hall and, glancing over her shoulder, notices he seems to be more than she'd remembered. Watching the sheriff turn into the kitchen, she smiles to herself as his belly arrives before the rest of him.

"Coffee, iced tea? Got some pigs in a blanket." Bridget pours them both coffees and loads a plate with the warm, pastry-wrapped sausages. She can't help but smile at Don's sudden interest in food.

He fills his plate and slurps half the coffee before putting his mug down. "Well, Bridget, you've called a few times, and I'm betting you want to know something on the investigation."

Bridget nods, sitting stiffly in front of her untouched mug. She laces her fingers on the bar and gives the sheriff her full attention. "What can you tell me?"

"Well..." Don rubs the back of his neck like he'd slept wrong. "There's a lot of moving parts here."

Bridget pins him with a stare. "What does that mean?"

"Means several names have come up."

"Like?"

"Oh... a long list of pissed-off husbands, boyfriends, old flames and... don't get me started on the irate fathers talking castration." Don takes a sip of coffee, raises his eyebrows, and looks straight at Bridget. "And then, there's... *you*."

"Me?"

"I've heard from more than one about the big scene at the feed mill... and what you said." Bridget's mouth drops open, and he adds, "'Bout wishing TC dead."

"I had a reason." Bridget sputters. The memory of that terrible day still tender, she takes a deep gulp of air, pushing back tears. "But Don... you don't believe I-I did this?"

"Not saying you did or didn't, but I got an earful from my little cousin—Darleen."

"What?"

"My cousin's cousin, actually. Guess that's what, second cousin?"

"Well, that's embarrassing," Bridget mumbles and traces a fingertip around the edge of her mug as she tries to stare a hole into the counter. "Did... did you know about her and TC?"

Don shakes his head. "But the whole town knows now."

"So, where are you with this?"

"Hell, I can't arrest half the county, Bridget. I've got a small force, limited budget." He chuckles. "We ain't the FBI here. Talk about motive. Shoot, more folks got one than days on your calendar. Look, I know you've been through a lot. But don't it make sense to... accept your blessing?"

"You're not saying, let somebody just get away with it?"

"I can say with confidence, whoever did this had a dog in the fight."

"How do you know?"

"Passion. Someone filled with rage and passion. The revenge in this case? Very personal."

"But I can't just let this go, like his life was worth nothing." Bridget doubles her fist and pounds the bar. Her emotion rising like cream, the room is suddenly uncomfortable. "I... I hated him for what he did, but he was my husband, father to our girls." On the verge of losing it, she stands and retreats to the kitchen window. She sniffs back tears, stares into the bright daylight, and dreams of the past. There was a time when she knew who she was—a confident, loving wife. This spot had been her favorite place at the end of each day. Making supper, she'd watch for TC. Her heart raced even now, just like it did each time she looked out and saw his truck climbing the hill. "I was a good wife to him," she manages before breaking down.

Don comes close, and she clutches him, sobbing into his shoulder. After a long moment, Bridget pushes back, reaching for a stack of dish towels. Drying her face, she addresses the sheriff with a new thought. "But TC was your friend, Don. Doesn't he deserve justice?"

"That's what I'm trying to tell you, Bridget. General opinion is... justice was served."

forty-six

THE SUN BALANCES on the horizon, a fireball on a seesaw, ready to call it a night. Still Jodie hasn't shown. Today when he'd passed by the house, she'd waved from the porch for him to stop then invited him to their secret place. It's been a while since they'd met at the clearing to share secrets beside the creek. And although Bunny is eager for company, he's terrified Jodie knows. Knows what he did.

After TC's death, Bunny had been afraid to approach the Conway family. It wasn't guilt that kept him away. No, it had to be done. And even though he'd been careful, the thought never left that he could be hauled to jail at any moment. So Bunny kept to himself, stayed away, and allowed the rituals of grief to play out. He'd seen them, a train of cars and trucks, nosy neighbors and friends visiting the Conway house on the hill to pay respects. He couldn't bring himself to go there, pretending sadness and offering comfort. Not when what he'd done seemed so *right*. Bunny Boy Potts at last felt complete and whole. His tortured nights vanished along with Nan's voice from the grave, pushing him to do something about TC. The house now silent, Bunny sleeps peacefully.

Now the sun has disappeared, and several of the cows walk close. That's when the familiar black truck appears through the gate.

Bunny watches it approach and an uncomfortable coldness creeps inside him. TC will never drive it again. It'd been sitting idle. No one would dare touch it.

When the truck gets close, the music volume is a tip-off to who's driving. Of course it's Jodie, and somehow, it seems only right. She'd be the one to claim her dad's truck. "Hey loser—no crutches," she yells from the window before hopping down on unencumbered feet.

"Looky, looky, the girl's got legs!" Bunny gives a fist pump.

"Yes, and... I've got something for you." She dangles a chain from one finger, a tiny golden rabbit's head, and heart swinging freely at the end. "Found this under my bed. Thought you might like to have it back."

Bunny grabs the necklace and shoves it into his pocket. He kicks the dirt, stirring up a cloud, and quickly looks away. "Thanks... I guess."

"Saw her yesterday," Jodie says. "She was sitting in Mean Man's car after school."

"Why are you telling me this?" He steams, heat rushing up his collar. "Don't care."

"Sounds like you kinda do." She frowns. "Her loss, Red. That guy's a giant muscular douche."

"That's another thing. I'm not going by Red any longer." Jodie eyes him. "Just... Bunny." He tries to soften his sharp reply and touches her arm. "Please... I'm just Bunny."

She shrugs. "Never thought it suited you anyway. Come on." Jodie takes the lead, walking toward the creek, and Bunny falls in behind. They weave through the thick growth of tree trunks with anticipation, confident their secret place has remained untouched since their last visit. When they reach the clearing, they each claim a spot near the steep drop of the sandy bank. The winding, dark line of the creek snakes below.

"So, your ankle good?"

"Well," Jodie snorts, lifting her leg. "Screws holding it together. Sometime, I'll have to get them removed, probably."

Bunny makes a face. "Sounds... painful."

"Yeah, probably won't be playing volleyball anytime soon." She rubs at the red, uneven scars. "Guess I'm a real nobody at school now."

"Don't feel bad. They won't let me on the archery team," Bunny says.

"We're a couple of nobodies doing nothing."

"Don't say that." His voice is almost a shout. "Don't get down on yourself."

Her eyes blink like Bunny has thrown ice water in her face.

"I think you're... special," Bunny mumbles and keeps an eye open, gauging if he should duck or grin.

"Really?" Jodie flashes a bright smile. "Speeeeecial?" she mocks as Bunny's face turns bright red. The awkward silence that follows is filled with a symphony from nearby tree frogs. "I, uh, like you, too, Bunny." Jodie's reply is almost a whisper. And when he looks up, she adds, "I mean, lots has happened, but you've come a long way in a few months."

"That's for sure."

"You dress better, got a truck, and I believe you're building some muscle." She laughs and squeezes the bicep he flexes.

"All those heavy hay bales, I guess."

"Hardly resemble Ronald McDonald at all now."

"Bummer. He's such a stud muffin."

"Reminds me, Mom said to tell you thanks for stepping up and taking the lead with the ranch." Jodie's voice cracks.

She must be thinking of TC. Bunny wonders if she'd feel the same way if she knew what a shit he really was. That's one cowboy who never saw it coming. But the tearful girl beside him causes Bunny to scoot close and put an arm around her thin body. Immediately, she lays her head against his shoulder, just as natural as kicking off shoes.

"Missing my dad," she says, with a small sniff. Yes, she'd love her dad no matter what. Easy for Bunny to understand. After all, he'd grown up with Nan.

The closeness of Jodie's body, warm against his side, reignites a pleasant feeling. Her hair smells like strawberries, and turning his head, he breathes in the sweetness. His fingers feel light and warm against her dewy arm, but a disturbing thought quickly derails the perfect moment.

"So your mom knew you were meeting me, here?" Jodie nods, rubbing against his chin. "And she didn't mind?"

"Why would she?" Jodie raises her head. "You've been a big help."

Seeing an opportunity, Bunny pushes for information. "I saw the sheriff's car at your house."

"Boy, was that worthless. He says there're too many people who could've done it. You know, had a grudge against Dad."

"What?"

"Yeah, stupid sheriff plans to do nothing."

"He say that?"

"In so many words." Jodie, absent-mindedly bending to rest an elbow on the ground, draws in the sand with a finger.

Her news is shocking, but the relief makes him so giddy he has to suppress a laugh. Existing on high alert for the last two weeks has been draining. He huffs out a sigh of relief. Maybe if the truth got out, they'd give him a medal or something. Don't mess with Texas or that badass Bunny Boy Potts. He breathes deep, swelling with pride, and ducks his head to hide a smile.

"Since I'm off my crutches, we can start working with your horse. Teaching you how to cowboy, Potts." Jodie smirks. "Yes sir, you and I gonna be like this." Jodie giggles, presses two fingers together, and rocks up, bumping his shoulder.

"Are you up for that?"

"Hey, I'll be the girl on the fence giving instructions. You, uh, ready to hear my secret, Potts?" Jodie presses her lips tight, keeping it in. She seems bursting with news.

Bunny nods and holds his breath, his own fear rising. *What is she going to tell me?*

"We're friends, right?" Jodie says slowly. He returns a wide-eyed nod. "Maybe we could be good friends or... something more," Jodie says and quickly goes back to her sand writing. Her exposed words hang, a total surprise and relief, but Bunny is quite lost and unsure. Bridget's warning words about his real father still ring in his ears.

Anxious, Jodie looks up. "What?" she snaps. "No law against it. Not like we're brother and sister or something."

Yes, a glimmer of hope...

He hungrily waits for more, but she only lifts her chin and focuses on his face. Jodie demands an answer. Sweat pops on Bunny's lip. He hates the spotlight. The surprise of her secret admission leaves him confused. "I didn't think you really even... *liked* me," he stammers.

"Cause you're blind." Jodie bugs her eyes. "You've been so dopey lovesick on Raquel. I knew that mess was going nowhere."

"You could have told me." Bunny shakes his head.

"You're too different. Besides, she's too pretty. Now you and me?" Jodie's face brushes against his own. "Imagine how cute we are together?"

Jodie likes him... all-the-way-to-boyfriend likes him. The idea makes him dizzy and excited. But it's hard to wrap his head around that.

"So, Potts, what's your secret for me?"

He gives her a sideways glance and bites his lip. Just days before, he had burned alive the man she called Dad. But looking into Jodie's soft blue eyes, Bunny knows that information will remain inside him.

"Oh, no you don't," she warns. "None of that loser action. You understand how this works. I give, then you give, Potts."

If he could just know what she knows, what Bridget knows. It's like crawling across a minefield, but Jodie storms forward, going for it. He loves her stubborn push, her expectations. The girl is not afraid to be honest, and they do fit well together. Maybe it doesn't matter. What ya don't know can't hurt, or something like that.

He leans, fumbling inside his pocket, and pulls the gold chain out between two fingers. "I'd like to be good friends or something." He smiles. "Can I give you this, good friend?"

Jodie plucks the necklace from his palm, brings it close, and studies the tiny gleaming charms. "Thanks," she says flatly, then closes her fist around the chain and slings it like a center fielder straight into the creek. "I don't do leftovers. I'm not my momma."

Bunny's mouth drops open. "You knew?"

"About Dad? Sure. I knew. I hated them both. Dad for doing it, Mom for taking it." Her anger grows with the telling, and her voice goes shrill. Now, she buries her face in her hands and mumbles through her fingers. "Do you know what that's like? Having your own father slobber over your friends like some scary old man?"

"No but, kids at school laughed at Nan, calling her the Crazy Cat Lady."

"Been meaning to ask... why did you call your own mother 'Nan'?"

"Her name." He shrugs. "She told me to call her Nan. I don't think being a mom was something she was proud of."

"Bummer," says Jodie. "But Potts, we're alike. You and me, we make sense. Almost like one brain."

Bunny nods, "You and me... comfortable."

"You said you wanted to be really good friends." She crooks fingers into air quotes and smiles brightly. "Then get out there, Bunny Boy, and buy your girl something special. After all, that's the way it's supposed to be done, isn't it?"

acknowledgments

The story of *The Forgotten Son* has lived inside me for many years. It came alive through the help and encouragement of the wonderful members of DFW Writer's Workshop and All Writers Online Workshop. In particular I would like to thank Daryle McGinnis for his edits, Colin Holmes for his encouragement, Larry Enmon with his wise advice, Gary Scott with his welcome humor, and LK Simonds with her practical and useful knowledge. A special thank you to my publisher, Jodi Thompson, and editor, Twyla Beth Lamber, of Fawkes Press, who believed enough to make it happen. Lastly, my husband Steve, who always takes time to spitball ideas, make me laugh, and spell obscure words.

If you enjoyed this book, please do one or more of the following:

- Leave a review on your favorite book review site
- Tell a friend about *The Forgotten Son*
- Ask your local library to put BJ Sloan's work on the shelf
- Recommend Fawkes Press books to your local bookstore

VISIT US ONLINE
WWW.FAWKESPRESS.COM

WWW.BJSLOANWRITES.COM

FAWKES PRESS

Milton Keynes UK
Ingram Content Group UK Ltd.
UKHW031953281024
450365UK00009B/565